Say Your Goodbyes to the Light

M.B. Whittington

© Copyright 2024 - All rights reserved.

The content contained within this book may not be reproduced, duplicated or transmitted without direct written permission from the author or the publisher.

Under no circumstances will any blame or legal responsibility be held against the publisher, or author, for any damages, reparation, or monetary loss due to the information contained within this book, either directly or indirectly.

Legal Notice:

This book is copyright protected. It is only for personal use. You cannot amend, distribute, sell, use, quote or paraphrase any part, or the content within this book, without the consent of the author or publisher.

Disclaimer Notice:

Please note the information contained within this document is for educational and entertainment purposes only. All effort has been executed to present accurate, up to date, reliable, complete information. No warranties of any kind are declared or implied. Readers acknowledge that the author is not engaged in the rendering of legal, financial, medical or professional advice. The content within this book has been derived from various sources. Please consult a licensed professional before attempting any techniques outlined in this book.

By reading this document, the reader agrees that under no circumstances is the author responsible for any losses, direct or indirect, that are incurred as a result of the use of the information contained within this document, including, but not limited to, errors, omissions, or inaccuracies.

Table of Contents

CHAPTER 1: THE OBSESSION..............................1

CHAPTER 2: CHOOSING THE VICTIM...............39

CHAPTER 3: THE KILL..92

CHAPTER 4: SIGNS OF HAUNTING...................145

CHAPTER 5: THE GHOST APPEARS..................199

CHAPTER 6: ESCALATION...............................251

CHAPTER 7: LOSING CONTROL......................303

CHAPTER 8: THE GHOST'S ULTIMATUM............336

CHAPTER 9: DESCENT INTO MADNESS............359

CHAPTER 10: THE FINAL CONFRONTATION...382

EPILOGUE: THE HAUNTING NEVER ENDS 403

Chapter 1:
The Obsession

Introduction to Elliot's Apartment

Elliot Marsh's apartment was not a home in the traditional sense. It wasn't a place of comfort or refuge. Instead, it was a shrine to obsession, a space meticulously curated to suit his dark needs. From the moment one stepped inside, it was clear that this was a world unto itself—a world that reflected the fractured mind of its sole occupant.

The Atmosphere of the Apartment

The first thing anyone would notice was the dimness. The curtains were perpetually drawn, shutting out the outside world. The few beams of light that managed to slip through the fabric created strange patterns on the walls, like jagged scars etched into the room. A single desk lamp, its bulb flickering faintly, cast a pale glow across the space. It illuminated only what Elliot deemed necessary: his desk, his chair, and, most importantly, the corkboard.

The air inside the apartment was heavy, a stagnant mix of stale coffee and the faint metallic tang of the knife Elliot had sharpened earlier that evening. The refrigerator hummed in the background, its sound a steady drone that seemed louder than it should have been. Every so often, the old building groaned, the creak of wooden beams and pipes shifting as if the place itself were alive.

And then there was the clock. It hung on the wall opposite the corkboard, its face plain and utilitarian. The ticking was relentless, a constant reminder of time slipping away. To Elliot, it wasn't a nuisance—it was a companion, a metronome that matched the rhythm of his thoughts. But to anyone else, it might have been maddening, a sound that underscored the unsettling atmosphere of the room.

The Cluttered Workspace

Elliot's workspace was both chaotic and precise, a reflection of his dual nature. The desk, positioned directly beneath the lamp, was cluttered with notebooks, pens, and scraps of paper covered in hastily scrawled notes. A stack of books teetered precariously on one side, their titles revealing the depths of his obsession: *Mindhunter: Inside the FBI's Elite Serial Crime Unit*, *The Anatomy of Violence*, and *Profiling the Psychopath* were just a few of the volumes that had shaped his thinking.

Despite the apparent disorder, there was a method to the madness. Every item had its place, every piece of paper its purpose. Elliot knew exactly where to find what he needed, and woe to anyone who dared disrupt his system—not that anyone ever did. The workspace was an extension of Elliot himself: private, untouchable, and deeply unsettling.

The Central Fixture: The Corkboard

The corkboard was the heart of the apartment, the axis around which Elliot's world revolved. It dominated the far wall, stretching nearly six feet across and covered from edge to edge with a collage of photos, maps, articles, and diagrams. Red string crisscrossed the board in an intricate web, connecting certain pieces to others in ways that only Elliot could understand. To an outsider, it might have looked like madness. To Elliot, it was art.

At the center of the board was the most important piece: a photograph of Delyla. It was larger than the others, its corners pinned down meticulously. Around it were maps of her neighborhood, schedules detailing her daily routine, and candid photos Elliot had taken during his surveillance. Each string that radiated from her photo connected to another piece of the puzzle—a bus stop where she waited every morning, the café she visited every Friday, the alley behind her apartment building.

Elliot often found himself standing in front of the corkboard, staring at it for hours. It wasn't just a tool; it was a living thing, a manifestation of his control and precision. Each thread represented a connection, each photo a piece of the story he was constructing. And at the center of it all was Delyla, the axis of his obsession.

Sensory Details of the Space

The sensory experience of Elliot's apartment was almost oppressive. The stale air seemed to cling to the skin, a reminder of how rarely the windows were opened. The faint smell of coffee was ever-present, mingling with the sharper scent of metal from the tools Elliot kept on his desk. On some days, there was another smell, subtler but unmistakable: the faint, acrid tang of sweat, a byproduct of Elliot's endless pacing and obsessive work.

The sounds of the apartment were equally unsettling. The hum of the refrigerator was a constant background noise, broken only by the occasional clink of glass as Elliot reached for a bottle of water or the creak of floorboards beneath his weight. The clock's ticking was loudest of all, a rhythmic beat that seemed to grow louder in the stillness of the night.

Even the lighting added to the atmosphere. The desk lamp cast long shadows across the room, exaggerating the shapes of the clutter on Elliot's desk and the chaotic lines of the corkboard. In the dim light, the red strings seemed to pulse faintly, as if alive, their vibrant color a stark contrast to the muted tones of the apartment.

The Sense of Isolation

Elliot's apartment was not just a physical space—it was a fortress, a barrier that kept the outside world at bay. The curtains were always drawn, their thick fabric blocking out both sunlight and the prying eyes of neighbors. The windows themselves were locked tight, the frames sealed with layers of grime that spoke to how long it had been since they were last opened.

The isolation was palpable. Elliot had no visitors, no friends who might stop by unannounced. His interactions with the outside world were limited to fleeting moments: a nod to the mail carrier, a brief exchange with the cashier at the corner store. Even those interactions felt like intrusions, unwelcome disruptions to the carefully controlled environment he had created.

The apartment was a reflection of Elliot's inner world. It was a place of silence and solitude, a space where he could retreat from the chaos of the city and lose himself in his thoughts. But it was also a prison, a self-imposed exile that mirrored the walls Elliot had built around his mind.

The Tension of Detachment

Despite its quiet and solitude, the apartment was not a place of peace. There was a tension in the air, a sense of something lurking just beneath the surface. The cluttered desk, the flickering lamp, the relentless ticking of the clock—all of it combined to create an atmosphere that was both oppressive and electric.

Elliot thrived in this environment. The isolation gave him the space to think, to plan, to perfect every detail of his work. But it also fed his darker impulses, amplifying the obsessive thoughts that drove him. The corkboard, the notes, the red string—they were not just tools of his obsession; they were manifestations of it, physical representations of the control he craved.

As the hours passed and the light from the desk lamp grew dimmer, Elliot would sit in his chair, staring at the corkboard. The world outside his apartment ceased to exist. There was only the room, the board, and the ticking of the clock—a metronome counting down to the moment when his plans would become reality.

Elliot's apartment was more than just a living space. It was a reflection of his mind, a place where obsession and isolation intertwined to create an atmosphere that was as unsettling as it was fascinating. Every detail, from the cluttered desk to the overwhelming presence of the corkboard, spoke to the meticulous nature of its occupant. The apartment was a world apart, a fortress that kept the outside world at bay while nurturing the dark thoughts that consumed Elliot. And in the heart of this world, at the center of the corkboard, was Delyla—a silent reminder of the plans that would soon be set into motion.

Elliot's Corkboard: A Symbol of Control

The corkboard wasn't just an object in Elliot's apartment—it was an extension of his mind. It dominated the far wall, a sprawling testament to his meticulous nature and obsessive tendencies. Its presence in the room was almost overpowering, the red strings crisscrossing its surface like veins, pulsing with purpose and precision. To Elliot, it was more than a tool. It was a masterpiece, the ultimate representation of his desire for control.

The Physical Presence of the Corkboard

The corkboard stretched nearly six feet across, its surface covered from edge to edge with photographs, articles, maps, and diagrams. It loomed over the rest of the apartment, its chaotic appearance belying the careful planning that had gone into every detail. The photos were pinned in neat rows, their edges perfectly aligned. The articles were clipped with precision, their titles underlined in red ink. The maps, tacked to the corners, were annotated with Elliot's handwriting, the lines and symbols revealing routes, times, and connections only he could decipher.

The red string was the most striking element. It snaked across the board, connecting seemingly unrelated pieces of information with an almost mathematical exactitude. Each thread represented a thought, a connection Elliot had uncovered through hours of research and observation. To an outsider, the board might have looked like chaos, a madman's attempt to make sense of the incomprehensible. But to Elliot, it was perfection.

Years of Research and Obsession

The corkboard was the product of years of work, a culmination of Elliot's obsession with understanding control and manipulation. It had started modestly, with a few clippings from newspapers and printouts from online articles. At first, Elliot had used the board to study the methods of history's most infamous serial killers. Photos of Ted Bundy, Jeffrey Dahmer, and the Zodiac Killer still occupied the top left corner, surrounded by articles detailing their crimes.

Elliot's research wasn't limited to their actions. He delved into their psychology, reading books and articles about what drove them, how they chose their victims, and how they evaded capture. Each photo and article on the board represented countless hours spent in libraries, on forums, and in the shadowy corners of the internet. He wasn't just studying killers—he was learning from them, dissecting their methods and cataloging their mistakes.

As his obsession grew, so did the board. It expanded to include unsolved cases, maps of crime scenes, and profiles of victims. Elliot used colored pins to denote different categories: red for killers, blue for victims, yellow for locations. The red string connected these elements, forming a web that mapped not only the killers' actions but Elliot's own understanding of their methods.

Delyla: The Centerpiece

At the center of the corkboard was the most important piece: a photograph of Delyla. It was larger than the others, its edges neatly trimmed and its corners secured with precision. The photo showed Delyla sitting on a park bench, her head tilted slightly to one side, her faint smile illuminated by sunlight. To anyone else, it was an ordinary image, unremarkable in every way. But to Elliot, it was the axis around which his entire world now revolved.

Surrounding Delyla's photograph were maps of her neighborhood, detailed schedules of her daily routine, and candid photos Elliot had taken during his surveillance. Each map was marked with red and yellow pins, highlighting the routes she took to work, the bus stops she frequented, and the café she visited on Fridays. Notes in Elliot's meticulous handwriting filled the gaps between the photos and maps, documenting everything from the time Delyla left her apartment to the way she stirred her latte.

The red string radiated from Delyla's photograph like spokes on a wheel, connecting her to every other piece on the board. It linked her to the alley behind her apartment, to the bus stop three blocks away, and to the café where she spent exactly twenty-three minutes every Friday evening. To Elliot, these connections weren't just data points—they were proof of his control, evidence that he had mastered her routine and could predict her every move.

Elliot's Obsessive Need for Precision

Elliot's relationship with the corkboard was as obsessive as the research it contained. He spent hours standing in front of it, adjusting the pins and strings with a surgeon's precision. If a photo was even slightly crooked, he would straighten it immediately, his hands moving with a practiced ease. If a string sagged or a pin felt loose, he would fix it without hesitation, ensuring that the board remained a perfect reflection of his mind.

His need for precision extended to every aspect of the board. He measured the spacing between the photos with a ruler, ensuring they were equidistant. He color-coded his notes, using red ink for observations, blue for theories, and black for confirmed facts. Even the pins were arranged methodically, their colors forming a pattern that only Elliot could see.

The act of maintaining the board was almost meditative for Elliot. As he adjusted the strings and aligned the photos, he felt a sense of calm wash over him. It was a ritual, a way to assert control over his world and quiet the chaos in his mind. The board wasn't just a tool—it was a sanctuary, a place where everything made sense.

Internal Monologue: The Masterpiece

Elliot often referred to the corkboard as his "masterpiece," a term he didn't use lightly. To him, it was more than just a collection of information—it was a work of art, a manifestation of his intellect and precision. As he stood before it, his arms crossed and his head tilted slightly, he would reflect on its significance.

"This is what separates me from the rest," Elliot thought as he traced the red string with his eyes. "The others—Bundy, Dahmer, the Zodiac—they were brilliant, but they were flawed. They let their impulses cloud their judgment, and they made mistakes. But I won't. This board is proof of that."

The corkboard was a source of pride for Elliot, but it was also a source of pressure. It reminded him of the expectations he had placed on himself, the perfection he demanded. Each pin, each photo, each string was a promise—a commitment to his plan, to his legacy. Failure wasn't an option, not with the board standing as a testament to his work.

But there were moments, fleeting and rare, when Elliot felt a flicker of doubt as he stared at the board. What if something went wrong? What if Delyla noticed him watching her? What if the plan unraveled before it even began? These thoughts were quickly dismissed, buried beneath layers of logic and determination. The board was his masterpiece, and masterpieces didn't fail.

The Duality of the Corkboard

While the corkboard represented control and precision, it also hinted at the chaos lurking beneath Elliot's surface. The web of red string, though meticulously arranged, resembled the tangled thoughts that raced through his mind. The photos and notes, though organized, spoke to an obsession that had consumed him entirely.

The board was both a reflection of Elliot's mind and a window into it. It revealed his need for order but also his fear of disorder. It showed his intellect but also his madness. To anyone else, it would have been a warning sign, a glimpse of the darkness that had taken root within him. But to Elliot, it was a source of comfort, a reminder that he was in control.

Elliot's corkboard was more than a tool—it was a symbol, a physical manifestation of his obsession with control. Every photo, every pin, every string was a testament to his meticulous nature and his determination to master the chaos of the world around him. But beneath the surface of the board's precision lay a darker truth: it was also a reflection of Elliot's unraveling mind, a portrait of a man who had sacrificed everything—his humanity, his sanity—for the illusion of control.

And at the center of it all, surrounded by maps and strings and notes, was Delyla. The corkboard was Elliot's masterpiece, but it was also his prison. It held his thoughts, his plans, and his fears, binding him as tightly as the red string that crisscrossed its surface. And as the days ticked by, the board's presence grew heavier, a silent reminder of the moment that was fast approaching—the moment when his obsession would be put to the ultimate test.

Introducing Delyla: The Perfect Target

Elliot didn't believe in coincidence. His world was a mosaic of patterns, each piece placed with purpose, each movement deliberate. He watched people like a predator stalking prey, observing their habits, their weaknesses, their vulnerabilities. And Delyla Cooper, whether she knew it or not, was perfect.

She had emerged into his world one crisp October morning, stepping off the bus in her quiet, unassuming way. Elliot had been walking through her neighborhood, eyes scanning the streets for... something. He didn't know exactly what he was looking for until he saw her. She was ordinary in every sense of the word—brown hair tied back in a loose ponytail, a black tote bag slung over her shoulder, headphones in place as if to tune out the world.

But to Elliot, she was extraordinary. She moved with quiet precision, her steps deliberate, her posture relaxed yet purposeful. She didn't hesitate or glance around nervously. She didn't seem to notice anyone watching her. And that, to Elliot, made her the perfect target.

The First Sight

She crossed the street toward a small café, her eyes downcast, her focus entirely inward. Elliot stopped, instinctively pulling back into the shadows of a doorway, and watched her.

He told himself it was curiosity, the kind that came naturally to someone like him—an observer, a student of human behavior. But even then, he knew better. He knew what she was.

The café door jingled faintly as Delyla entered, and Elliot lingered outside, watching her silhouette through the frosted glass. She didn't look up as she approached the counter, didn't engage the barista in small talk. She simply placed her order, took her drink, and found a seat by the window. From where Elliot stood, he could see the faint steam rising from her cup, could see the way she stirred it slowly, almost absentmindedly, her gaze fixed on her phone.

"She's perfect," Elliot whispered, the words escaping before he could stop them. His breath formed small clouds in the crisp autumn air, but his focus was entirely on her.

He didn't know her name then, didn't know where she lived or what she did. But he knew she was the one.

A Creature of Habit

From that moment on, Delyla became the center of Elliot's world. He learned her name, her routine, the rhythms of her life. It was almost too easy. Delyla was a creature of habit, her days a predictable loop that played out like clockwork.

At exactly 8:00 a.m., she left her apartment, her tote bag slung over her shoulder, her headphones firmly in place. She walked three blocks to the bus stop, her pace steady, her focus on the sidewalk ahead of her. She always stood in the same spot, leaning slightly against the metal pole of the bus sign as she scrolled through her phone. At 8:12 a.m., the bus arrived. Delyla boarded without hesitation, taking a seat in the middle row on the left side. By 8:45 a.m., she was at her office, a gray, boxy building downtown.

Elliot followed her several times, blending into the crowd as she walked from the bus stop to her workplace. He watched her through the glass doors, noting how she interacted—or didn't interact—with her coworkers. Delyla was polite but distant, offering nods and faint smiles but rarely engaging in conversation. During her lunch breaks, she crossed the street to a small park, always sitting on the same bench, her phone in hand, a sandwich balanced on her knee. By 5:15, she was back on the bus, heading home, her day a mirror image of the one before.

Fridays were the only exception. At 6:30 p.m., Delyla visited the café near her apartment. She ordered a caramel latte with extra foam, her voice soft and measured, and took a seat by the window. She sat there for exactly twenty-three minutes, stirring her drink slowly as she scrolled through her phone. Elliot had timed her visits with precision, his stopwatch ticking softly in his pocket.

Her predictability was intoxicating. To Elliot, it wasn't just convenient—it was a challenge, a puzzle he was determined to solve. Each movement, each habit, each deviation from her routine was a piece of the picture he was constructing. And the more he watched her, the more perfect she became.

Delyla Through Elliot's Eyes

Elliot didn't see Delyla as a person. He didn't wonder about her thoughts or feelings, didn't consider what she might dream about or fear. To him, she was data, a collection of patterns and behaviors that he could manipulate and control. Her humanity was irrelevant. What mattered was her routine, her vulnerability, her invisibility.

She was the kind of person who didn't draw attention, who moved through the world without leaving a mark. Her neighbors barely seemed to notice her. She didn't linger in conversations or make friends at work. Even the barista at the café barely looked up when she ordered her drink. She was, in Elliot's mind, invisible.

And that made her perfect.

The Notes and the Board

Back at his apartment, Delyla's life unfolded on Elliot's corkboard. Her photograph was pinned at the center, surrounded by maps of her neighborhood, schedules of her daily routine, and candid photos Elliot had taken during his surveillance. Red string connected her to the places she frequented: the bus stop, the office, the café, the alley behind her apartment building. Each connection was a testament to Elliot's control, proof that he could predict her every move.

He spent hours standing in front of the board, his arms crossed, his eyes scanning the threads and pins. Every detail had to be perfect, every piece in its proper place. He adjusted the pins with a surgeon's precision, straightened the strings, and added notes in his careful handwriting. The board wasn't just a tool—it was a manifestation of his mind, a living, breathing representation of his obsession.

As he stared at Delyla's photograph, Elliot felt a strange mix of emotions. Satisfaction, certainly—he had found the perfect target, the culmination of years of research and preparation. But there was something else, too, something he couldn't quite name. It wasn't guilt—Elliot had trained himself to suppress that long ago. But it wasn't triumph, either. It was something deeper, something that unsettled him.

A Flicker of Humanity

There were moments when Delyla's humanity threatened to break through Elliot's carefully constructed image of her as a target. As he watched her sip her latte at the café or pause to adjust her tote bag on her shoulder, he would catch himself wondering, just for a moment, what she was thinking. Did she enjoy her job? Did she feel lonely in her apartment? Did she dream of something more?

These thoughts were fleeting but persistent. They lingered at the edges of Elliot's mind, a faint whisper that he tried to ignore. He reminded himself that Delyla wasn't a person—she was a means to an end, a puzzle to be solved. But the whisper remained, growing louder with each passing day.

The Illusion of Control

Despite his meticulous planning, Elliot couldn't shake the feeling that something was slipping out of his control. He dismissed it as nerves, the natural tension that came with executing a plan of this magnitude. But the feeling lingered, a faint unease that gnawed at the edges of his mind.

As he stared at Delyla's photograph, he whispered to himself, "I can do this. I have to do this." The words were steady, confident. But deep down, Elliot knew they were more for himself than for anyone else.

Delyla's life was a puzzle he believed he had solved, a routine he thought he had mastered. But what Elliot didn't realize—what he couldn't realize—was that beneath the surface of her quiet, predictable existence lay a complexity he hadn't accounted for. And that complexity would become his undoing.

Elliot's Planning and Doubts

The corkboard loomed over Elliot like a silent judge, its web of red strings and meticulously arranged photos a testament to the hours he had spent perfecting his plan. It was the culmination of years of study, months of surveillance, and countless sleepless nights.

Every detail had been accounted for. Every variable controlled. Yet as Elliot stood before his masterpiece, the faint tendrils of doubt began to creep into his mind.

Step-by-Step Perfection

Elliot prided himself on his precision. Planning wasn't just a necessity; it was an art form. His notebook, filled with dense handwriting and carefully drawn diagrams, lay open on the desk beside him. He flipped through the pages, his eyes scanning every line of his timeline.

"8:00 a.m.—leaves apartment.
8:12 a.m.—boards bus.
8:45 a.m.—arrives at office."

He had mapped out Delyla's entire day, reducing her life to a series of predictable movements. It wasn't just her morning routine that he knew by heart—he could recite her Friday café visits and her evening walks home as if they were lines from a favorite play. He had rehearsed this plan in his mind so many times it felt as though he had already lived it.

Yet he reviewed it again, his pen tapping against the desk in a steady rhythm. The tapping was a habit, a way to focus his restless energy. Every detail of the plan was replayed in his mind, each step a cog in the machine he had built.

"The bus stop. The alley. The knife."

The alley behind Delyla's apartment was the perfect location—dark, secluded, and rarely traveled after sundown. He had chosen it with care, timing his visits to confirm its emptiness. He had even measured the time it would take to move from his hiding spot to intercept her. Eleven seconds. Just enough time for him to emerge from the shadows and act.

The Knife: A Tool of Control

The knife rested on the desk in front of him, its six-inch blade gleaming under the pale glow of the desk lamp. It wasn't just a weapon—it was an extension of his will, a tool of precision and control. Elliot picked it up, feeling its weight in his hand. He had chosen this particular knife after hours of research, reading reviews and studying videos that demonstrated its capabilities. Sharp, balanced, and easy to handle—it was everything he needed.

He ran his thumb along the flat of the blade, his skin prickling at its coolness. The edge caught the light as he tilted it, a faint, almost imperceptible rainbow glinting along its surface. It was beautiful in its simplicity, a tool designed for a singular purpose.

Elliot stood and moved to the center of the room, holding the knife in front of him. He adjusted his grip, testing the way it felt in his hand. His movements were fluid, practiced. He had spent hours rehearsing, stabbing at an old pillow until the fabric was shredded and the stuffing spilled onto the floor.

But even as he moved, doubts flickered at the edges of his mind. His grip faltered for a moment, the knife slipping slightly in his hand. He tightened his hold, forcing the thought away. This was just preparation, he told himself. Practice made perfect.

Replaying the Timeline

Elliot set the knife down and returned to his desk, his focus shifting back to the timeline. He closed his eyes, leaning back in his chair, and replayed the sequence of events in his mind.

"6:30 p.m.—Delyla leaves the café.
6:45 p.m.—she walks through the alley.
6:46 p.m.—she's gone."

The steps were simple, elegant in their efficiency. He had thought of everything, from the gloves he would wear to the quickest escape route. There was no room for error, no margin for failure. And yet, as he played the scene in his mind, a faint whisper of doubt crept in.

What if she notices you? What if she fights back? What if someone sees?

Elliot's hands clenched into fists, his nails digging into his palms. He opened his eyes, staring at the corkboard as if it could provide him with the answers. Failure wasn't an option. He had spent too much time, too much effort, to let it all fall apart now.

Hesitation and Humanity

Despite his resolve, there were moments when Elliot's mind wandered. As he stared at Delyla's photograph, he found himself wondering about the life behind the image. What did she think about as she sipped her latte at the café? Did she enjoy her job? Did she dream of something more?

These thoughts were dangerous, Elliot knew. They threatened to humanize her, to transform her from a target into a person. He couldn't allow that. He couldn't afford to see Delyla as anything more than a piece of the puzzle he was solving.

But the thoughts persisted. He remembered the way she had smiled at the barista one Friday evening, a small, genuine expression that lingered for only a moment. It was a smile that had no place on his corkboard, no place in his plans. And yet, it stayed with him, a faint echo in the recesses of his mind.

Elliot shook his head, forcing the memory away. He turned his attention back to the knife, picking it up again and testing its weight. The blade was sharp, the edge perfect. It was a reminder of what mattered—control, precision, and the plan.

The Fear of Failure

Elliot's greatest fear wasn't being caught. It wasn't the idea of prison or punishment or even death. His greatest fear was failure. The idea that he might hesitate, might falter at the critical moment, filled him with a gnawing sense of dread.

He had studied the mistakes of others, dissecting the flaws that had led to their capture. Ted Bundy's arrogance, the Zodiac Killer's taunting letters, Jeffrey Dahmer's carelessness—they had all let something slip, something that had led to their downfall. Elliot was determined not to make the same mistakes.

But the fear lingered, a shadow at the edge of his mind. He imagined the moment when he stepped out of the shadows, the knife in his hand, and Delyla turned to face him. What if she screamed? What if she ran? What if he couldn't go through with it?

These thoughts were a betrayal, a crack in the foundation of his plans. Elliot clenched his jaw, his fingers tightening around the knife. He wouldn't fail. He couldn't. He had worked too hard, planned too carefully, to let doubt destroy him.

The Mantra

To silence the doubts, Elliot turned to his mantra. He had repeated the words so many times they had become a part of him, a steady rhythm that matched the ticking of the clock on the wall.

"I can do this. I have to do this."

The words were simple, almost banal, but they held power. They reminded him of his purpose, of the control he craved and the legacy he wanted to leave. Each repetition was a nail driven into the coffin of his doubt, sealing it away where it couldn't reach him.

Elliot stared at the corkboard as he whispered the mantra under his breath. Delyla's photograph was at the center, her faint smile illuminated by the soft glow of the desk lamp. She was the axis of his world, the reason for every decision he had made. And in less than twenty-four hours, she would be gone.

As the words filled the room, the tension in Elliot's chest began to ease. The doubts didn't disappear entirely, but they retreated, pushed to the back of his mind by the force of his will. He placed the knife back on the desk, its blade gleaming in the light, and sat down, his hands steady once more.

"I can do this," he whispered, his voice firm. "I have to do this."

The clock on the wall ticked steadily, its rhythm matching the beating of his heart. Outside, the city was quiet, the streets empty under the glow of the streetlights. And inside the apartment, surrounded by the evidence of his obsession, Elliot prepared for the moment that would define him.

Foreshadowing and Suspense

Elliot's apartment, once his sanctuary, was beginning to feel like something else entirely. The heavy air, once comforting in its staleness, now seemed to press against him like an invisible weight. Shadows, long and undefined, clung to the corners of the room, and the steady hum of the refrigerator had begun to sound more like a low growl than a mundane background noise. He told himself it was nothing. It was the same apartment he had lived in for years, the same walls, the same furniture, the same corkboard. Yet, as he sat at his desk, staring at Delyla's photograph pinned at the center of his carefully constructed web, he couldn't shake the feeling that something had changed.

The Shifting Shadows

It started with the shadows. They were nothing, Elliot told himself—just tricks of the light, the product of his overworked mind. But no matter how much he rationalized it, he couldn't ignore how they seemed to move when he wasn't looking directly at them.

He would catch them out of the corner of his eye, subtle shifts that made him turn his head sharply, only to find everything in its place. At first, he blamed the flickering desk lamp. The bulb was old, and its light had begun to stutter unpredictably, creating fleeting moments of darkness that he could have sworn weren't there before.

One evening, as he sat reviewing Delyla's routine for the hundredth time, he noticed the shadow of the chair in the corner move—not a gentle sway, but a deliberate shift. His breath caught, and for a moment, he sat frozen, his eyes locked on the chair. The shadow was perfectly still now, its edges sharp against the wall.

Elliot shook his head and forced a laugh, though the sound was hollow. "I need more sleep," he muttered, though he knew that wasn't true. Sleep was a luxury he hadn't indulged in for weeks, not with the weight of his plans pressing down on him. He turned back to the corkboard, ignoring the faint chill that crept up his spine.

The Cold Draft

The chill was the next thing he noticed—a sudden, inexplicable draft that seemed to snake through the room despite the sealed windows and locked door. It came at random, a cold brush against his skin that made the hairs on his arms stand on end.

One night, as he stood in front of the corkboard, adjusting a thread that had gone slack, the draft hit him so suddenly that he shivered. He glanced at the window, but the heavy curtains were drawn tight, and the glass beyond them was undisturbed.

Elliot moved toward the door, checking the lock, then the seams where air might be slipping through. There was nothing. The apartment was as secure as it had always been. Yet the chill lingered, wrapping itself around him like an icy hand.

"Just the temperature dropping," he whispered to himself, though the reassurance felt thin. It wasn't the kind of cold that came with winter air. It was different—sharper, heavier, almost unnatural. He rubbed his arms and returned to his desk, his eyes darting to the corners of the room where the shadows gathered.

The Feeling of Being Watched

The sensation of being watched was the hardest to ignore. It followed him everywhere in the apartment, a constant pressure against the back of his neck. He would turn quickly, expecting to see someone standing behind him, only to find the room empty.

At first, he convinced himself it was paranoia. He was alone—he had always been alone. The walls of his apartment were his fortress, shielding him from the chaos of the outside world. No one could get in. No one even knew about the corkboard, let alone his plans.

But the feeling persisted, growing stronger each day. It wasn't just a vague unease—it was specific, targeted, as if unseen eyes were tracking his every move. Sometimes, as he sat at his desk, he swore he could hear faint whispers, low and indistinct, coming from the corners of the room. The sound was too soft to make out any words, but it was enough to set his nerves on edge.

One night, as he lay in bed staring at the cracks in the ceiling, the feeling became so overwhelming that he sat up abruptly, his chest heaving. His eyes scanned the room, lingering on the darkened corners where the light from the streetlamps didn't quite reach.

For a moment, he thought he saw movement—a faint flicker, like someone shifting their weight. He blinked, and it was gone.

The Weight of the Plan

As the strange occurrences in the apartment grew more frequent, the weight of Elliot's plan began to settle heavily on him. The corkboard, once a source of pride, now felt like a silent judge, its meticulously arranged threads and photographs demanding perfection. Every time he looked at Delyla's photograph, he felt the pressure mounting.

She stared back at him with that faint, unassuming smile, her face illuminated by the soft light of the desk lamp. She had no idea how much of her life he had dissected, how thoroughly he had studied her every move. To Elliot, she wasn't just a person—she was a symbol, a test of his ability to control every variable.

But as the hours ticked by, doubt began to creep into his mind. He found himself wondering about Delyla in ways he hadn't allowed before. Did she have dreams? Regrets? Did she ever feel the weight of her own existence pressing down on her the way he did now?

These thoughts were dangerous, Elliot knew. They threatened to humanize her, to transform her from a target into something more. He tried to push them away, focusing on the timeline, the knife, the alley. But no matter how much he concentrated, the questions lingered, nagging at the edges of his consciousness.

The Atmosphere Grows Heavier

The apartment itself seemed to change as Elliot's doubts grew. The air, once heavy with stale coffee and the faint metallic tang of the knife, now felt oppressive, almost suffocating. The walls seemed to close in on him, their shadows stretching longer and darker as the days went by.

Even the corkboard, his masterpiece, began to feel like a burden. The red strings that once symbolized control now seemed tangled and chaotic, their connections fraying in his mind. He spent hours adjusting them, his fingers trembling as he tried to restore the order that had always come so easily to him.

The desk lamp flickered again, casting the room into brief moments of darkness. Elliot's breath hitched as the shadows seemed to pulse with life, their edges blurring and shifting. He shook his head and forced himself to focus, his gaze locking onto Delyla's photograph.

"I can do this," he whispered, his voice trembling slightly. "I have to do this."

The words felt hollow, like a prayer offered to a god he no longer believed in. The room grew colder, the shadows pressing closer, and for a moment, Elliot thought he heard a faint, distant laugh. He turned sharply, but there was nothing—only the ticking of the clock on the wall and the hum of the refrigerator.

The Final Whisper

As the night deepened, Elliot sat at his desk, his hands gripping the edges of the table so tightly that his knuckles turned white. The corkboard loomed before him, Delyla's photograph at its center, surrounded by the web of connections he had spent so long constructing.

The apartment was silent, save for the ticking of the clock and the faint rustle of paper as

Elliot flipped through his notes. Yet the silence wasn't comforting—it was charged, electric, as if the room itself was holding its breath.

Elliot closed his eyes and took a deep, shuddering breath. The doubts, the unease, the strange sensations—they were all in his head. They had to be. He had planned for everything, accounted for every variable. This was just the natural tension of preparing for something monumental.

"I can do this," he whispered again, his voice firmer this time. "I have to do this."

As the words left his lips, the atmosphere in the room seemed to shift. The air grew heavier, colder, pressing against him like a tangible force. The shadows in the corners of the room stretched longer, their edges bleeding into the light. For a moment, Elliot thought he saw a figure in the corner, its shape indistinct but undeniably present.

He blinked, and it was gone.

Elliot exhaled slowly, his breath visible in the now-frigid air. He turned back to the corkboard, his gaze fixed on Delyla's photograph. The room was silent again, the shadows still. But the feeling of being watched lingered, stronger than ever.

And somewhere, just beyond the edge of his awareness, he thought he heard a whisper.

Chapter 2: Choosing the Victim

Elliot's Criteria for the Perfect Victim

Elliot didn't view the world the way most people did. To him, humanity wasn't a collection of unique individuals with dreams, fears, and identities. Instead, people were patterns—predictable, repetitive, and subject to the laws of routine. His methodical mind had spent years dissecting those patterns, refining his ability to see past the distractions of personality and focus on the underlying mechanisms that made people tick.

It was with this mindset that he approached the most critical decision of his life: choosing the perfect victim. Elliot knew this wasn't a task that could be approached haphazardly. Mistakes weren't an option. His success, his legacy, depended on this first selection. And so, he devised a system—a framework built on three essential criteria: predictability, isolation, and control.

Predictability: The Anchor of His Plan

For Elliot, predictability wasn't just important; it was the foundation of everything. A predictable target was like a well-rehearsed play—every movement scripted, every action anticipated. Predictability meant control, and control was the essence of Elliot's plan.

The first step was observation. Elliot spent hours in crowded cafés, train stations, and parks, watching the ebb and flow of human behavior. He carried a small notebook where he jotted down notes about the strangers who caught his eye. Most were dismissed almost immediately—too chaotic, too inconsistent, too unpredictable. These were the people who paused to chat with strangers, who changed their routes on a whim, who lived lives filled with spontaneity. Elliot had no use for them.

What he needed was someone whose life was governed by routine, someone whose movements could be anticipated with precision. He looked for patterns: the woman who always sat on the same bench during her lunch break, the man who left his apartment at exactly 7:45 a.m. each morning. He noted these details carefully, cataloging them as if they were pieces of a larger puzzle.

"Predictability," Elliot wrote in his notebook, "is the most reliable form of weakness. People are creatures of habit, and those habits are their vulnerabilities."

He spent weeks studying the same people, cross-referencing his observations to confirm their consistency. He tested his theories, following them from a distance to ensure their routines were as rigid as they appeared. It was tedious, grueling work, but Elliot thrived on it. Each confirmed pattern was a victory, a small piece of evidence that his methods were sound.

But predictability alone wasn't enough. A person's routine might be flawless, but if they were too visible—too integrated into their surroundings—they posed a risk Elliot couldn't afford. That's where isolation came in.

Isolation: The Shield Against Detection

The second criterion was isolation. A target couldn't just be predictable; they had to be detached, disconnected from the world around them. Isolation wasn't just about physical solitude—it was about a lack of meaningful connections. Elliot needed someone who could vanish without immediate alarm, whose absence wouldn't trigger a cascade of inquiries and investigations.

He developed a checklist to evaluate isolation:

1. **Social Interactions:** Did they engage with others frequently, or did they keep to themselves?
2. **Routine Contacts:** Were they greeted by neighbors or coworkers, or did they go unnoticed?
3. **Family and Friends:** Did they appear to have strong personal relationships, or were they alone in the world?

Elliot watched for the subtle signs of loneliness: the man who ate lunch alone every day, the woman who avoided eye contact with her coworkers, the teenager who walked home from school without ever pulling out a phone to text someone. He noted these behaviors with clinical detachment, ranking potential targets based on how isolated they appeared.

"Isolation is a buffer," Elliot wrote. "The fewer connections a person has, the less likely anyone is to notice when they're gone. Loneliness is their vulnerability, and my opportunity."

It was this criterion that eliminated most of the people Elliot observed. Even those with predictable routines often had too many connections—friends who met them for drinks after work, families who waited for them at home, coworkers who depended on them for tasks and deadlines. These people were anchors in their communities, and their absence would be noticed almost immediately.

What Elliot needed was someone who moved through the world like a ghost, unseen and unremarkable. Someone who could disappear without causing a ripple.

Control: The Key to Execution

The final and perhaps most critical criterion was control. Predictability and isolation might make a target easier to identify, but control determined whether they were feasible. A person's routine had to intersect with opportunities that allowed Elliot to act without interference. Control wasn't just about knowing where someone would be—it was about ensuring he could manipulate their environment to his advantage.

Elliot analyzed the logistics of each target's routine with the precision of a military strategist. He looked for weaknesses in their patterns, moments when they were most vulnerable. Did they walk through secluded areas on their way home? Did they linger in quiet places, away from prying eyes? Did their habits create openings that he could exploit?

He studied escape routes and evaluated the risk of witnesses. He measured the distances between locations, timing himself as he walked the same paths they did. His plans were so detailed that he even accounted for environmental factors, noting the placement of streetlights, the density of foliage, and the likelihood of stray dogs barking at a sudden noise.

"Control," Elliot wrote, "is the difference between success and failure. The perfect target isn't just predictable and isolated—they're accessible. Their routine must offer windows of opportunity that I can exploit with precision."

A Clinical Approach

Elliot's method was as cold and emotionless as the man himself. He viewed his targets as data points, their lives reduced to a series of charts, maps, and notes. He didn't think about their hopes or fears, didn't consider their humanity. To Elliot, they were puzzles to be solved, problems to be eliminated.

He created spreadsheets to track his observations, using color-coded columns to rank potential targets based on their predictability, isolation, and accessibility. Green meant ideal, yellow meant possible, red meant disqualified. Delyla's name, when it finally appeared in his notebook, was marked in bold green, surrounded by annotations and exclamation points.

But even as he refined his system, Elliot knew that perfection was a moving target. Every plan, no matter how meticulously crafted, contained variables he couldn't control. And it was this knowledge—the possibility of failure—that drove him to work tirelessly, eliminating every potential flaw.

"Emotion clouds judgment," Elliot reminded himself whenever doubt crept into his mind. "This is a process, not a decision."

The Dismissal of Humanity

One of Elliot's greatest strengths—and greatest weaknesses—was his ability to detach himself from the humanity of his targets. He deliberately avoided learning personal details that might make them feel real. Names were irrelevant, except as labels for his notes. Faces were unimportant, except as identifiers in photographs.

He avoided targets who evoked sympathy or reminded him of someone from his past. If he felt even a flicker of emotion while observing someone, he crossed them off his list. His process demanded absolute objectivity, and sentimentality was a liability he couldn't afford.

"Emotion is the enemy of control," Elliot wrote. "The moment I see them as people is the moment I fail."

The Selection of Delyla

When Elliot first noticed Delyla stepping off the bus one chilly October morning, he didn't know her name. He didn't know where she lived, where she worked, or what kind of person she was. But he knew, within seconds of watching her walk down the street, that she was perfect.

Delyla moved through the world with a quiet efficiency that fascinated Elliot. She followed the same routes, took the same buses, and carried herself with a calm detachment that mirrored his own. She was polite but distant, her interactions with others brief and unremarkable. She seemed to drift through life without leaving a trace, her presence as unobtrusive as a shadow.

Elliot spent weeks observing her, mapping her routines and cataloging her movements. By the time he pinned her photograph to the center of his corkboard, he knew more about her life than most of the people she worked with. He knew when she woke up, when she left for work, when she returned home. He knew the exact time she ordered her caramel latte at the café on Fridays, the way she stirred it three times clockwise before taking her first sip.

She was, in Elliot's mind, flawless. Predictable. Isolated. Accessible. The perfect target.

The Illusion of Perfection

Despite his confidence in Delyla's selection, Elliot couldn't ignore the faint whispers of doubt that lingered in the back of his mind. What if he had overlooked something? What if her routine wasn't as rigid as it seemed? What if she wasn't as isolated as he thought?

These questions gnawed at him, their edges sharp and unrelenting. But Elliot silenced them with logic, reminding himself of the criteria he had so painstakingly developed. Delyla wasn't just a target—she was the product of a process, a symbol of his ability to control the uncontrollable.

"Perfection is a myth," Elliot thought as he stared at Delyla's photograph, her faint smile illuminated by the glow of his desk lamp. "But this... this is as close as it gets."

And with that, he turned back to his notebook, his pen moving across the page as he refined the final details of his plan.

First Observations

Elliot had a system. Observation, he called it, though others might have referred to it as stalking. For Elliot, the word stalking carried unnecessary connotations, emotions that had no place in his work. His task was simple: to study, to understand, to identify. People were puzzles, each a collection of habits, routines, and quirks waiting to be deciphered.

Every morning, just after sunrise, Elliot would leave his apartment and begin his routine. He had no set destination—he preferred to let the streets guide him. His path wound through busy intersections, quiet residential neighborhoods, and bustling parks, the rhythm of the city providing a steady backdrop to his thoughts. To the world, he looked like any other pedestrian: unremarkable, invisible. But Elliot was anything but ordinary.

The Notebook: His Companion in Observation

Elliot carried a small, black notebook with him wherever he went. Its pages were lined and neat, each one filled with tight, meticulous handwriting. The notebook was his most important tool, a repository for the observations he made during his daily walks. He didn't trust his memory—details could be forgotten, distorted over time. The notebook, however, was infallible.

Each entry followed a strict format: the time, the location, a brief description of the individual, and any notable patterns in their behavior. Elliot recorded everything: the way a woman adjusted her scarf before stepping onto a bus, the route a man took as he walked his dog, the exact number of seconds a teenager spent waiting at a crosswalk.

Most of these entries were discarded after a day or two, the subjects deemed unworthy of further attention. But a select few were underlined, circled, or marked with a small star in the margin. These were the individuals who interested Elliot, the ones who showed potential.

The Search for Patterns

Elliot's walks weren't aimless. He wasn't looking for just anyone—he was searching for the perfect target. Predictability was his first and most important criterion. A person's habits had to be consistent, their movements governed by routine. He watched for patterns, following potential targets for days or even weeks to confirm their predictability.

One afternoon, Elliot noticed a man who left his apartment at precisely 7:30 a.m. every morning. The man walked the same route to the train station, his pace steady, his gaze fixed on the sidewalk ahead of him. Elliot followed him twice, staying far enough back to avoid detection, and noted that the man even took the same seat on the train each day.

But on the third day, the man deviated. He stopped at a coffee shop, lingering inside for nearly twenty minutes before continuing to the station. Elliot frowned as he wrote in his notebook, crossing out the man's name with a single, sharp line. The deviation was minor, but it was enough to disqualify him. Predictability, Elliot reminded himself, had to be absolute.

Flaws in the Patterns

Most of the people Elliot observed failed to meet his standards. Their routines were too chaotic, their movements too erratic. Some were surrounded by too many people, their interactions frequent and unpredictable. Others lived lives so dull and unstructured that there was no routine to analyze. These individuals frustrated Elliot—they were noise, static that cluttered the clean lines of his observations.

One woman caught his attention for several days. She left her house at the same time every morning, walked the same route to her office, and returned home by the same path each evening. But as Elliot followed her one afternoon, he noticed something he hadn't seen before: a young boy, perhaps her nephew, running up to greet her. The boy stayed with her for the rest of the evening, their laughter echoing through the quiet street.

Elliot closed his notebook with a sigh. People with attachments were unreliable. Their lives were influenced by external factors, variables Elliot couldn't predict or control. He crossed her name off the list and moved on.

The Influence of Public Spaces

The locations people frequented were just as important as their routines. Elliot avoided individuals who spent too much time in crowded, public spaces. Parks, coffee shops, and busy intersections were fertile grounds for observation, but they were also risky. A target who spent their days in such places was likely to attract attention from others, and attention was the last thing Elliot wanted.

One man stood out for his regular visits to a small park near Elliot's apartment. He arrived every afternoon, carrying a book and a thermos of coffee. He always sat on the same bench, under a tree that provided shade from the afternoon sun. Elliot followed him for three days, noting his movements in meticulous detail.

But on the fourth day, the man was joined by a woman—someone Elliot hadn't seen before. The two of them laughed and talked, their conversation animated. The presence of another person shattered the man's predictability, introducing a variable Elliot couldn't account for. Another name was crossed off the list.

The Weight of Disappointment

Every time Elliot disqualified a potential target, he felt a pang of frustration. He had been at this for weeks, walking the streets, watching, waiting, and yet no one had met his criteria. The perfect target seemed elusive, a ghost he could never quite catch.

He began to doubt himself. Was he being too selective? Was his system too rigid? He replayed the disqualifications in his mind, questioning whether he had dismissed some individuals too quickly. But each time, he reminded himself of the importance of perfection. A single mistake—a deviation in routine, an unexpected attachment, a flaw in his observations—could unravel everything.

Elliot leaned against a lamppost one evening, staring down at his notebook. The pages were filled with names, descriptions, and crossed-out lines. He flipped through them, his frustration mounting. This was supposed to be the easy part. The observation phase was meant to confirm what he already knew: that people were predictable, controllable, reducible to patterns. But so far, they had all been disappointments.

A Glimpse of Perfection

And then there was Delyla. She appeared in his notebook like a breath of fresh air, her routine so flawless it almost seemed artificial. Elliot first noticed her on a Wednesday morning, stepping off the bus in her quiet, unassuming way. She carried herself with a calm efficiency, her movements deliberate and precise.

For the next week, Elliot followed her obsessively, cataloging every detail of her life. She left her apartment at the same time every morning, took the same bus to work, and returned home by the same route each evening. Her Friday visits to the café were the only deviation, but even those were consistent: the same time, the same drink, the same table by the window.

As Elliot wrote in his notebook that evening, his frustration melted away. For the first time, he felt a glimmer of hope. Delyla wasn't just another potential target. She was something more—a person whose routine was so predictable, so perfect, that it seemed almost designed for him.

He underlined her name in his notebook, circling it twice for good measure. The pieces were finally falling into place.

Elliot's daily walks were a study in discipline and patience. He had spent weeks observing the people around him, searching for the patterns that would lead him to the perfect target. Most of his observations ended in disappointment—flaws in routines, attachments he couldn't account for, and variables he couldn't control.

But Delyla was different. She represented everything Elliot had been searching for: predictability, isolation, and control. As he closed his notebook that evening, a faint smile played at the corners of his lips. The search was over. The puzzle was complete.

And now, the real work could begin.

The Discovery of Delyla

Elliot wasn't looking for Delyla. He hadn't even expected to find anyone worth noting on that particular morning. His walks had become monotonous, a ritualistic exercise in disappointment as he sifted through the endless stream of faces and routines that never quite met his criteria. But on that chilly October day, with the sharp bite of autumn in the air and the faint hum of the city around him, she stepped into his world, and everything changed.

The Morning That Changed Everything

Elliot had woken early, as he always did, and followed his usual route through the city streets. His path was erratic by design, ensuring he never lingered too long in one place, never fell into a routine that might make him noticeable. He had already passed a coffee shop where a group of young professionals were engaged in animated conversation and a park where a woman jogged in tight loops around a small pond. Neither scene held his attention. They were noise, irrelevant to his search.

He was just about to turn onto a quieter street when he saw her.

The bus had just pulled up to the curb, its doors hissing open with a mechanical sigh. A handful of people stepped off; each one absorbed in their own world. Some clutched phones, others adjusted bags or scarves. But one figure stood out—a woman who moved with a calm, unhurried grace that caught Elliot's eye immediately.

She wore a plain black coat and carried a simple tote bag slung over her shoulder. Her brown hair was pulled back into a loose ponytail, and a pair of headphones rested over her ears. She wasn't striking or ostentatious in any way. In fact, her ordinariness was part of what made her so captivating to Elliot. She was understated, unassuming, and entirely predictable.

Delyla Cooper.

Elliot didn't know her name yet. He didn't know where she was going or what she did. But as she stepped off the bus and began walking down the street, he felt something he hadn't felt in weeks: a flicker of hope.

First Impressions

Delyla moved with purpose but not urgency. Her steps were steady, her posture relaxed. She wasn't distracted by her phone like so many others, nor did she glance around nervously as if expecting someone to approach her. She existed in a bubble of calm that seemed impervious to the chaos of the city around her.

Elliot's eyes followed her as she crossed the street, her tote bag swinging gently at her side. He noted the way she glanced briefly at the crosswalk signal before stepping forward, the way she adjusted her headphones as she walked, the faint expression of focus on her face. There was no hesitation in her movements, no wasted effort. She was a creature of habit, and Elliot knew instantly that he needed to know more.

He kept his distance, blending into the crowd as he trailed her. His steps matched hers, his movements careful and deliberate. He had done this enough times to know how to remain invisible, to become just another faceless presence in the background. As Delyla turned onto a side street, Elliot followed, his heart pounding with a mix of anticipation and curiosity.

The First Walk

Delyla's route was simple, unremarkable. She walked three blocks to a small office building with gray, nondescript architecture. The sign on the door indicated that it housed a variety of businesses—accounting firms, marketing agencies, consulting services. Elliot watched from across the street as Delyla entered the building, her figure disappearing behind the tinted glass doors.

He didn't follow her inside. That would come later, once he had more information. For now, he was content to observe. He made a note in his small black notebook: *8:12 a.m.—Woman steps off the 42nd Street bus. Walks three blocks to 418 Greenview Avenue. Appears calm, focused.*

The rest of the day was spent retracing her steps, piecing together her routine. Elliot followed the same path she had taken from the bus stop to the office, noting the landmarks and the potential blind spots. He lingered near the building for a while, watching as other employees came and went. None of them seemed to notice Delyla, and she didn't seem to notice them.

"Isolated," he murmured to himself as he wrote the word in his notebook. It was a promising detail, one that added weight to his initial impression.

The Second Encounter

The following morning, Elliot returned to the same spot. He arrived fifteen minutes early, positioning himself at a café across the street from the bus stop. The staff there had seen him enough times not to pay attention, which was precisely why he chose the location. He ordered a coffee he wouldn't drink and sat by the window, his gaze fixed on the street.

At exactly 8:12 a.m., the bus arrived, its doors hissing open as a small group of passengers disembarked. Once again, Delyla was among them. She wore the same black coat, her tote bag slung over her shoulder. Her headphones were in place, and her expression was as calm and focused as it had been the day before.

Elliot's pulse quickened. He leaned forward slightly, watching as she crossed the street and began her walk to the office. Her movements were identical to the day before, her pace steady and unhurried. It was as if she were following a script, each step perfectly choreographed.

"Predictable," Elliot whispered, jotting the word down in his notebook.

The Sense of Triumph

By the end of the week, Elliot was certain. Delyla was everything he had been searching for. Her routine was flawless, her movements precise and unwavering. She took the same bus at the same time every morning, walked the same route to the same building, and returned home in the same unremarkable way each evening. Even her Friday visit to the café—a brief deviation from her usual routine—was consistent, down to the exact table she chose by the window.

Elliot felt a sense of triumph unlike anything he had experienced before. Delyla wasn't just a potential target—she was the perfect target. She was the missing piece of the puzzle he had been trying to solve for so long, the embodiment of everything he had been working toward.

"She's it," he murmured to himself as he stared at her photograph, which he had pinned to the center of his corkboard. The image was a candid shot he had taken earlier that week, capturing her as she walked toward the office. Her face was calm, her posture relaxed, her focus entirely inward.

Elliot adjusted one of the red strings on the board, connecting Delyla's photo to a map of her neighborhood. The lines crisscrossed the board like veins, creating a web that represented weeks of observation and planning. As he stepped back to admire his work, a faint smile tugged at the corners of his mouth.

"This is it," he whispered. "This is the beginning."

The Quiet Chaos of Delyla

Though Elliot was meticulous in his observations, he couldn't help but feel an undercurrent of chaos as he pieced together Delyla's life. Her movements were predictable, her routine unchanging, but there was something about her that felt different from the others he had studied. She wasn't loud or attention-seeking, but her presence lingered in his mind in a way he couldn't quite explain.

Elliot dismissed the feeling as a byproduct of his excitement. He had been searching for so long, and now that he had found someone who met his criteria so perfectly, it was natural to feel a sense of attachment. But deep down, he couldn't shake the thought that there was more to Delyla than he had seen so far.

The Final Confirmation

By the end of the second week, Elliot's certainty had solidified into resolve. He had followed Delyla every day, cataloging her movements with the precision of a scientist conducting an experiment. There were no deviations, no surprises. Her life was a pattern, a perfectly constructed loop that Elliot could predict down to the second.

He added the final details to his notebook, his pen moving steadily across the page. The entries were neat and concise, each one a testament to the hours he had spent watching, analyzing, and planning.

"8:12 a.m.—Disembarks from bus. Walks three blocks to 418 Greenview Avenue.
5:15 p.m.—Leaves office. Walks to bus stop. Takes same route home.
Friday, 6:30 p.m.—Visits café. Orders caramel latte. Sits by window for 23 minutes."

Elliot closed the notebook and set it aside, his gaze shifting to the corkboard. Delyla's photograph stared back at him, surrounded by maps, notes, and red strings. She was the center of his world now, the axis around which everything revolved.

"She's perfect," he whispered to himself, his voice filled with quiet conviction. "Absolutely perfect."

The discovery of Delyla was a turning point for Elliot. After weeks of fruitless observation and countless disappointments, he had finally found someone who met his criteria with uncanny precision. Delyla wasn't just another potential target—she was the embodiment of everything he had been searching for.

As Elliot stared at her photograph that evening, a sense of triumph washed over him. The puzzle was complete, the pieces perfectly aligned. And for the first time in weeks, he felt a sense of clarity.

This was it. This was the moment he had been waiting for. And nothing would stand in his way.

Initial Surveillance

Elliot was not a man who believed in shortcuts. He understood that true mastery required patience, diligence, and a relentless commitment to detail. Delyla, his perfect puzzle, was no exception. To Elliot, her life was a map waiting to be drawn, each step a line on the page, each movement a dot marking a critical point. He began the painstaking process of charting her routine, memorizing her route home, and noting the smallest details of her existence.

The First Follow

It started the evening after he first noticed her stepping off the bus. Elliot had spent the day observing her walk to work and return to the same bus stop at 5:15 p.m. As she boarded the bus, he followed at a safe distance, ensuring there was always at least one other person between them. She sat in the middle of the bus, near the window, her headphones still in place, her focus entirely inward.

When Delyla disembarked near her apartment building, Elliot waited a moment before following. His heart raced—not from nerves, but from the thrill of discovery. This was the first time he would see the route she took home, the way she interacted with her surroundings when she thought no one was watching.

Delyla's path was straightforward. She walked two blocks from the bus stop to her building, her tote bag swinging gently at her side. She didn't pause to chat with anyone or glance at her phone. Her pace was steady, unhurried, and entirely predictable. She entered her building through a side door, unlocked it with a quick swipe of her keycard, and disappeared inside.

Elliot lingered outside, studying the building. It was an older structure, four stories tall, with peeling paint and narrow windows. A security camera hung above the main entrance, its lens cracked and dusty. The side door Delyla used didn't appear to have any surveillance, a detail that Elliot filed away for later.

Memorizing Her Route

Over the next several days, Elliot followed Delyla home religiously. He varied his approach, sometimes taking different routes to ensure he wasn't seen repeatedly in the same places. He noted every detail of her journey: the streets she crossed, the shops she passed, the way she hugged the edge of the sidewalk rather than walking in the middle. Her routine was as consistent as clockwork, each step aligning perfectly with the one before.

He drew maps in his notebook, marking the landmarks along her path. There was a small corner store where she occasionally stopped to buy water or gum, a laundromat with a broken neon sign, and a streetlight near her building that flickered faintly at dusk. Elliot even timed her walk, noting that it took exactly seven minutes and twenty-three seconds for her to travel from the bus stop to her apartment.

"Predictable," he muttered to himself one evening as he reviewed his notes. It was a word he had written over and over again in connection with Delyla. Her predictability wasn't just reassuring—it was intoxicating. It gave him the sense of control he craved, the belief that he could anticipate her every move.

The Small Details

Elliot's observations weren't limited to Delyla's route. He studied the way she interacted with her environment, cataloging every gesture and habit. She carried her tote bag over her left shoulder, her hand resting lightly on the strap as if to keep it from slipping. She often adjusted her headphones, tilting them slightly forward as she walked, though she never seemed to change the volume or track on her phone.

There was a faint tension in her posture, a subtle stiffness in the way she held herself. Elliot couldn't tell if it was the result of stress or simply the way she carried her body, but he found it fascinating. It was as though she were bracing herself against the world, erecting a wall between herself and her surroundings.

He noticed other small details as well: the way she avoided walking too close to parked cars, the faint hesitation before she crossed the street, the quick glance she gave to the windows of her apartment building as she approached. These habits told a story, one that Elliot was determined to understand.

The Evening Ritual

Delyla's evenings followed a routine that was just as predictable as her commute. After entering her apartment building, she usually disappeared for about an hour before re-emerging to take out her trash or retrieve her mail. Elliot waited nearby, blending into the shadows as he watched her move.

On one occasion, she paused at the mailbox longer than usual, flipping through a small stack of envelopes. Elliot's breath caught as he observed her expression—was it annoyance? Concern? Whatever it was, it passed quickly, her face returning to its usual calm neutrality as she turned and headed back inside.

Elliot began to speculate about what her evenings looked like behind the closed doors of her apartment. Did she cook dinner? Watch TV? Work on some project he couldn't yet fathom? The thought of her private life intrigued him, though he knew it was secondary to his purpose. What mattered most was her routine—the moments when she stepped out into the world where he could observe her.

Testing the Waters

Elliot wasn't content to simply watch. He needed to test the consistency of Delyla's routine, to see how she reacted to small disruptions. One evening, as she walked from the bus stop to her apartment, he dropped his keys on the sidewalk several yards behind her, the sound sharp and deliberate. Delyla glanced back briefly, her eyes flickering over him for only a moment before she continued walking.

Another time, he positioned himself in front of the corner store as she approached, pretending to check his phone. She didn't so much as glance at him as she walked past, her focus fixed on the path ahead. These experiments reassured Elliot. Delyla's predictability wasn't just a product of habit—it was deeply ingrained, a part of who she was.

"Unshakable," he wrote in his notebook after the second test. "No reaction to minor disruptions. Focused on routine."

The Growing Obsession

As the days turned into weeks, Elliot's surveillance of Delyla became an obsession. Her life was a puzzle, each piece fitting together with satisfying precision. But the more he observed her, the more he found himself drawn to the small, human details that he had initially tried to ignore.

He noticed the way she sometimes bit her lip when she was deep in thought, the faint smile that flickered across her face when she passed a bakery near her building. He saw her pause to adjust her bag strap, her movements quick and efficient, and the way she tilted her head slightly to the side when she listened to something through her headphones.

Elliot tried to suppress these observations, to remind himself that Delyla wasn't a person in his eyes—she was a target, a means to an end. But the details lingered, tugging at the edges of his mind in ways he couldn't entirely control.

Final Preparations

By the end of the second week, Elliot felt he had memorized every aspect of Delyla's routine. He knew her route by heart, could anticipate her movements with uncanny accuracy. He had drawn detailed maps of her neighborhood, marking every intersection, every blind spot, every potential escape route.

He also began preparing for the moment when observation would no longer be enough. The knife he had chosen rested on his desk, its blade sharp and gleaming under the glow of the desk lamp. He held it in his hand one evening, testing its weight, imagining the way it would feel in the moment of action.

But even as he planned, a small voice in the back of his mind whispered doubts. Delyla's predictability, her calm demeanor—these were strengths as much as they were weaknesses. What if she noticed him watching? What if she broke her routine at the last moment? The thought of failure gnawed at him, but he pushed it aside.

He returned to his notebook, flipping through the pages of notes he had taken over the past weeks. Each entry was a reminder of his control, his ability to anticipate and adapt. Delyla's life wasn't just predictable—it was a system, and Elliot was its master.

The Perfect Puzzle

As he sat at his desk that night, Elliot stared at the corkboard where Delyla's photograph was pinned at the center. The red strings connecting her to the maps and notes seemed to pulse faintly in the dim light, a visual representation of the web he had woven around her.

"She's perfect," Elliot murmured to himself, his voice barely audible. His fingers traced the edge of her photograph, his touch light and deliberate.

Every detail, every moment of surveillance, had led him to this point. Delyla was more than just a target—she was the culmination of all his work, the embodiment of the control he had spent his life seeking. And soon, she would become something more.

But for now, Elliot was content to watch, to wait, and to memorize every last detail of her routine. The puzzle wasn't complete yet, but it was close—so close he could almost feel the pieces snapping into place.

The thought filled him with a quiet, almost euphoric sense of anticipation. The waiting was almost over. And when the time came, Elliot knew, he would be ready.

Doubt Creeps In

Elliot thrived on control. His world was built on routine, order, and precision. Every step of his plan had been carefully calculated, every detail meticulously accounted for. Delyla was supposed to be no different—another piece in the grand puzzle he had spent years constructing. Yet, for reasons Elliot couldn't fully articulate, cracks were beginning to form in his resolve. Doubt, an unwelcome intruder in his otherwise pristine mind, had begun to creep in.

The First Flicker of Doubt

It started as a fleeting thought, barely more than a whisper at the edges of his consciousness. Elliot had been watching Delyla for weeks, following her predictable routine with a precision that bordered on obsession. He knew her schedule, her habits, even the subtle quirks in her posture. But one evening, as he stood in the shadows near her apartment building, he found himself wondering: *What if she isn't as simple as she seems?*

The thought was unnerving. Delyla was supposed to be perfect—a predictable, isolated target whose life fit neatly into the framework Elliot had designed. Her calm demeanor, her unwavering routine, her apparent lack of close connections—all of it had made her the ideal choice. Yet now, as he replayed her movements in his mind, he felt an unfamiliar pang of uncertainty.

Elliot shook his head, as if to physically dispel the thought. *This is just fatigue,* he told himself. He had been working tirelessly, barely sleeping, consumed by the details of his plan. Doubt was a natural byproduct of exhaustion, nothing more. But the whisper persisted, faint yet insistent, like the ticking of a clock in a silent room.

The Humanizing Moments

As much as Elliot tried to suppress it, the doubt was fueled by small, seemingly inconsequential moments. Delyla's life, while predictable, wasn't entirely devoid of personality. She wasn't a blank slate, no matter how much Elliot wanted her to be.

He remembered the way she had smiled at the barista in the café one Friday evening, a genuine, fleeting expression that lit up her otherwise reserved demeanor. It was the kind of smile that suggested kindness, a warmth Elliot hadn't expected. For a moment, he had found himself wondering what had prompted it. Had the barista said something funny? Was Delyla thinking about something pleasant? Did she have a life beyond the routine he had meticulously documented?

Another time, as she walked home from the bus stop, she had paused to help an elderly man who had dropped his bag of groceries. Elliot had watched from a distance as she crouched to gather the fallen items, her movements quick and efficient, her expression soft but focused. It was a small act of kindness, one that most people would have overlooked. But to Elliot, it was a disruption—a reminder that Delyla wasn't just a target; she was a person.

These moments were dangerous. They chipped away at the detachment Elliot had so carefully cultivated, forcing him to see Delyla in a way he hadn't intended. She was supposed to be predictable, isolated, and unremarkable. Yet these glimpses of humanity threatened to complicate the narrative he had constructed around her.

The Hesitation

The doubt culminated one evening as Elliot sat in his apartment, staring at the corkboard where Delyla's photograph was pinned at the center. The web of red strings connecting her to maps, notes, and timelines was as precise as ever, a testament to his meticulous nature. But as he traced the lines with his eyes, he felt an inexplicable sense of unease.

"What if I'm wrong?" The thought surfaced unbidden, a rogue wave crashing against the carefully constructed walls of his mind. What if Delyla wasn't as simple as he believed? What if her routine was a facade, hiding complexities he hadn't accounted for? What if she noticed him watching, sensed his presence, and altered her behavior?

The questions spiraled in his mind, each one feeding the next. For the first time, Elliot found himself questioning the very foundation of his plan. It wasn't just Delyla's predictability that he doubted—it was his own ability to control every variable, to anticipate every outcome.

He clenched his fists, his nails digging into his palms. "Stop," he muttered under his breath. This wasn't him. He didn't make mistakes. He didn't let emotion cloud his judgment. Doubt was a weakness, and weakness was unacceptable.

The Struggle for Detachment

Elliot's greatest strength had always been his ability to detach. He didn't see people as individuals; he saw them as data points, pieces of a larger puzzle. Emotions had no place in his work. Yet now, as he thought about Delyla, he couldn't entirely suppress the flicker of humanity that had begun to intrude on his thoughts.

He tried to refocus, reminding himself of the facts. Delyla's life was a routine, a loop that played out with mechanical precision. She took the same bus at the same time every morning, walked the same route to the same office, and returned home by the same path each evening. She was polite but distant, her interactions with others brief and superficial. Everything about her fit the profile of a perfect target.

But then there were the details he couldn't ignore: the way she bit her lip when she was deep in thought, the faint smile that occasionally crossed her face, the kindness she had shown to the elderly man. These were the cracks in her predictability, the moments that made her feel real in a way Elliot hadn't anticipated.

He pushed back against these thoughts, forcing himself to focus on the corkboard. "She's just a target," he said aloud, his voice firm. "Nothing more."

Rationalizing the Doubt

Elliot wasn't the type to ignore a problem. If doubt had crept into his mind, he needed to address it head-on. He spent the next several days revisiting his observations of Delyla, scrutinizing every detail with renewed intensity. He followed her more closely, testing her reactions to minor disruptions. He even lingered outside her office building longer than usual, watching the way she interacted with her coworkers.

The results were reassuring. Delyla's routine remained consistent, her demeanor unchanged. She didn't seem to notice him or anyone else watching her. Her life was as predictable as it had always been. And yet, the doubt lingered, a faint but persistent shadow in the back of his mind.

Elliot tried to rationalize it. Doubt, he told himself, was a natural response to the gravity of his plan. It wasn't a sign of failure; it was a sign of his commitment to perfection. If anything, it made him more cautious, more thorough. And caution, he reminded himself, was the key to success.

The Mantra

To silence the doubt, Elliot returned to his mantra. It was a simple phrase, one he had repeated to himself countless times during the planning process: "I can do this. I have to do this."

The words were a reminder of his purpose, a way to ground himself in the logic of his actions. Delyla wasn't a person in his eyes—she was a puzzle, a means to an end. Her humanity was irrelevant. What mattered was the plan, the control, the legacy he was building.

Elliot repeated the mantra under his breath as he stood in front of the corkboard, his fingers tracing the edges of Delyla's photograph. "I can do this," he said again, his voice steady. "I have to do this."

The doubt didn't disappear entirely, but it receded, pushed to the edges of his mind by the force of his resolve. He wasn't wrong. He couldn't be wrong. Delyla was the perfect target, and his plan was flawless.

Doubt was a foreign emotion to Elliot, but in the weeks leading up to his planned act, it became an unwelcome companion. Delyla, who had once seemed so predictable and unremarkable, had begun to reveal flashes of humanity that threatened to disrupt Elliot's carefully constructed narrative. These moments of kindness, warmth, and complexity forced him to confront the possibility that she might be more complicated than he had believed.

Yet Elliot refused to let doubt take root. He suppressed his hesitation, rationalizing it as a byproduct of exhaustion and the weight of his plan. Through sheer force of will, he refocused on the facts, on the routine he had so painstakingly documented. Delyla wasn't a person to him—she was a target, a puzzle to be solved.

As Elliot stared at the corkboard that night, the doubt lingered at the edges of his mind, but his resolve remained unshaken. He couldn't afford to falter now. The plan was in motion, and there was no turning back.

Foreshadowing the Chaos

Elliot was a man who trusted logic above all else. His world was built on precision, predictability, and control. Patterns governed his life, and Delyla was the perfect embodiment of those patterns: predictable, orderly, and blissfully unaware of his presence. But as the days passed and his plan edged closer to its conclusion, Elliot began to notice things—small, unsettling moments that didn't fit into his neat, carefully constructed world. Shadows seemed to shift where they shouldn't, and a persistent, unshakable sensation of being watched began to claw at the edges of his mind.

The First Unsettling Incident

It began one evening as Elliot was following Delyla home from the bus stop. The sky was a dull gray, the air thick with the damp chill of an approaching storm. Elliot kept his distance, his footsteps deliberately quiet on the pavement as he watched her navigate the familiar streets. She moved as she always did—calm, composed, and oblivious to his presence.

But as she neared the corner of her street, Elliot noticed something strange. A shadow darted across the wall of a building ahead of her, its movement sharp and deliberate, like a figure slipping out of sight. He froze mid-step, his heart pounding. The shadow had no clear source. There was no one else nearby, no vehicle passing to cast such a fleeting image.

Elliot glanced around, his eyes scanning the street for any sign of movement. But the sidewalk was empty, save for Delyla, who continued on as if nothing had happened. He shook his head and forced himself to focus, dismissing the incident as a trick of the light. He had been following her for weeks without issue. There was no reason to believe anything had changed now.

The Feeling of Being Watched

Over the next few days, the sensation began to build—a persistent, creeping awareness that he wasn't alone. Elliot had always been careful, his movements calculated to ensure he remained invisible. But now, as he watched Delyla from across the street or trailed her discreetly through the alleys near her apartment, he couldn't shake the feeling that someone was watching him.

The sensation was subtle at first, a faint prickling at the back of his neck. It often struck him when he was stationary, waiting for Delyla to emerge from her office or return to the bus stop. He would glance over his shoulder, scanning the area for anything out of place, but there was never anyone there.

Elliot tried to dismiss the feeling, rationalizing it as nerves. His plan was nearing its culmination, and it was natural to feel a heightened sense of awareness. But the sensation refused to fade. It followed him everywhere, growing stronger with each passing day.

The Shadow That Shouldn't Be

The next incident was impossible to ignore. Elliot had taken up his usual position near the café where Delyla spent her Friday evenings, timing her visit to the second. He stood across the street, partially concealed by the shadow of a shop awning, his notebook in hand as he observed her through the café window.

Everything about Delyla was as predictable as ever. She stirred her caramel latte three times clockwise, as she always did, before taking a sip. Her phone sat on the table in front of her, her fingers idly scrolling through the screen. But as Elliot focused on her, he became aware of something out of place—a shadow cast on the wall behind her, darker and sharper than the others.

The shadow moved slowly, deliberately, as if it belonged to a figure standing directly behind Delyla. But there was no one there. Elliot's breath caught, his pulse quickening as he stared at the impossible image. The shadow shifted slightly, almost imperceptibly, before disappearing altogether.

For a long moment, Elliot stood frozen, his mind racing. Had he imagined it? Was it a trick of the light, the result of the café's dim interior and the glare from the streetlamps outside? He forced himself to take a deep breath, his fingers tightening around the edge of his notebook. Whatever it was, it didn't matter. Delyla was the focus, not some fleeting shadow.

The Unseen Presence

The feeling of being watched grew more intense with each passing day, an oppressive weight that seemed to press against Elliot's chest. It wasn't just limited to the times he followed Delyla—it began to creep into his own space, invading the sanctuary of his apartment.

One night, as he sat at his desk reviewing the notes on Delyla's routine, he became acutely aware of the stillness around him. The usual sounds of the city—muffled voices, distant traffic, the occasional creak of the building's old pipes—seemed to fade, replaced by an eerie, suffocating silence.

Elliot glanced over his shoulder, half-expecting to see someone standing behind him. The room was empty, the shadows in the corners of the apartment as still as ever. But the sensation lingered, an unshakable certainty that he wasn't alone.

He turned back to his desk, his eyes darting to the corkboard where Delyla's photograph was pinned at the center. For a moment, it seemed as though the photograph had shifted, her faint smile now a grimace. Elliot blinked, and the image was normal again.

"This is ridiculous," he muttered to himself, running a hand through his hair. He wasn't one to believe in the supernatural, and the idea that anything otherworldly could be happening was absurd. He was just tired, overworked, his nerves fraying under the weight of his plan.

Unexplained Sounds

The disturbances escalated. Objects in Elliot's apartment began to shift inexplicably—a pen rolling off his desk, a book falling from its shelf. The noises were subtle at first, easy to attribute to the natural settling of the building or a misplaced item. But as they grew more frequent, they became harder to ignore.

One evening, as Elliot was sharpening the knife he had chosen for his plan, he heard a faint whisper. It was indistinct, more a vibration than a sound, but it sent a chill down his spine. He paused, the blade held steady in his hand, and listened. The whisper came again, faint but persistent, like someone speaking just out of earshot.

"Who's there?" Elliot demanded, his voice sharp and commanding. The room remained silent, the shadows unchanged. But the whisper lingered in his mind, a faint echo that refused to fade.

Dismissal and Denial

Despite the growing unease, Elliot refused to let these incidents derail him. He had worked too hard, planned too carefully, to let himself be distracted by what he considered irrational fears. Every time doubt crept into his mind, he pushed it aside, focusing instead on the logic and precision of his plan.

"These are just distractions," he told himself as he adjusted the strings on the corkboard. "Nothing more."

He reminded himself of Delyla's routine, her predictability, her isolation. She was the perfect target, the culmination of months of work. Whatever strange occurrences were happening around him, they were irrelevant to the task at hand.

But the unease remained, a constant undercurrent that he couldn't entirely suppress. The shadows in the corners of his apartment seemed to grow darker, their edges blurring as if they were alive. The whispers became more frequent, their indistinct murmurs impossible to ignore. And always, there was the feeling of being watched, an unseen presence that seemed to grow stronger with each passing day.

The Lingering Doubt

For all his attempts to dismiss the incidents, Elliot couldn't shake the feeling that something was slipping out of his control. His plan, once so meticulously crafted, now felt fragile, as though it could collapse under the weight of these unexplained occurrences.

He began to question himself in small, quiet moments. What if these incidents weren't just distractions? What if they were signs of something more, something he couldn't understand or control? The thought was unsettling, a direct challenge to the logical, ordered worldview Elliot had always relied on.

But even as the doubt lingered, Elliot forced himself to focus. He couldn't afford to falter now, not when he was so close to achieving his goal. Delyla's life was a puzzle, and he was determined to solve it, no matter what strange forces seemed to be conspiring against him.

The unsettling moments Elliot experienced were more than distractions—they were harbingers of the chaos to come. The moving shadows, the whispers, and the feeling of being watched all hinted at a force beyond Elliot's control, a crack in the foundation of his carefully constructed world.

Despite his efforts to dismiss these incidents, they lingered in his thoughts, gnawing at the edges of his mind. Elliot had always prided himself on his ability to anticipate and adapt, but as the strange occurrences escalated, he began to realize that there were forces at play that defied his understanding.

And yet, he pressed on, clinging to the logic and precision that had always guided him. For Elliot, the plan was everything. But as the shadows deepened and the whispers grew louder, he couldn't ignore the growing sense that his perfect plan was unraveling—and that something far more sinister was watching him, waiting for the moment to strike.

Chapter 3: The Kill

The Build-Up

Elliot's life had always been defined by preparation. He prided himself on leaving nothing to chance, crafting plans so precise they felt infallible. Now, standing on the precipice of his ultimate act, he devoted every waking moment to ensuring perfection. Delyla, his chosen target, was the centerpiece of his plan, and Elliot was determined that nothing—not even his own mounting doubts—would derail what he had spent months constructing.

But as the day drew closer, cracks began to form in his confidence. For the first time in years, Elliot found himself doubting his ability to maintain control.

Meticulous Preparation

Elliot's preparations began with the timeline. He had mapped out every second of the day he intended to act, building a framework that left no room for improvisation. From the moment Delyla stepped off the bus in the morning to the instant she walked into the alley behind her apartment that evening, Elliot had planned it all.

His notebook became a battleground for his thoughts, pages filled with diagrams, lists, and annotations. The timeline was broken down into fifteen-minute increments, each marked with exacting detail. He wrote and rewrote the sequence until the words blurred on the page, driven by the belief that perfection was the only safeguard against failure.

"6:30 p.m.—Delyla leaves the café.
6:45 p.m.—Delyla approaches the alley.
6:46 p.m.—Action initiated."

Elliot's pen hovered over the final entry, his hand trembling slightly. He clenched his jaw and forced himself to write it out again, as if the act of committing it to paper would solidify his resolve. But the doubt remained, lingering just beneath the surface.

Running Through the Scenario

Elliot rehearsed the timeline obsessively, walking Delyla's route over and over again to ensure he knew every inch of it. He timed himself with a stopwatch, pacing the length of the alley until he could predict with near-perfect accuracy how long it would take for her to reach the critical point.

The knife, his chosen weapon, became an extension of himself. He practiced gripping it, testing its weight, imagining the feel of it in his hand at the moment of action. The blade was sharp, gleaming under the pale light of his desk lamp as he honed it nightly. Elliot whispered to himself as he worked, reciting the timeline like a mantra.

"Thirty seconds from the café to the crosswalk. Another fifteen to the alley entrance. Ten seconds to emerge from cover. Eleven seconds to act."

But no matter how many times he ran through the scenario, the same question gnawed at him: *What if something goes wrong?*

The Worst-Case Scenarios

Elliot's mind began to betray him, conjuring images of failure that refused to be silenced. He imagined Delyla noticing him as he stepped out of the shadows, her eyes widening in fear as she screamed for help. He saw her running, faster than he had anticipated, her footsteps echoing in the alley as she escaped into the night. He pictured bystanders appearing out of nowhere, their faces turning toward him with expressions of shock and horror.

The images grew darker. Elliot saw himself caught, his hands trembling as he dropped the knife and tried to flee. He imagined police officers surrounding him, their voices cold and commanding as they demanded he surrender. He saw the inside of a cell, the walls closing in as the weight of his failure suffocated him.

These thoughts haunted him, creeping into his mind at the most inopportune moments. He would wake in the middle of the night, his heart racing, the worst-case scenarios playing out in vivid detail behind his eyes. He told himself it was just his overactive mind, that these fears were the price of his meticulous nature. But the doubt refused to fade.

The Struggle to Reassure Himself

Elliot fought back against the doubt with logic. He reminded himself of the facts—the months of preparation, the precision of his timeline, the countless hours spent studying Delyla's routine. He had accounted for every variable, planned for every contingency.

Delyla was predictable, isolated, and oblivious to his presence. The plan was flawless.

But logic couldn't silence the unease that gnawed at the edges of his mind. There were too many unknowns, too many factors he couldn't control. He thought about the alley itself, its flickering streetlights casting erratic shadows on the walls. What if someone else was there? A passerby taking a shortcut or a homeless person seeking shelter?

He visited the alley every night, pacing its length, memorizing its layout. He studied the placement of the streetlights, the position of the dumpsters, the sounds of the city beyond its walls. But no matter how familiar he became with the space, the doubt remained. The alley felt alive, its shadows shifting and whispering as if mocking his attempts at control.

Physical and Mental Exhaustion

The strain of preparation began to take its toll on Elliot. His nights were restless, filled with fitful dreams and sudden awakenings. During the day, his focus wavered, his thoughts consumed by the plan and the nagging sense that it might unravel.

His body mirrored his mental state. His hands trembled as he adjusted the strings on the corkboard, and his chest felt tight as if the weight of his plan was pressing down on him physically. He stopped eating regularly, his meals reduced to hastily consumed snacks that did little to sustain him. The dark circles under his eyes grew more pronounced, a visual reminder of the toll his obsession was taking.

Elliot stared at himself in the bathroom mirror one morning, his reflection pale and gaunt. For a moment, he didn't recognize the man staring back at him. The confident, meticulous planner he had always been seemed to have disappeared, replaced by someone haunted, someone uncertain.

"You're fine," he whispered to his reflection, his voice firm despite the tremor in his hands. "You've done the work. You're prepared."

But the reassurance rang hollow, and the doubt lingered.

The Knife as a Focal Point

The knife became both a source of comfort and a symbol of his growing unease. Elliot spent hours sharpening it, testing its edge against strips of paper and soft blocks of wood. The act of preparing the blade was meditative, a way to channel his restless energy. He imagined the moment when he would use it, the precision and control it would require.

But the knife also reminded him of the stakes. Its gleaming blade was a physical manifestation of the plan, a tangible reminder that there was no turning back. Every time he held it, he felt a surge of adrenaline mixed with fear. What if his hand slipped? What if he hesitated?

Elliot forced himself to grip the knife tightly, his knuckles white against the handle. He practiced moving with it, stepping into the shadows of his apartment and mimicking the motions he had rehearsed in the alley. The more he practiced, the more confident he became. But the fear never truly disappeared.

Refining the Timeline

Despite his doubts, Elliot continued to refine the timeline, obsessing over every detail. He adjusted the timing of Delyla's walk, accounting for the possibility that she might linger at the café or pause to check her phone.

He calculated the exact number of steps it would take for him to emerge from the shadows and intercept her.

The timeline became an anchor, a way for Elliot to cling to the belief that he could control the outcome. He wrote it out over and over again, each iteration more detailed than the last. But as he stared at the pages, the words began to blur together, their meaning lost in the haze of his doubt.

Envisioning the Moment

Elliot spent hours envisioning the moment of action, replaying it in his mind like a scene from a film. He saw himself stepping out of the shadows, the knife steady in his hand, his movements precise and controlled. He imagined the look on Delyla's face, the shock and confusion that would give him the advantage.

But the vision didn't always go as planned. Sometimes, in the quiet of his apartment, Elliot's mind turned against him, conjuring images of failure. He saw Delyla fighting back, her screams echoing in the alley as she struggled against him. He imagined her escaping, her figure disappearing into the night while he stood frozen, the knife useless in his hand.

These visions left him shaken, his confidence eroded by the weight of his imagination. He tried to push them aside, to focus on the logic and precision of his plan. But the doubt was always there, lurking in the shadows, waiting to pounce.

As the day of the planned attack approached, Elliot's meticulous preparations were overshadowed by the growing weight of his doubts. Despite his obsessive attention to detail, his confidence wavered, his mind plagued by visions of worst-case scenarios. He clung to his timeline, his corkboard, and his knife, desperate to maintain control in the face of uncertainty.

But the doubt was relentless, an unshakable presence that gnawed at the edges of his resolve. Elliot told himself that he was prepared, that he had accounted for every variable. Yet, deep down, he knew that no amount of planning could eliminate the unknown.

The build-up to the act became a battle between Elliot's need for control and the chaos threatening to break through. And as the day drew nearer, the cracks in his confidence widened, foreshadowing the chaos that was about to engulf his carefully constructed world.

The Approach

The evening was perfect. Elliot had planned for this moment with painstaking precision, and as the hours ticked closer to his chosen time, he felt a strange mix of excitement and dread. Tonight, everything would come to fruition. All the weeks of preparation, the endless hours of surveillance, and the meticulous crafting of his plan had led him to this moment.

Delyla was just finishing her latte inside the small café, seated at her usual table by the window. Elliot stood across the street, partially hidden in the shadows of a storefront, his eyes fixed on her. His breathing was steady, his heartbeat deliberate. He had practiced this moment in his mind so many times that it felt as though he were reliving a memory rather than stepping into uncharted territory.

The streets were unusually quiet. The hum of the city, typically a constant backdrop to Elliot's nocturnal observations, seemed muffled tonight. The usual chorus of distant sirens, the murmur of passing conversations, and the clatter of footsteps on the pavement were absent, replaced by an eerie stillness that amplified every sound. It was as if the city itself were holding its breath.

Delyla Leaves the Café

Elliot's pulse quickened as Delyla rose from her seat, slipping her phone into her bag and donning her coat. She moved with the same calm efficiency he had come to expect, her gestures precise and unhurried. She walked to the counter, exchanged a polite smile with the barista, and stepped out onto the street.

Elliot watched as she paused briefly outside the café, adjusting the strap of her tote bag before beginning her walk home. She turned left, her pace steady, and Elliot waited three full seconds before following. It was crucial to maintain the right amount of distance—not so far that he might lose sight of her, but not so close that she might sense his presence.

His footsteps fell into rhythm with hers, the faint echo of his soles on the pavement blending with the sound of hers. He matched her pace perfectly, his body tense but controlled. His eyes never left her figure as she moved through the quiet streets, her silhouette illuminated by the soft glow of the streetlights.

The Eerily Quiet Streets

The silence was unnerving. The streets, usually bustling with activity at this hour, were nearly deserted. A lone car rolled by, its headlights cutting through the darkness before disappearing around a corner. A gust of wind rustled the leaves in the trees lining the sidewalk, the sound unnaturally loud in the stillness.

Elliot's senses were heightened, every noise and movement amplified by the quiet. He could hear the faint hum of the streetlights overhead, the soft shuffle of Delyla's steps on the pavement, and the rhythmic swish of her coat as she walked. His own breathing seemed too loud, an intrusive sound that broke the fragile silence.

The stillness wasn't just a backdrop—it was a character in the scene, adding a layer of tension that Elliot hadn't anticipated. It made every step feel significant, every moment charged with an almost unbearable weight.

Matching Her Movements

Elliot's focus was absolute. He mirrored Delyla's movements with a precision that bordered on mechanical. When she slowed to cross the street, he slowed. When she adjusted her bag, he adjusted his own posture, as if to mimic her actions without thinking. It was a dance, one he had rehearsed countless times in his mind.

He stayed close enough to keep her within his sight but far enough that she wouldn't hear his footsteps. He avoided the pools of light cast by the streetlamps, sticking to the shadows where he blended seamlessly into the background.

Delyla walked with her usual calm, her gaze fixed ahead. She didn't check her phone or look over her shoulder. She seemed completely unaware of Elliot's presence, her body language relaxed and unguarded. To her, it was just another Friday night, another walk home through familiar streets.

But to Elliot, every step was a test of his control. His heart pounded in his chest, each beat a reminder of the stakes. He couldn't afford a single misstep, a single moment of hesitation. This was the moment he had been preparing for, and failure wasn't an option.

The Shadows Begin to Shift

As they moved deeper into the quieter part of the neighborhood, the shadows seemed to take on a life of their own. Elliot noticed them out of the corner of his eye—subtle movements that didn't align with the stillness of the environment. At first, he dismissed them as tricks of the light, the result of his heightened nerves and the flickering streetlamps overhead.

But as they approached the alley near Delyla's apartment, the shadows grew more pronounced. They clung to the walls and pavement like living things, their edges shifting and blurring as if responding to an unseen force. Elliot's breath hitched, but he forced himself to stay focused.

"It's just your mind playing tricks on you," he muttered under his breath. He couldn't afford distractions, not now. The plan was all that mattered.

The Weight of the Knife

Elliot's hand brushed against the pocket of his coat where the knife rested, its weight both reassuring and ominous. He had chosen it carefully, selecting a blade that was sharp, balanced, and easy to handle. It was a tool of precision, an extension of the control he had worked so hard to achieve.

But now, as the moment drew closer, the knife felt heavier than it should have, its presence a constant reminder of what was about to happen. Elliot's fingers twitched, a faint tremor betraying the nerves he had tried so hard to suppress. He clenched his hand into a fist, forcing himself to focus.

"This is what you've been preparing for," he reminded himself. "You've accounted for everything. There's no reason to hesitate."

The Final Stretch

Delyla turned onto the street leading to her apartment, her pace unchanged. Elliot followed, his steps precise, his eyes locked on her figure. The alley was just ahead, its entrance marked by a flickering streetlamp that cast erratic patterns of light and shadow on the ground.

Elliot felt his pulse quicken as they neared the alley. This was it—the point of no return. His breath came in shallow bursts, the sound loud in his ears. He adjusted his grip on the strap of his bag, his fingers brushing against the edge of the knife hidden inside.

Delyla reached the entrance to the alley and paused briefly, glancing up at the streetlamp as it flickered above her. Elliot froze, his heart pounding. For a moment, it felt as though she had sensed his presence, her body tensing as she hesitated.

But then she stepped forward, disappearing into the shadows of the alley.

The Threshold of Action

Elliot stood at the edge of the alley, his body rigid with anticipation. The plan was simple:

step into the shadows, close the distance, and act with precision. He had rehearsed it so many times that it felt like second nature. But now, standing on the threshold of action, doubt began to creep in.

His mind raced with questions. What if she heard him approaching? What if she fought back? What if someone else appeared, shattering the carefully constructed silence of the night?

Elliot clenched his fists, his nails digging into his palms. He couldn't afford to think about what might go wrong. He had spent months preparing for this moment, and there was no turning back.

He took a deep breath, his eyes fixed on the darkness ahead. The shadows seemed to pulse and shift, their edges alive with movement. But Elliot ignored them, focusing instead on the faint sound of Delyla's footsteps as she moved deeper into the alley.

"This is it," he whispered to himself. "Stay in control."

The Weight of the Silence

The silence of the alley was suffocating. Every sound, no matter how small, felt amplified in the stillness. Elliot could hear the rustle of Delyla's coat, the soft scuff of her shoes on the pavement. He could hear his own breathing, shallow and uneven, as he forced himself to take the first step into the shadows.

The weight of the moment pressed down on him, a physical force that made his movements slow and deliberate. He felt the knife in his pocket, its presence both reassuring and oppressive. His fingers brushed against the handle, and he gripped it tightly, drawing strength from its cold, unyielding surface.

But as he moved deeper into the alley, the doubt returned, stronger than before. The shadows seemed to close in around him, their edges blurring and shifting as if alive. The silence grew heavier, the air thick with tension.

For the first time, Elliot felt the fragility of his plan. He had spent months crafting every detail, but now, in the darkness of the alley, he realized that control was an illusion. The chaos he had fought so hard to suppress was waiting for him, lurking in the shadows, ready to strike.

And as he took another step forward, the feeling of being watched returned, stronger than ever.

The Moment of Action

Elliot's heart pounded so loudly that it seemed to echo off the alley walls, a rhythm that matched the tension tightening every muscle in his body. He gripped the knife tightly in his hand, the blade gleaming faintly in the dim light filtering through the flickering streetlamp at the mouth of the alley. This was the moment. Every meticulous plan, every sleepless night, every careful step he had taken had led to this point. And yet, as he stood there, hidden in the shadows with the knife raised, poised to strike, a faint tremor ran through him.

He told himself it was adrenaline, a natural response to the enormity of the act he was about to commit. But somewhere, deep in the recesses of his mind, doubt began to take root.

The Perfect Setting

The alley was as familiar to Elliot as the layout of his own apartment. He had walked its length countless times, memorizing every crack in the pavement, every detail of the graffitied walls. It was narrow and poorly lit, the perfect place for an ambush. The single streetlamp at the entrance cast an erratic glow, its flickering light creating a dance of shadows that made it impossible to see clearly from the street. To anyone passing by, the alley would appear empty.

Elliot had chosen this spot precisely for its seclusion. Delyla walked this route every Friday evening, a predictable pattern he had confirmed over weeks of surveillance. She never deviated, never glanced over her shoulder. Her routine was a script, and tonight, Elliot intended to write the final scene.

But as Delyla moved deeper into the alley, her silhouette illuminated briefly by the streetlamp before disappearing into the shadows, the weight of the silence pressed down on Elliot. The world around him felt unnaturally still, as if the city itself were holding its breath.

The Knife in His Hand

The knife in Elliot's hand felt heavier than it should have, its cold metal pressing against his palm. He had chosen it carefully, spending hours researching blades that were sharp, reliable, and easy to wield. It was a tool, nothing more—a means to an end. Yet now, as he gripped it tightly, it seemed to carry a weight far beyond its physical presence.

He adjusted his grip, his fingers wrapping more securely around the handle. The action was meant to reassure him, but instead, it amplified the growing tension coursing through his body. He felt a faint tremor in his hand and clenched his fist, willing it to stop. This was not the time for hesitation.

"This is what you've prepared for," Elliot whispered to himself, his voice barely audible over the sound of his own breathing. "You're in control."

But even as he spoke the words, he felt the first pang of doubt—a sharp, unwelcome intrusion that cut through his carefully constructed resolve.

Delyla Pauses

Delyla was halfway down the alley when she stopped. The motion was so sudden, so unexpected, that Elliot froze in place. She tilted her head slightly, as if listening for something, her body tensing ever so slightly. The faint glow of the streetlamp caught the edge of her profile, highlighting the curve of her jaw and the furrow in her brow.

Elliot's breath hitched. Had she sensed him? He had been so careful, so silent. He remained perfectly still, his body pressed against the rough brick wall of the alley, the knife poised in his hand. The air around him felt charged, the silence broken only by the faint hum of the streetlamp and the distant sound of traffic.

For a moment, time seemed to stretch, the seconds dragging on interminably as Elliot watched her. His mind raced with possibilities. Had she heard him? Had she seen something in the shadows? Or was this just a momentary hesitation, an unconscious reaction to the eerie stillness of the alley?

The First Crack of Doubt

As Delyla stood there, unmoving, Elliot felt the first crack in his confidence. He had spent weeks convincing himself that she was the perfect target—predictable, isolated, and oblivious. But now, as she paused in the middle of the alley, he began to question everything.

What if he had been wrong? What if she wasn't as unaware as she seemed? What if, somehow, she knew he was there?

The thought sent a shiver down his spine, and for the first time, the knife in his hand felt like a foreign object. His grip slackened slightly, and he had to force himself to tighten it again. He couldn't afford to hesitate. Not now. Not when he was so close.

But the doubt lingered, a faint whisper in the back of his mind that he couldn't silence.

A Shift in Perspective

Elliot's doubt wasn't just about Delyla. It was about himself. For weeks, he had viewed her as a target, a puzzle to be solved, a means to an end. He had stripped her of her humanity, reducing her to a series of patterns and data points. But now, as he watched her standing in the alley, something shifted.

She wasn't just a figure in his plans anymore. She was a person—a living, breathing individual who existed beyond the confines of his notebook and corkboard. The realization unsettled him, throwing his carefully constructed narrative into disarray.

Elliot tried to push the thought away, focusing instead on the logic and precision that had always guided him. Delyla's routine was predictable. Her presence in the alley was expected. Everything about this moment was exactly as he had planned.

And yet, as he raised the knife higher, his body tensed for action, the doubt refused to fade.

The Weight of the Moment

The weight of the moment was almost unbearable. Elliot's breathing grew shallow, each inhale and exhale loud in his ears. His muscles ached from the tension of holding himself so still, and his heart pounded in his chest like a drumbeat.

He glanced at Delyla again, her figure still frozen in the middle of the alley. She had turned slightly, her head angled as if listening for something, her body poised to move. The streetlamp flickered overhead, casting shadows that danced around her like restless spirits.

Elliot's mind raced with conflicting thoughts. This was the moment he had been preparing for, the culmination of all his work. He couldn't let doubt derail him now. But the longer he stood there, the heavier the knife felt in his hand, and the more the silence pressed down on him.

The Flicker of Humanity

For a brief, fleeting moment, Elliot felt a pang of something he couldn't quite name. It wasn't regret or guilt—not exactly. It was more like a faint flicker of humanity, a reminder that Delyla wasn't just a target. She was a person.

He thought about the small details he had observed over the weeks: the way she smiled at the barista, the way she adjusted her bag strap, the way she had paused to help an elderly man retrieve his groceries. These moments, so insignificant at the time, now loomed large in his mind.

What was he about to do? Was this act really about control, or was it something else entirely? The question hung in the air, unspoken but heavy, as Elliot stood frozen in the shadows.

The Final Decision

Elliot knew he couldn't hesitate any longer. The longer he stood there, the greater the risk of being discovered. He tightened his grip on the knife, his knuckles white against the handle. His breath came in sharp, shallow bursts as he forced himself to focus.

"This is what you've been preparing for," he whispered to himself. "You can't stop now."

But even as he stepped forward, the knife raised, the doubt lingered. It was a crack in his confidence, a fracture in the foundation of his plan. And as he closed the distance between himself and Delyla, he couldn't shake the feeling that he had already lost control.

The moment of action was supposed to be the culmination of Elliot's meticulous planning, the perfect execution of a flawless plan. But as he stood in the shadows, the knife poised to strike, doubt began to creep in. Delyla's pause in the alley, her subtle tension, and the quiet humanity she exuded all worked to unsettle him, shaking his confidence and forcing him to question everything.

Elliot had always prided himself on his ability to maintain control, to suppress emotion and focus on the task at hand. But in this moment, as he prepared to act, he realized that control was an illusion. The chaos he had worked so hard to avoid was already beginning to unravel his carefully constructed world.

And as he took that final step forward, the knife glinting in the faint light, Elliot couldn't help but wonder if he was truly ready—or if he was about to step into a nightmare of his own making.

The Sudden Kill

The alley was quiet—eerily so. The dim streetlamp at its entrance flickered erratically, casting shifting shadows that danced along the brick walls. Elliot stood poised in the darkness, his body tense, the knife in his hand feeling heavier than it ever had before. He had rehearsed this moment endlessly in his mind, every step carefully calculated, every variable accounted for. But as he stood there, hidden in the shadows, watching Delyla pause in the middle of the alley, a strange unease crept over him.

Delyla turned her head slightly, as if sensing something. Her hesitation was subtle, but it sent a ripple through Elliot's carefully maintained resolve. His grip on the knife tightened, his knuckles whitening as he struggled to regain control. This was it. This was the moment he had planned for. All he needed to do was step forward, close the distance, and act.

But before he could move, a sudden sound shattered the fragile silence—a sharp, jarring noise that cut through the night like a blade.

The Disruption

The sound was deafening in the stillness. A car alarm blared from somewhere nearby, its shrill wail echoing through the narrow alley. The noise startled both Elliot and Delyla, breaking the tension in an instant. Delyla froze, her body stiffening as she turned her head sharply toward the source of the noise.

Her posture, once relaxed and unguarded, became tense and alert.

Elliot felt his heart leap into his throat. The noise wasn't part of the plan. It was an intrusion, a chaotic variable that threatened to unravel everything he had worked for. He remained motionless, his back pressed against the cold brick wall, his breath shallow as he watched Delyla.

For a moment, she seemed unsure of what to do. Her eyes darted toward the entrance of the alley, then back to the path ahead of her. Her hand tightened on the strap of her tote bag, her fingers clenching as if preparing to bolt. Elliot knew he couldn't wait any longer. The window of opportunity was closing, and if he hesitated now, it would be lost forever.

The Attack

Adrenaline surged through Elliot's body as he pushed himself off the wall and stepped forward. His movements were quick but unsteady, driven more by instinct than by the careful precision he had envisioned. He closed the distance between himself and Delyla in a matter of seconds, his shoes scuffing against the pavement as he moved.

Delyla turned at the sound, her eyes widening in shock as she saw him emerge from the shadows. She opened her mouth to scream, but Elliot didn't give her the chance. He lunged forward, raising the knife in his hand and bringing it down with more force than he intended.

The blade struck her side, piercing through the fabric of her coat and into flesh. Delyla let out a sharp cry, her body jerking as she staggered backward. Her bag slipped from her shoulder, falling to the ground with a dull thud. Elliot pulled the knife free and struck again, his movements frantic and uncoordinated. Blood spattered onto the pavement, the metallic scent filling the air as Delyla collapsed to her knees.

The Chaos of the Moment

Nothing about the attack went as Elliot had planned. In his mind, the act had always been clean and efficient—a single, precise strike followed by a swift escape. But the reality was far messier. The knife felt awkward in his hand, its handle slick with sweat. His breathing was ragged, his chest heaving as he struggled to maintain control.

Delyla's movements were chaotic, her body writhing as she fought against the attack. Her hands clawed at the ground, her fingers scraping against the pavement as she tried to push herself up. Her eyes locked onto Elliot's, wide with a mixture of fear and confusion.

Elliot hesitated for a moment, frozen by the intensity of her gaze. It wasn't supposed to be like this. She wasn't supposed to look at him, wasn't supposed to fight back. She was supposed to be an object, a puzzle piece that fit neatly into his plan. But now, in the chaos of the moment, she felt undeniably real.

The car alarm continued to blare in the distance, its piercing wail mingling with the sound of Delyla's ragged breaths. Elliot raised the knife again, his hands trembling as he brought it down one final time. The blade struck her chest, and Delyla's body went limp, collapsing onto the ground in a motionless heap.

The Aftermath

For a long moment, Elliot stood frozen, his chest heaving as he stared down at Delyla's lifeless body. Blood pooled around her, seeping into the cracks of the pavement and staining the hem of her coat. The knife hung limply in his hand, its blade slick and glinting faintly in the dim light.

He felt a strange mix of emotions—triumph, fear, and something he couldn't quite name. This was what he had been working toward, what he had planned for so meticulously. And yet, as he stood there, he didn't feel the satisfaction he had expected. Instead, he felt hollow, his body trembling with the weight of what he had done.

The car alarm continued to blare, the noise grating against his nerves. Elliot's eyes darted toward the entrance of the alley, his mind racing with the need to escape. But his legs refused to move, his body paralyzed by the enormity of the moment.

Humiliation and Self-Loathing

As the adrenaline began to fade, humiliation crept in. Elliot's hands, still gripping the knife, trembled uncontrollably. He had imagined this moment so many times, always with the same image of precision and control. But the reality had been far from perfect. The attack had been clumsy, frantic, and filled with hesitation. He had let the car alarm distract him, allowed Delyla's resistance to shake his resolve.

"You were sloppy," he muttered to himself, his voice barely audible over the din of the alarm. "You let it get out of hand."

The words echoed in his mind, feeding a growing sense of self-loathing. Elliot had always prided himself on his meticulous nature, his ability to maintain control in even the most chaotic situations. But tonight, he had failed. He had let the chaos dictate his actions, and the result was a messy, humiliating scene that felt entirely out of his control.

The Need to Escape

The weight of the moment finally broke through Elliot's paralysis. He knew he couldn't stay in the alley any longer. The car alarm was drawing too much attention, and the risk of someone discovering him was growing with every passing second.

He wiped the blade of the knife on Delyla's coat, his movements hurried and mechanical. His hands were slick with sweat and blood, and he struggled to slip the knife back into his pocket. His breath came in short, panicked bursts as he scanned the alley for any sign of movement.

The silence that followed was oppressive, broken only by the distant sound of the alarm. Elliot forced himself to move, stepping over Delyla's body as he made his way toward the entrance of the alley. He kept his head down, his shoulders hunched, trying to make himself as inconspicuous as possible.

Every step felt like an eternity, the sound of his shoes on the pavement loud in the stillness. He reached the mouth of the alley and paused, glancing back one last time at Delyla's body. Her figure was barely visible in the dim light, a motionless shadow against the bloodstained pavement.

Elliot swallowed hard and turned away, disappearing into the night.

The Weight of the Kill

As Elliot walked away from the scene, the weight of what he had done settled heavily on his shoulders. His mind raced with conflicting thoughts—relief that it was over, shame at how poorly it had gone, and a growing fear of what might come next.

He had imagined this moment as the pinnacle of his work, a testament to his precision and control. But instead, it felt like a failure, a reminder of his own fallibility. The image of Delyla's lifeless body lingered in his mind, her wide, terrified eyes staring up at him even in death.

Elliot clenched his fists, his nails digging into his palms as he tried to push the memory away. This wasn't the time for reflection. He needed to focus on the next steps—disposing of the knife, cleaning himself up, and ensuring there was no trace of his presence at the scene.

But no matter how hard he tried, the doubt remained. The chaos of the moment had shaken him, forcing him to confront the possibility that he wasn't as in control as he had always believed. And as he disappeared into the shadows of the city, Elliot couldn't shake the feeling that this was only the beginning of something far darker than he had ever anticipated.

Elliot's Aftermath

The walk back to his apartment felt like an eternity. Each step dragged against the weight of his thoughts, and the world around him blurred into an oppressive haze of shadow and sound. Elliot had never known shame like this. It was visceral, clawing at him from the inside out, a constant reminder of how miserably he had failed his own expectations.

The streetlights flickered as he passed beneath them, their dim glow barely illuminating the empty streets. The muffled sound of a distant car engine echoed faintly, but the world otherwise felt abandoned, as if it too recoiled from the chaos Elliot had unleashed. His hands were clammy and trembling, his coat heavy with the memory of the alley. The knife in his pocket was an unbearable weight, its cold metal a physical reminder of his clumsy failure.

He didn't look at anyone. He didn't think about anything but his destination. He needed to get home—back to his sanctuary, back to the place where he could confront himself away from the prying eyes of a world that now seemed so much more hostile.

The Storm Within

When Elliot finally reached his apartment building, he fumbled with his keys, his hands shaking so violently that it took several attempts to fit the key into the lock. He pushed the door open with more force than necessary, the creak of the hinges echoing unnaturally loud in the quiet hallway.

The space inside was as dim and cluttered as he had left it, but tonight it felt different. The comforting hum of the refrigerator and the ticking of the wall clock were no longer familiar sounds—they were an assault, reminders of the life he had tried to construct around his obsession, a life that now seemed fragile and meaningless.

He slammed the door shut behind him and threw his bag onto the floor, the sound jarring in the otherwise still apartment. His breathing was uneven, his chest heaving as he paced the length of the room, his hands pulling at his hair in frustration.

"This wasn't supposed to happen," he muttered to himself, his voice shaking with anger. "It wasn't supposed to be like this."

He turned toward the corkboard, the centerpiece of his life for the past several months. Delyla's photograph still hung in the center, surrounded by maps, notes, and red strings meticulously arranged to tell the story of her life. It was supposed to have been a testament to his precision, his control. But now, it felt like a cruel mockery, a reminder of everything that had gone wrong.

The Corkboard's Collapse

With a sudden, furious motion, Elliot tore Delyla's photograph from the board. The sound of the pin ripping free was sharp and satisfying, but it wasn't enough. He crumpled the photograph in his hand, his knuckles whitening as he squeezed it tightly.

His rage grew with every passing second. He grabbed at the strings, yanking them loose in one violent motion. They came undone easily, falling to the floor in tangled heaps. The maps and notes followed, ripped from their tacks and scattered across the room like confetti.

Elliot's movements were wild and uncoordinated, driven by pure frustration. The corkboard, once his greatest source of pride, was reduced to a bare and battered frame, its surface pockmarked with holes. He stared at it for a moment, his chest heaving, before slamming his fist against it with a force that sent it crashing to the floor.

The room fell silent, save for Elliot's ragged breathing. He stood in the middle of the chaos he had created, his hands trembling at his sides. For the first time in years, he felt powerless, his carefully constructed world crumbling around him.

Hesitation's Haunting Echo

As the adrenaline began to fade, the anger gave way to something far worse: shame. Elliot sank to the floor, his back against the wall, surrounded by the remnants of his corkboard. He ran his hands through his hair, his fingers pulling at the strands as he replayed the events of the alley in his mind.

The hesitation had been brief, but it had cost him everything. He had frozen in the critical moment, his confidence shattered by the sudden noise of the car alarm and Delyla's unexpected pause. Instead of the clean, precise kill he had envisioned, the act had been frantic and sloppy, a chaotic mess that left him feeling exposed and vulnerable.

He clenched his fists, his nails digging into his palms as he tried to suppress the memories. But they wouldn't fade. The image of Delyla's wide, terrified eyes haunted him, her gaze locking onto his in the final moments before the knife struck. She hadn't been a target in that moment—she had been a person, alive and desperate. And he had faltered.

"Why did you hesitate?" he whispered to himself, his voice barely audible. The question echoed in his mind, growing louder with each repetition. Why had he faltered? Why hadn't he been able to maintain control?

The Knife's Burden

Elliot's eyes drifted to the knife, which lay on the floor where he had dropped it in his frenzy. Its blade was still smeared with Delyla's blood, the dark stains a stark reminder of his actions. He reached for it hesitantly, his fingers brushing against the cold metal before pulling back.

The knife, which had once been a symbol of his precision and control, now felt like an accusation. It was proof of his failure, a tangible representation of the chaos he had allowed to consume him. He hated it. He hated himself for needing it, for relying on it, for failing to wield it with the skill and confidence he had spent months cultivating.

Elliot finally picked it up, his hand trembling as he turned it over in his palm. He wanted to clean it, to erase the evidence of his mistake. But the thought of touching the blade, of confronting what it represented, was too much. He set it back down, his fingers lingering on the handle for a moment before letting go.

The Weight of Isolation

The apartment felt suffocating, its walls closing in around him as the silence stretched on. Elliot had always thrived in isolation, finding solace in the solitude of his meticulously controlled world. But now, that same solitude felt oppressive, amplifying the weight of his failure.

He thought about Delyla, about the life he had taken and the mess he had left behind. He had chosen her because she was predictable, isolated, and seemingly insignificant. But in the end, it hadn't been about her at all—it had been about him. His need for control, his desire to prove himself, his obsession with perfection.

And he had failed.

Elliot buried his face in his hands, his shoulders shaking as he fought back the tears threatening to spill. He didn't cry—he hadn't cried in years—but the weight of his emotions was almost unbearable. He had spent so much time convincing himself that he was different, that he was in control. But tonight, he had been just as chaotic and flawed as everyone else.

The Lingering Gaze

As Elliot sat in the wreckage of his apartment, a strange sensation crept over him. It was subtle at first—a faint prickling at the back of his neck, a sense of being watched. He froze, his breath catching in his throat as his eyes darted toward the shadows in the corner of the room.

There was nothing there. The apartment was empty, just as it had always been. But the feeling didn't fade. It clung to him, an oppressive weight that made his skin crawl.

Elliot shook his head, forcing himself to look away. He was imagining things. The events of the night had shaken him, and his mind was playing tricks on him. There was no one else in the apartment. There couldn't be.

But even as he tried to dismiss the sensation, it lingered, a constant reminder that he was no longer alone with his thoughts.

The Beginning of Obsession

As the hours stretched on, Elliot's anger gave way to obsession. He couldn't stop replaying the events of the alley in his mind, analyzing every detail, every misstep. The hesitation, the chaos, the sloppy execution—it all consumed him, a fire that burned hotter with each passing moment.

He needed to understand why he had failed. He needed to confront the part of himself that had faltered, to dissect it and strip it away so that it could never happen again. The corkboard might have been destroyed, but his obsession remained intact, stronger now than it had ever been.

Elliot pushed himself to his feet, his movements slow and deliberate. He began to gather the scattered remnants of the corkboard, his hands shaking as he sorted through the papers and strings. He didn't know what he was building, but he knew he couldn't stop. The plan had failed, but there would be another. There had to be.

Because failure wasn't an option. Not again.

The aftermath of Elliot's failed kill was more than just a moment of reckoning—it was a catalyst. His rage and shame at his hesitation shattered the illusion of control he had worked so hard to create, forcing him to confront the chaos within himself. The destruction of the corkboard was a symbolic act, a reflection of the turmoil consuming him as he struggled to process what had happened.

But even in the depths of his despair, Elliot's obsession persisted. The need for control, for perfection, refused to be silenced. And as he stood in the ruins of his apartment, surrounded by the fragments of his carefully constructed world, he knew that this was only the beginning.

The failure would haunt him, but it would also drive him. Because Elliot wasn't just running from his mistakes—he was running toward something darker, something he could no longer control.

Subtle Supernatural Hints

The apartment was eerily quiet. Elliot sat on the edge of his bed, staring blankly at the dimly lit room, his thoughts swirling in a chaotic storm of shame and anger. The events of the alley replayed in his mind on an endless loop—the hesitation, the car alarm, the sloppy execution, and Delyla's lifeless eyes staring up at him in those final moments. The weight of the knife in his hand, the smell of blood in the air, and the slick pavement beneath his feet felt as vivid now as they had in the moment.

But now, in the suffocating stillness of his apartment, the world seemed different. The hum of the refrigerator, the ticking of the clock, the faint creaks of the aging building— all the usual noises that Elliot had once ignored—felt louder, more invasive. The air was thick, heavy with something he couldn't name. And though he was alone, he couldn't shake the sensation that he was being watched.

The Knife Falls

The knife sat on the desk across the room, its blade cleaned of blood but still carrying the memory of what had transpired. Elliot had placed it there after returning home, its precise position carefully chosen as if to restore some semblance of order to his shattered world. It sat perfectly parallel to the edge of the desk, its handle pointing toward the corkboard where Delyla's torn photograph once hung.

Elliot's eyes drifted toward the blade, its gleaming surface catching the faint light from the desk lamp. It was just an object—a tool. It had no power, no agency. And yet, as he stared at it, a flicker of unease crept into his mind. The knife felt different now, almost as though it carried the weight of the act it had been used to commit.

He forced himself to look away, running a hand through his hair and letting out a long, shaky breath. But as he turned his gaze back toward the corkboard, the sound of metal hitting wood shattered the silence.

The knife had fallen.

Elliot froze, his body stiffening as his eyes darted to the desk. The knife now lay on the floor, the blade reflecting the dim light in sharp, jagged angles. He stared at it, his mind racing. He had placed it carefully—he was sure of it. There was no reason for it to have fallen.

His first thought was that the desk had shifted, but the surface was level, and there was nothing nearby that could have knocked it over. He remained seated, his breathing shallow, his gaze locked on the knife as if expecting it to move again.

"It's just the angle," he muttered to himself, his voice hollow in the stillness. "Nothing more."

He stood slowly, his footsteps cautious as he approached the desk. His hand trembled slightly as he reached down to pick up the knife, his fingers brushing against the cold metal. For a moment, he thought he felt a faint vibration, but it stopped as quickly as it had started. He set the knife back on the desk, this time securing it more firmly against the wooden surface.

"It's nothing," he repeated, though the words felt empty.

The Corkboard Moves

Elliot's attention turned to the corkboard, now stripped of its strings, maps, and most of its notes. Only a few pieces of paper remained tacked to its surface, including a smaller, crumpled photograph of Delyla he had retrieved from the chaos of his earlier outburst. He had pinned it back to the board, unable to fully let go of the obsession that had consumed him for months.

As he stood there, staring at the photograph, something caught his eye. The edges of the photo seemed to shift ever so slightly, as though the paper were trembling in an invisible breeze. Elliot blinked, leaning closer to inspect it. The photograph remained still, its faintly smiling subject staring back at him with the same detached expression she always had.

He took a step back, shaking his head. "I'm just tired," he told himself. "I need sleep."

But as he turned away, the photograph shifted again, this time sliding slightly downward. The tack holding it in place tilted, and the photo hung crookedly, as though it had been disturbed by an unseen hand. Elliot whipped around, his eyes wide, his pulse racing.

The room was still. The air felt heavy, almost oppressive, but there was no movement, no sound except for the faint hum of the refrigerator. He approached the corkboard slowly, his footsteps tentative, and reached out to straighten the photograph. His fingers hesitated just before touching it, as if expecting the paper to move again.

"It's just the tack," he said aloud, his voice shaky. "It wasn't secure."

He pressed the tack more firmly into the corkboard, ensuring the photograph was perfectly aligned. But as he stepped back, the unease in his chest refused to dissipate.

The Feeling of Being Watched

The sensation of being watched had been with Elliot since the moment he returned to the apartment, but now it was stronger, more palpable. It was as if the shadows in the corners of the room had eyes, silent and unblinking, fixed on his every move. He turned quickly, scanning the space, but there was nothing there—just the familiar furniture, the cluttered desk, the bare walls.

Still, the feeling persisted, wrapping around him like a cold, invisible hand. He moved to the window, pulling back the curtain and peering out into the street below. It was empty, the only movement coming from the flickering streetlamp at the corner. Yet the sensation remained, pressing against him like a weight he couldn't shake.

Elliot closed the curtain and stepped away, his movements stiff and mechanical. He tried to convince himself that it was paranoia, a natural reaction to the stress of the night. But deep down, he knew it was something more. The air in the apartment felt different now—charged, as though it carried an energy he couldn't explain.

Dismissal and Denial

Elliot returned to the corkboard, his eyes scanning the few remaining notes and photographs. He needed to focus, to ground himself in the logical world he had spent his life building. The knife falling, the photograph shifting, the oppressive feeling in the air—these were just coincidences, he told himself. Tricks of the mind brought on by exhaustion and stress.

"You're imagining things," he said firmly, though the tremor in his voice betrayed his unease. "This is all in your head."

He gathered the scattered remnants of his earlier outburst, sorting through the papers and placing them in neat stacks on the desk. The act of organizing calmed him slightly, giving him a sense of control amidst the chaos. But the unease lingered, gnawing at the edges of his mind like a faint, persistent whisper.

The Whisper of Doubt

As the hours stretched on, the silence in the apartment grew heavier. Elliot tried to distract himself, reviewing his notes and re-reading the timeline he had so meticulously crafted.

But no matter how hard he tried to focus, his thoughts kept returning to the strange occurrences of the night.

The knife falling. The photograph moving. The feeling of being watched. They weren't part of the plan, weren't part of the ordered, logical world Elliot had created for himself. And the more he thought about them, the more they unsettled him.

He glanced at the corkboard again, his eyes drawn to Delyla's photograph. Her face seemed different now, her faint smile taking on a quality he couldn't quite define. It was as if she were mocking him, her expression a silent reminder of his failure.

Elliot shook his head, tearing his gaze away from the photograph. "It's just a picture," he muttered, but the words felt hollow.

The Growing Unease

By the time the first rays of dawn began to filter through the curtains, Elliot was still awake, his body heavy with exhaustion but his mind too restless to find sleep. The apartment, once his sanctuary, now felt like a prison, its walls closing in around him with every passing moment.

He paced the room, his hands clenching and unclenching at his sides as he struggled to make sense of what was happening. The knife, the photograph, the oppressive air—it all felt connected somehow, part of a larger pattern he couldn't yet see. And though he tried to dismiss it as paranoia, a small, insistent voice in the back of his mind whispered otherwise.

Something was wrong. Something had changed. And for the first time in his life, Elliot wasn't sure if he was in control.

The night after the botched kill marked the beginning of a shift in Elliot's carefully ordered world. The subtle supernatural hints—the knife falling inexplicably, Delyla's photograph seeming to move on its own, and the oppressive feeling of being watched—were easy enough to dismiss on their own. But together, they created a sense of unease that Elliot couldn't ignore.

He told himself it was all in his head, a product of exhaustion and stress. But deep down, he knew the truth. The world he had so meticulously constructed was beginning to unravel, and something far darker was waiting in the shadows, ready to consume him.

Chapter 4:
Signs of Haunting

Unexplained Movements

Elliot's apartment had always been his sanctuary. A place of routine, control, and order, it was a reflection of the meticulous precision that governed his life. Every object had a purpose, every surface was carefully maintained, and nothing was ever out of place. But now, in the wake of Delyla's death, that sense of control was unraveling.

The air inside his apartment felt different, heavier somehow, as though it carried the weight of something unseen. The usual hum of the refrigerator and the faint ticking of the wall clock no longer provided comfort; instead, they grated on his nerves, their rhythms out of sync with the disarray in his mind. And then, slowly but unmistakably, the objects around him began to move.

The First Sign

It started innocuously enough—a book falling from his desk. Elliot had been pacing the room, his thoughts consumed by the events of the previous night. The memory of the botched kill, of Delyla's wide, terrified eyes and the chaotic mess he had made, played on an endless loop in his mind. His hands clenched and unclenched at his sides as he muttered to himself, trying to regain some semblance of control.

The sound of the book hitting the floor startled him. He froze mid-step, his head snapping toward the desk where the book had been. It lay on the floor now, splayed open, its pages crumpled where they pressed against the hardwood.

For a moment, Elliot stared at it, his mind struggling to process what he was seeing. He was certain he hadn't touched it. The book had been sitting neatly on the edge of the desk, exactly where he had left it. There was no breeze, no sudden movement, nothing that could explain how it had fallen.

"It must have been the angle," he muttered to himself, walking over to pick it up. "I must have knocked it earlier without realizing."

He placed the book back on the desk, aligning it carefully with the edge. But as he stepped back, a faint unease settled in his chest. The book felt heavier in his hands than it should have, its presence more significant than he could explain.

The Knife Moves

The next incident was harder to dismiss. Elliot had placed the knife on his desk earlier that evening, its blade cleaned and its position carefully chosen. It was a tool, an object of purpose, and its placement was deliberate—a way for him to reclaim the control he had lost in the alley.

But when he returned to the desk later that night, the knife was gone.

Panic flared in his chest as he scanned the surface of the desk, his eyes darting over the cluttered papers and scattered notes. The knife wasn't where he had left it. His heart raced as he began searching the room, his movements frantic and uncoordinated.

He found it on the kitchen counter.

The sight of the knife, lying there as though it had been casually placed, sent a chill down his spine. He hadn't moved it. He was certain of that. He had left it on the desk, its blade parallel to the edge, its handle pointing toward the corkboard. There was no reason for it to be in the kitchen.

Elliot picked it up slowly, his fingers brushing against the cold metal. He turned it over in his hand, inspecting it for any sign that it had been disturbed. But the knife was unchanged, its blade still sharp, its surface unmarked.

"Exhaustion," he whispered to himself, his voice barely audible. "That's all this is. You're exhausted."

But even as he tried to dismiss the incident, a flicker of paranoia began to take root.

The Growing Unease

The movements continued. Objects that had been in one place when Elliot went to bed would be somewhere else when he woke up. A chair pushed slightly away from the table. A pen that had been on his desk now lying on the floor. A photograph of Delyla, pinned to the corkboard, tilted at an angle as though someone had touched it.

At first, Elliot tried to rationalize it. He told himself that he was tired, that his mind was playing tricks on him. He had been under a great deal of stress—anyone would start to lose track of small details under such circumstances.

But the incidents were becoming harder to ignore. Each time something moved, it felt deliberate, purposeful, as though it was meant to catch his attention. And the more it happened, the more Elliot felt the presence of something he couldn't explain.

The air in the apartment grew heavier with each passing day, the silence more oppressive. The sensation of being watched, which had first appeared the night after Delyla's death, became a constant companion. It followed him everywhere, wrapping around him like an invisible shroud.

Paranoia Takes Root

Elliot began to question everything. His once-orderly apartment now felt alien to him, its familiar corners and shadows transformed into places of unease. He double-checked the placement of every object before leaving the room, memorizing their positions so that he could tell if they had moved. But even this provided little comfort. No matter how careful he was, something always seemed to change.

The sensation of being watched grew stronger. It wasn't just a vague feeling anymore—it was tangible, oppressive. Elliot found himself glancing over his shoulder constantly, his eyes scanning the room for any sign of movement. But there was never anything there. Just the empty apartment, silent and still.

At night, the unease became unbearable. Elliot lay in bed, his body tense, his eyes fixed on the ceiling as he listened for the faintest sound. The creak of the floorboards, the hum of the refrigerator, the rustle of papers on the desk—every noise felt significant, a reminder that he was no longer alone.

The Corkboard Comes Alive

One evening, as Elliot sat at his desk trying to focus on his notes, the corkboard caught his attention. It was still in disarray from his earlier outburst, its surface bare except for a few scattered photographs and scraps of paper. Delyla's photograph remained pinned at the center, its edges slightly frayed from being torn and re-pinned multiple times.

As Elliot stared at the photograph, he thought he saw it move. It was subtle, almost imperceptible—a faint shift, as though the paper had trembled in an invisible breeze. He blinked, leaning closer to inspect it, but the photograph remained still.

"Just my imagination," he muttered, shaking his head.

But then it moved again. This time, it slid downward slightly, the tack holding it in place tilting at an angle. Elliot froze, his breath catching in his throat. His eyes darted to the other papers on the board, but they were unchanged. Only Delyla's photograph had moved.

His hand trembled as he reached out to straighten it, his fingers brushing against the smooth surface of the paper. The air around the corkboard felt colder than the rest of the room, a faint chill that raised goosebumps on his skin.

"It's just the tack," he said aloud, his voice shaky. "It wasn't secure."

He pressed the photograph back into place, ensuring the tack was firmly embedded in the cork. But as he stepped back, he couldn't shake the feeling that it was watching him.

A World Out of Control

Elliot's world, once defined by order and precision, was slipping through his fingers. The movements of the objects, the oppressive silence, the subtle shifts in the corkboard—all of it pointed to something he couldn't explain, something that defied the logical framework he had built his life around.

He tried to dismiss it as exhaustion, as paranoia brought on by the stress of the kill. But deep down, he knew the truth. Something was happening. Something he couldn't control.

The unease grew with each passing day, a constant presence that gnawed at the edges of his mind. Elliot's sanctuary had become a prison, its walls closing in around him as the objects within seemed to conspire against him. And though he tried to hold onto the belief that he was in control, that belief was slipping away.

The unexplained movements in Elliot's apartment were more than just minor disruptions—they were a manifestation of the chaos that had begun to consume his life. The book falling, the knife moving, the photograph shifting on the corkboard—each incident chipped away at his sense of control, feeding the paranoia that had taken root in his mind.

Elliot tried to dismiss the events as coincidences, as tricks of an exhausted mind. But the growing unease in his chest, the oppressive feeling of being watched, and the undeniable sense that something was wrong told him otherwise. His world, once defined by order and precision, was unraveling. And as the movements continued, Elliot began to realize that he was no longer the master of his own domain.

Something else was at work, and it was only just beginning.

Auditory Disturbances

Elliot had always thrived in silence. To him, silence was order; it was clarity. His apartment was a sanctuary, a place where the chaos of the outside world was kept at bay, and every sound carried purpose—a drawer opening, a page turning, the click of a pen against paper. But now, the silence was gone, replaced by something far more insidious.

It started with faint whispers late at night, barely perceptible over the ambient hum of the refrigerator or the muffled ticking of the wall clock. At first, Elliot dismissed them, chalking it up to his overactive imagination or the remnants of stress clawing at his subconscious. But as the nights stretched into days, and the whispers grew louder and more persistent, Elliot realized he was no longer alone.

The First Whispers

The first time Elliot noticed the whispers, it was just past midnight. He was sitting at his desk, surrounded by the remnants of his corkboard and scattered notes, the dim glow of his desk lamp casting long shadows across the room. The air was thick with the tension of his thoughts as he reviewed the details of his failed kill, the moments of hesitation that had cost him control.

At first, he thought the sound was coming from outside—a faint, almost rhythmic murmuring that ebbed and flowed like a distant conversation. He stood, moving to the window and peering out into the darkened street below. The city was quiet, the only movement the flicker of a streetlamp at the corner. There was no one outside, no voices to explain the sound.

Elliot returned to his desk, the faint whispers still audible. They were so soft, so indistinct, that they could have been mistaken for the rustling of leaves or the creak of the building settling. But as he sat there, straining to listen, he realized the sound wasn't coming from outside—it was inside the apartment.

Persistent and Unsettling

The whispers became a nightly occurrence, faint and fleeting at first but growing more persistent with each passing day. They seemed to come from nowhere and everywhere at once, echoing through the apartment as if carried on an unseen breeze. The words were indistinct, a jumble of sounds that Elliot couldn't quite make out, but their presence was undeniable.

He tried to ignore them, focusing instead on his notes and the plans he had begun to piece back together. But the whispers refused to be silenced. They crept into his thoughts, disrupting his concentration and pulling his attention away from the task at hand.

Elliot's sleep, already restless, became even more fractured. He would wake in the middle of the night to the faint sound of murmuring, his body tense and his heart racing. He lay in bed, staring at the ceiling as the whispers filled the room, their cadence rising and falling like the tide.

The Words Begin to Take Shape

The turning point came on the fifth night, when the whispers began to form words.

Elliot had been pacing the apartment, unable to sleep, his nerves frayed by the weight of the unease that had settled over him. The whispers had been faint and indistinct as usual, a low murmur that seemed to come from the walls themselves. But then, as he passed by the corkboard, he heard it—a single, clear word cutting through the haze of sound.

"Why?"

The word stopped Elliot in his tracks. He turned sharply, his eyes scanning the room for any sign of movement. But the apartment was still, the shadows in the corners unchanged. The whispers faded for a moment, and Elliot wondered if he had imagined it. But then they returned, louder this time, and the words became clearer.

"You knew."

The voice was soft, almost gentle, but it sent a chill down Elliot's spine. He felt his chest tighten as the words echoed through the apartment, their meaning heavy with accusation. He clenched his fists, his nails digging into his palms as he tried to steady his breathing.

"This isn't real," he muttered to himself. "It's just your mind playing tricks on you."

But even as he said the words, he knew they weren't true. The whispers were real. They were inside the apartment, and they were speaking to him.

Desperate Rationalization

Elliot spent the following days trying to rationalize the whispers. He told himself it was exhaustion, the result of too many sleepless nights and the stress of his failed kill. He read articles about auditory hallucinations, convincing himself that his mind was simply reacting to the trauma of the past week.

But no matter how hard he tried to dismiss the whispers, they persisted. They grew louder at night, filling the apartment with their faint, accusatory words. "Why?" they would ask, their tone both curious and condemning.

"You knew." The phrases repeated like a mantra, their cadence slow and deliberate.

Elliot began to feel as though the whispers were probing him, searching for something he couldn't define. They seemed to know him, to see through the carefully constructed facade he had built around himself. The sensation was unbearable, a constant reminder that he was no longer in control.

A Shifting Presence

The whispers weren't the only thing that changed in the apartment. The air itself seemed to carry a weight, a subtle pressure that pressed against Elliot's chest and made it difficult to breathe. The shadows in the corners grew darker, their edges blurring as if they were alive. And always, there was the feeling of being watched—a sensation that had begun as a faint unease but had now become a constant presence.

Elliot tried to combat the paranoia by throwing himself into his work, reconstructing his corkboard and refining his plans. But the whispers followed him everywhere. They interrupted his thoughts, weaving their way into his mind like a persistent thread that refused to be unraveled.

One night, as Elliot sat at his desk, the whispers grew louder than ever. They seemed to come from directly behind him, their words clear and insistent.

"You knew. You knew."

Elliot whipped around, his chair scraping against the floor as he searched the room for the source of the sound. But there was nothing there—just the empty apartment, silent except for the ticking of the clock on the wall.

His chest heaved as he tried to catch his breath, his mind racing. He clenched his fists, his nails biting into his palms as he fought to suppress the fear rising within him.

"You're losing it," he whispered to himself. "You're letting this get to you."

But the words felt hollow, a futile attempt to deny what he knew deep down: he wasn't alone.

The Growing Accusation

The whispers began to change, their tone shifting from curiosity to accusation. The words became sharper, their cadence more urgent. "Why?" they asked, their voices overlapping in a discordant chorus. "Why did you do it?"

Elliot covered his ears, trying to block out the sound, but it was no use. The whispers weren't coming from the apartment—they were inside his head, burrowing deep into his thoughts and amplifying his guilt.

"I didn't know," Elliot muttered, his voice trembling. "I didn't know."

But the whispers didn't stop. They grew louder, their voices echoing in his mind like a relentless tide. "You knew," they said again, their tone filled with quiet fury. "You always knew."

Elliot stumbled to the corner of the room, his back pressed against the wall as he sank to the floor. His breathing was shallow, his heart pounding as the whispers surrounded him, closing in like a storm. He felt as though he were drowning, the weight of their words pulling him under.

A Moment of Silence

And then, as suddenly as they had begun, the whispers stopped. The silence that followed was deafening, a stark contrast to the relentless noise that had filled the apartment moments before. Elliot sat frozen, his body trembling as he tried to process what had just happened.

The room felt colder now, the air heavy with an unspoken tension. The shadows in the corners seemed to pulse faintly, their edges flickering like dying embers. Elliot's gaze drifted to the corkboard, where Delyla's photograph still hung, slightly crooked. Her faint smile seemed different now—mocking, almost triumphant.

Elliot forced himself to his feet, his legs unsteady beneath him. He crossed the room slowly, his eyes fixed on the photograph. His hand trembled as he reached out to straighten it, his fingers brushing against the paper. For a moment, he thought he felt a faint vibration, as though the photograph were alive.

He pulled his hand back quickly, his chest tightening as a fresh wave of unease washed over him.

The whispers were more than just sounds—they were an invasion, a relentless reminder of the chaos Elliot had unleashed. Their faint, indistinct murmurs had grown into clear and accusatory words, probing at the guilt and fear that Elliot had tried so hard to suppress.

Though he tried to dismiss them as hallucinations or the product of exhaustion, the whispers refused to be silenced. They filled the apartment with their presence, transforming his sanctuary into a place of torment. And as the shadows deepened and the air grew heavier, Elliot realized that the whispers weren't just a product of his mind—they were something far more real, and far more dangerous.

The question now was whether Elliot could withstand their relentless assault—or whether they would drive him to the edge of madness, and beyond.

Physical Manifestations

The apartment had always been Elliot's sanctuary. A cocoon of solitude where control reigned supreme, its four walls were a reflection of his meticulously ordered mind. Every object had its place, every surface was deliberate in its composition. Yet, as the days stretched into nights and the whispers gave way to something far more tangible, Elliot began to feel as though his sanctuary was turning against him.

The air had shifted. What was once a quiet, predictable haven now carried an oppressive weight. Shadows lingered longer than they should, and the faint feeling of being watched, which had first unsettled him after Delyla's death, grew stronger, more invasive. Then came the physical changes—the scratches on the walls, the unsettling messages, and the cold, spectral touches that made Elliot question everything he thought he knew about reality.

The First Scratch

Elliot noticed it one morning as he sat at his desk, his fingers nervously fidgeting with a pen. The corkboard in front of him had been partially rebuilt, its bare surface now home to a few salvaged notes and a photograph of Delyla, still pinned at the center. He was staring at the board, lost in thought, when his gaze wandered to the wall beside it.

A thin, jagged scratch marred the otherwise smooth plaster.

It wasn't deep, but it was long, stretching diagonally from just above the baseboard to about waist height. The sight of it sent a jolt through Elliot's chest. He stood abruptly, his chair scraping against the floor as he moved closer to inspect it. His fingers hovered over the scratch, hesitant to touch it.

The plaster was cool to the touch, and the scratch felt rough beneath his fingertips. Elliot frowned. He didn't remember seeing it before, and he certainly hadn't caused it. The wall had been pristine the night before—he was certain of that.

"It's nothing," he muttered, pulling his hand away. "Probably just the paint chipping."

But even as he tried to dismiss it, he couldn't shake the unease settling in his chest.

More Scratches Appear

Over the next few days, more scratches began to appear. They were subtle at first—thin, barely noticeable lines that seemed to crop up overnight. Elliot would wake in the morning to find new ones on the walls, their erratic patterns crisscrossing like the marks of an unseen claw.

He tried to ignore them, convincing himself that they were the result of the building's age, the walls shifting and settling. But the scratches grew bolder, deeper, and more deliberate. One evening, as Elliot stood in the doorway of his bedroom, he noticed a particularly large scratch on the wall opposite his bed. It was long and curved, almost like a word that had been hastily scrawled but then abandoned midway.

The sight of it made his skin crawl. He moved closer, his breath hitching as he traced the mark with his fingers. It didn't feel random. There was intent behind it, as though someone—or something—had made it purposefully.

Elliot's pulse quickened. He stepped back, his mind racing with possibilities. Was someone breaking into the apartment? Had he done this in his sleep, unaware of his actions? The questions circled endlessly, feeding the paranoia that had taken root in his mind.

Delyla's Name on the Mirror

The first time it happened, Elliot was stepping out of the shower. The bathroom was thick with steam, the mirror fogged over to the point of opacity. He reached for the towel, running it over his face before wrapping it around his waist. As he moved to the sink to brush his teeth, something caught his eye—a faint disturbance in the fogged mirror.

At first, he thought it was nothing. But as he leaned closer, the disturbance became clearer. Letters, faint but unmistakable, were scrawled in the condensation.

Delyla.

Elliot froze, his heart pounding so hard he thought it might burst from his chest. The letters were jagged, uneven, as though written by a trembling hand. He reached out instinctively, swiping at the mirror with his hand to erase the word. The condensation smeared beneath his touch, but the letters remained, stark and unyielding.

His breath came in sharp, shallow bursts as he stumbled back, his mind reeling. He hadn't written it. He was certain of that. But if not him, then who—or what—had?

"Steam," he whispered to himself, his voice trembling. "It's just a trick of the steam."

But the explanation felt hollow, and as he turned to leave the bathroom, he couldn't shake the feeling that he wasn't alone.

The Cold Touch

The first time Elliot felt it, he was lying in bed, staring at the ceiling. Sleep had become an elusive companion, the whispers and scratches keeping him awake night after night. He lay there in the darkness, his body tense, his mind racing, when he felt it—a faint, icy touch on his arm.

The sensation was so light, so subtle, that he almost dismissed it as a draft. But then it came again, this time on his neck, a cold, deliberate caress that sent a shiver down his spine.

Elliot bolted upright, his chest heaving as he scanned the room. The darkness was impenetrable, the shadows in the corners thick and unmoving. He reached for the lamp on his bedside table, fumbling with the switch until the warm glow filled the room.

There was nothing there. The room was empty, just as it always was. But the sensation of the touch lingered, its cold imprint still fresh on his skin.

Over the next few days, the touches became more frequent. They came when he least expected them—a light brush against his hand as he sat at his desk, a faint pressure on his shoulder as he stood by the window. Each touch was fleeting, but it left him with a chilling sense of unease.

Escalation

As the physical manifestations grew more frequent, Elliot's paranoia reached a breaking point. The scratches on the walls became more intricate, forming patterns that seemed to taunt him. One morning, he woke to find a series of marks on the wall above his bed. They weren't random scratches—they were letters, jagged and uneven, spelling out a single word:

Why?

Elliot stared at the word, his body frozen with fear. He reached out to touch it, his fingers trembling, but the marks felt real, etched into the plaster as though carved with intent.

The cold touches, too, grew bolder. They lingered longer, their icy pressure more deliberate. One night, as Elliot sat at his desk, he felt a hand on his shoulder. The touch was unmistakable—firm and deliberate, as though someone were standing behind him. He spun around, his heart racing, but there was no one there.

"Stop it!" he shouted, his voice echoing through the empty apartment. "Leave me alone!"

But the apartment remained silent, its oppressive air pressing down on him like a weight.

Delyla's Name Returns

The bathroom mirror became a canvas for the unseen force that had invaded Elliot's apartment. Each time he showered, the steam would reveal new messages. At first, it was just her name, scrawled in the same jagged letters as before. But then the messages became more complex.

You knew.
Why did you do it?
She saw you.

The words sent chills through Elliot's body, their meaning heavy with accusation. He tried scrubbing the mirror, cleaning it with every product he could find, but the messages always returned, their presence an unyielding reminder of his guilt.

One morning, as he stepped out of the shower, he found a new message waiting for him: *Look behind you.*

Elliot froze, his body rigid with fear. He turned slowly, his breath hitching as he scanned the bathroom. The room was empty, but the oppressive feeling of being watched was stronger than ever.

The physical manifestations in Elliot's apartment were more than just signs of a haunting—they were a relentless assault on his sanity. The scratches on the walls, the messages on the mirror, and the cold, spectral touches all worked in concert to unravel his sense of control, reducing his once-meticulous world to chaos.

Elliot tried to dismiss the events as tricks of his mind, the product of exhaustion and paranoia. But the evidence was undeniable.

His sanctuary had been breached, and the force that had invaded it wasn't just haunting him—it was targeting him.

And as the manifestations grew more intense, Elliot couldn't shake the feeling that this was only the beginning. Whatever was happening in his apartment, it wasn't finished with him yet.

Nightmares

Sleep had never been a problem for Elliot. It was the one time his mind, usually so consumed by precision and control, could truly rest. His apartment's silence at night had always been a comfort, a cocoon in which he could escape the day's complexities. But now, the stillness that once lulled him into a deep sleep had turned against him. It was no longer a sanctuary—it was a trap.

The nightmares started subtly, creeping into his mind like whispers, faint and almost indistinct. But as the days stretched on, they grew darker, more vivid, and inescapable. Delyla, the woman whose life he had ended in an alley drenched in his failure, became the haunting centerpiece of these nocturnal terrors. Her face, once calm and detached in his memories of her routine, was now a mask of twisted anger and pain. In his dreams, she wasn't just a victim—she was a relentless pursuer.

The First Dream

The first dream came a week after the kill. Elliot had spent the day trying to reassemble the fragments of his corkboard, fighting the growing unease that permeated his apartment. Exhaustion finally overtook him, and he collapsed onto his bed, the weight of the past week dragging him into a restless sleep.

The dream began innocently enough. He was standing in the alley where it had all happened, the familiar sights and sounds surrounding him. The streetlamp flickered above, its light casting erratic shadows on the walls. A faint chill hung in the air, but Elliot felt no fear—only the calm detachment that had guided him during his surveillance.

But then, from the darkness, she emerged.

Delyla's figure was unmistakable, her silhouette backlit by the flickering light. At first, she looked as she always had: calm, composed, and indifferent to the world around her. But as she stepped closer, her face began to change. Her eyes, once unremarkable, were now wide and burning with anger. Her mouth twisted into a grimace of pain and accusation. Blood trickled from a wound in her chest, staining her coat and dripping onto the pavement.

Elliot tried to move, to step back, but his legs wouldn't respond. He was frozen in place as Delyla advanced, her footsteps echoing unnaturally loud in the narrow alley.

"Why?" she asked, her voice distorted and layered, as though a dozen voices spoke through her at once. "Why did you do it?"

Elliot opened his mouth to respond, but no sound came out. Delyla lunged toward him, her hands outstretched, and Elliot woke with a start, his chest heaving, his skin slick with sweat.

The Dreams Intensify

Each night, the dreams grew more vivid, more relentless. They no longer began in the alley but in a series of dark, twisting corridors that seemed to stretch on forever. The walls were cold and damp, their surfaces lined with scratches that mirrored the ones appearing in his apartment. The air was thick, oppressive, and filled with the faint sound of whispers—familiar phrases that had haunted his waking hours: *Why? You knew.*

Elliot would find himself running through the corridors, his breath ragged, his heart pounding in his chest. He didn't know where he was going or what he was running from, but the sense of dread was overwhelming. And then, inevitably, Delyla would appear.

She always came from the darkness, her movements deliberate and unyielding. Her face, twisted with rage and pain, was illuminated by an unnatural light that seemed to emanate from within her. Her eyes locked onto Elliot's, and he felt as though she could see straight through him, into the darkest corners of his soul.

"Elliot," she would whisper, her voice cold and accusing. "You can't run from me."

No matter how fast he ran, she was always just behind him, her footsteps echoing in perfect rhythm with his own. The walls of the corridors seemed to close in around him, forcing him into tighter and tighter spaces until he could hardly breathe. And then, just as her hands reached for him, he would wake.

The Blurring of Reality

The nightmares began to bleed into Elliot's waking life. He would wake drenched in sweat, his body trembling and his mind struggling to separate dream from reality. The oppressive feeling of the corridors lingered long after he opened his eyes, and the whispers seemed to follow him into the daylight hours.

One night, Elliot woke with a start, his chest heaving and his hands clutching at his sheets. The air in the room was cold, far colder than it should have been, and the faint sound of Delyla's voice still echoed in his ears.

He sat up, his eyes darting around the room, searching for any sign that he was still dreaming. The shadows in the corners seemed to shift and pulse, their movements subtle but unmistakable. His gaze fell on the corkboard, where Delyla's photograph hung slightly askew. For a moment, he thought he saw the image move, her faint smile twisting into something darker.

Elliot rubbed his eyes, trying to shake the feeling. "It's just the dreams," he muttered to himself. "It's all in your head."

But even as he said the words, he couldn't shake the feeling that the line between dream and reality was beginning to blur.

The Dark Corridor

The corridors in Elliot's dreams became more vivid with each passing night. Their walls, once undefined and shadowy, now seemed to take on a life of their own. They were lined with jagged scratches, the marks forming patterns that resembled letters, words, accusations.

Why? You knew. You saw.

Elliot would run, his footsteps echoing in the enclosed space, but the walls seemed to shift around him, rearranging themselves to trap him in an endless loop. The whispers grew louder, their cadence rising and falling like a sinister tide. And always, Delyla was there, her figure looming in the darkness, her voice cutting through the chaos.

"Elliot," she called, her tone sharp and relentless. "You can't hide."

In one dream, the corridor opened into the alley where it had all begun. The flickering streetlamp illuminated the bloodstains on the pavement, and Delyla stood at the center, her body broken and twisted but still impossibly alive. She reached out to him, her hand dripping with blood, her eyes filled with rage.

Elliot fell to his knees, his chest heaving as he tried to speak. "I didn't know," he stammered, his voice trembling. "I didn't know."

But Delyla only smiled, her expression cold and unforgiving. "You knew," she said, her voice echoing through the alley. "You always knew."

The Unending Chase

The dreams took on a horrifying consistency. Night after night, Elliot found himself trapped in the corridors, running endlessly from Delyla's relentless pursuit. No matter how fast he ran or how cleverly he tried to navigate the shifting walls, she was always there, her presence a constant, oppressive force.

Her voice haunted him, growing louder and more accusatory with each dream. "You can't escape," she would say, her tone mocking. "You're mine now."

Elliot's body grew heavier in the dreams, his movements slower and more labored. The corridors seemed to sap his strength, their walls pressing in on him until he could hardly breathe. And still, Delyla pursued him, her face a mask of rage and pain, her outstretched hands clawing at the air between them.

One night, the dream ended differently. Instead of waking just as Delyla reached him, Elliot found himself cornered, the corridor narrowing until there was nowhere left to run. Delyla loomed over him, her eyes burning with fury as she leaned in close.

"You're not the hunter," she whispered, her voice a cold breath against his skin. "You're the prey."

Elliot woke screaming, his body drenched in sweat, his heart pounding so hard he thought it might burst. The words echoed in his mind long after he opened his eyes, their meaning gnawing at the edges of his sanity.

The Descent

The nightmares became a relentless force, consuming Elliot's nights and leaving him exhausted and shaken during the day. He stopped sleeping altogether, fearing what awaited him when he closed his eyes. The line between dream and reality blurred further, the whispers and shadows of his dreams creeping into his waking hours.

His apartment, once a place of order and control, had become a prison. The walls seemed to close in around him, their surfaces marked by the same scratches that lined the corridors in his dreams. The oppressive feeling of being watched grew stronger, and Elliot began to see flashes of Delyla's face in the corners of his vision.

"I can't do this," he muttered to himself, his voice trembling. "I can't keep doing this."

But there was no escape. The dreams were a part of him now, as inescapable as the guilt that weighed on his chest. And as the days stretched into nights, Elliot realized that he was no longer in control. The hunter had become the hunted, and the nightmare was only just beginning.

The nightmares that plagued Elliot were more than just dreams—they were a descent into madness, a relentless reminder of the life he had taken and the chaos he had unleashed.

Delyla's presence, once confined to the shadows of his mind, had become a tangible force, pursuing him through the dark corridors of his subconscious and tearing apart the fragile sense of control he had worked so hard to maintain.

Each night, the dreams grew darker, more vivid, and more oppressive, blurring the line between sleep and reality. And though Elliot tried to escape them, he knew deep down that there was no running from the truth. The nightmare wasn't confined to his mind—it had become his reality.

Escalation of Tension

Elliot had once taken pride in his ability to control his environment. His apartment was his fortress, a sanctuary of meticulous order and precision. But now, it had turned on him. The walls that once sheltered him now felt like a cage, closing in with every passing moment. The disturbances, which began as subtle whispers and faint movements, had grown louder, more violent, and far harder to dismiss. What had started as an unsettling presence had now evolved into an all-out assault, and Elliot found himself trapped, fearing the space that had once been his sanctuary.

Objects in Motion

The first time an object was thrown, Elliot was sitting at his desk, staring blankly at the corkboard he had tried to reconstruct. His thoughts were a tangled mess of guilt, paranoia, and the creeping sense that he was no longer in control. His desk lamp flickered faintly, a reminder of the building's aging electrical system, as the air grew heavy around him.

It happened suddenly—a sharp, violent motion that shattered the silence. A book flew from the shelf across the room, crashing into the floor with enough force to send a plume of dust into the air. Elliot jumped, his chair scraping loudly against the hardwood as he turned toward the source of the noise.

The book lay open on the floor, its pages splayed out like wings. It had been on the shelf moments ago, neatly placed alongside its counterparts. Elliot stared at it, his heart pounding in his chest.

"You're imagining things," he muttered, though the words sounded hollow even to his own ears. He stood slowly, his legs unsteady as he approached the book. Picking it up, he placed it back on the shelf, his movements deliberate, almost ritualistic.

But as he turned away, another object—a framed photo of his parents—slid off the same shelf, hitting the ground with a dull thud. This time, Elliot didn't move. He stood frozen, the breath catching in his throat as the photo lay face down on the floor.

Doors Slam in the Night

The next escalation came late one evening, as Elliot paced the length of his apartment. Sleep had become impossible. Each time he closed his eyes, he was haunted by the vivid nightmares that had begun to bleed into his waking hours. His movements were restless, his footsteps a constant echo against the walls as he tried to shake the oppressive feeling that clung to him.

It was just after midnight when the first door slammed.

The sound was deafening in the stillness, reverberating through the apartment like a gunshot. Elliot stopped mid-step, his body stiffening as he turned toward the source. The bathroom door, which had been ajar moments ago, was now shut tight. The force of the slam had rattled the walls, causing a small framed painting to fall to the floor.

Elliot approached the door cautiously, his hand trembling as he reached for the handle. The air around him felt colder, heavier, and his chest tightened with each step. When he finally opened the door, the bathroom was empty, just as it had been before. The mirror, fogged with condensation despite the lack of recent use, reflected his pale, gaunt face.

As he stared into the mirror, another door slammed behind him. This time, it was the door to his bedroom. Elliot spun around, his pulse racing, but the hallway was empty. The sound of his own breathing filled his ears as he backed away, retreating into the living room.

The Apartment Turns Hostile

From that night forward, the disturbances became more frequent, more aggressive. Objects that had once been stationary were now in constant motion—books flew off shelves, chairs scraped against the floor as though dragged by unseen hands, and picture frames fell from the walls with no apparent cause. Doors no longer stayed open or closed; they slammed shut with such force that Elliot feared the hinges might snap.

The apartment had become a battleground, a place of chaos and hostility. Elliot tried to maintain some semblance of control, picking up the objects that had been thrown, straightening the chairs, and re-hanging the pictures. But it was a futile effort. The disturbances would undo his work within minutes, as though mocking his attempts to restore order.

One evening, as he sat on the couch, a glass he had left on the coffee table shattered spontaneously, the shards scattering across the floor. Elliot jumped, his body trembling as he stared at the remnants of the glass. The sound of the shattering echoed in his ears long after the pieces had settled.

"You're not real," he whispered, his voice shaking. "You're not real."

But the apartment seemed to respond, the air growing colder, the walls seeming to close in around him. The whispers, faint but unmistakable, began to fill the room.

Retreating to the Corner

Elliot's world shrank with each passing day. The apartment, once a place of refuge, had become a labyrinth of fear. He found himself retreating to the corner of the living room, the only space where he felt even a semblance of safety. He would sit there for hours, his knees pulled to his chest, his back pressed against the wall as he scanned the room for signs of movement.

The corner offered no real protection, but it gave him a sense of control—however fleeting. From there, he could see the entire room, every object, every shadow. He kept the lights on at all times, afraid of what might happen if darkness consumed the space.

But even in the corner, Elliot wasn't safe. The cold, spectral touches that had first appeared in his sleep now came during his waking hours. He would feel them on his arms, his neck, his face—light, fleeting brushes that sent chills through his body. Each touch was accompanied by the faint sensation of breath on his skin, as though someone were standing just behind him.

Delyla's Name Appears Again

The most chilling moment came one night as Elliot sat in the corner, his eyes fixed on the corkboard across the room. The board, once meticulously organized, was now a mess of torn photographs and discarded notes. Delyla's photograph still hung at the center, its edges curling as though burned.

As he stared at it, the lights flickered, plunging the room into brief moments of darkness. When the lights stabilized, Elliot's breath caught in his throat. Her name was scrawled across the far wall in jagged, uneven letters:

DELYLA

The letters were dark and smeared, as though written with blood. Elliot scrambled to his feet, his back pressing harder against the wall as his chest heaved. His mind raced, searching for an explanation, but none came. The letters hadn't been there moments ago, and there was no way they could have appeared without his noticing.

"Get out," he whispered, his voice trembling. "Leave me alone."

The apartment seemed to respond, the temperature dropping sharply as the lights flickered again. The whispers grew louder, more distinct, filling the room with overlapping voices that seemed to come from every direction.

Breaking Point

Elliot's breaking point came when the disturbances turned violent. He had been sitting in the corner, his body tense, when a chair across the room suddenly flipped over, crashing against the floor with enough force to splinter the wood. The sound was deafening, and Elliot flinched, his arms coming up to shield his face.

Before he could react, another object—a lamp this time—was hurled across the room, narrowly missing his head. It shattered against the wall, the pieces raining down onto the floor like glass raindrops.

Elliot bolted to his feet, his body trembling with fear and anger. "What do you want from me?" he screamed, his voice cracking. "What do you want?"

The apartment fell silent for a moment, the oppressive stillness almost worse than the chaos. Then, as if in response, a door slammed somewhere in the distance, the sound echoing through the walls like a thunderclap.

Elliot sank back to the floor, his body collapsing under the weight of his fear. The room seemed to close in around him, the shadows in the corners growing darker, more menacing. He buried his face in his hands, his mind racing with thoughts he couldn't control.

The escalating disturbances in Elliot's apartment were more than just an assault on his senses—they were an unraveling of his reality. The objects thrown, the doors slammed, and the spectral touches all served to strip away the last vestiges of control he had over his world. His once-orderly apartment had become a prison, a place of relentless torment where chaos reigned supreme.

As Elliot sat in the corner, trembling and broken, he realized that there was no escape. Whatever force had invaded his life wasn't just haunting him—it was consuming him, piece by piece. And as the whispers grew louder and the shadows closed in, Elliot knew that this was only the beginning. The escalation of tension was a prelude to something far darker, something he couldn't yet comprehend.

Delyla's Photo Changes

The corkboard had always been Elliot's anchor, his means of controlling the chaos in his mind by pinning it, literally, to something tangible. It was a map of his obsession, a visual representation of his calculated precision. Among the scattered notes and strings, Delyla's photograph remained the centerpiece, a constant amidst the disorder.

But lately, even the corkboard had begun to betray him. What had once been a monument to control now felt like a mocking testament to his failure, and Delyla's photo, once so ordinary and unassuming, was at the center of the growing strangeness in his world.

The First Change

It happened on a gray, overcast afternoon. Elliot sat at his desk, staring blankly at the corkboard. The apartment was silent, save for the faint hum of the refrigerator and the rhythmic ticking of the clock on the wall. His eyes, as they often did, wandered to Delyla's photograph. It was a candid shot, taken from a distance—her face partially turned, her faint smile aimed at someone or something out of the frame.

But today, something was different. Her smile—it wasn't there.

Elliot leaned closer, his breath catching in his throat. Delyla's expression had changed. The faint, detached smile he had memorized over weeks of observation was now a grimace, her lips pulled taut, her jaw clenched. Her eyes, once soft and unremarkable, seemed to glare at him with an intensity that made his chest tighten.

Elliot froze, his mind struggling to process what he was seeing. He blinked, his gaze fixed on the photograph, waiting for the image to shift back to the way he remembered it. But it didn't. The grimace remained, her expression etched with pain and anger, as though she were condemning him from beyond the grave.

The Photo Returns to Normal

Elliot sat there for what felt like hours, his eyes locked on the photograph. His breathing grew shallow, his hands trembling as he tried to make sense of what was happening. Was this real? Or was it another trick of his mind, a symptom of the growing paranoia that had consumed him since Delyla's death?

He forced himself to look away, his gaze darting to the scattered papers on his desk. He tried to focus on anything else—the details of his plans, the scratches on the walls—but his thoughts kept circling back to the photo.

When he finally mustered the courage to look again, Delyla's smile had returned. Her faint, detached expression was as it had always been, her features calm and unassuming. Elliot let out a shaky breath, his body sagging with relief.

"It's just your imagination," he whispered to himself, his voice trembling. "You're seeing things."

But the memory of her grimace lingered, the image burned into his mind. No matter how hard he tried to dismiss it, he couldn't shake the feeling that it had been real.

The Changes Become Subtler

Over the following days, Elliot began to notice other changes in the photograph. They were subtle, almost imperceptible—small shifts in her expression that seemed to mock him when he wasn't looking directly at her.

One morning, as Elliot sat sipping his coffee, he glanced at the corkboard and felt his stomach drop. Delyla's head was slightly tilted, her eyes fixed on him in a way that felt deliberate, intentional. He stared at the photo, his chest tightening as he waited for the image to shift back to normal. But it didn't.

Elliot stood abruptly, his chair scraping against the floor as he moved closer to the corkboard. The photograph seemed to change as he approached, her tilted head straightening, her gaze becoming neutral once more. By the time he was standing directly in front of it, her expression was as it had always been—calm, detached, and entirely ordinary.

He reached out hesitantly, his fingers brushing against the paper. The photograph felt normal, its surface smooth and cool to the touch. But as he stepped back, the unease in his chest refused to dissipate.

A Confrontation with the Corkboard

That evening, as Elliot sat at his desk, the air in the apartment felt heavier than usual. The oppressive silence that had become a constant presence was broken only by the faint sound of the clock ticking on the wall. Elliot's eyes wandered to the corkboard, drawn once again to Delyla's photograph.

Her expression had changed again. This time, her mouth was slightly open, her lips curled into what looked like a snarl. Her eyes, which had always been faintly unfocused, were now sharp and piercing, as though she were staring directly at him.

Elliot felt a wave of panic wash over him. He stood, his movements jerky and uncoordinated, as he approached the corkboard. His heart pounded in his chest, each beat echoing in his ears as he reached for the photograph.

"What do you want from me?" he whispered, his voice trembling. "Why won't you leave me alone?"

The photograph seemed to shift again as he spoke, her expression softening, her features returning to their original state. Elliot stumbled back, his breathing ragged as he tried to steady himself.

The Photo as a Living Thing

Elliot began to avoid looking at the photograph altogether, but it was impossible to ignore. No matter where he sat in the apartment, he felt its presence, as though her eyes were following him, watching his every move. The corkboard, once a tool of control, now felt like a trap—a portal through which Delyla's anger and pain seeped into his world.

He considered taking the photograph down, tearing it from the board and destroying it. But each time he reached for it, a wave of dread washed over him, paralyzing him with fear. What if destroying it made things worse? What if it was the only thing keeping her at bay?

Instead, Elliot began to cover the corkboard with a sheet, draping it over the surface in a desperate attempt to block out her gaze. But the sheet did little to ease his paranoia. He could still feel her eyes on him, piercing through the fabric, burning into his mind.

The Final Change

The breaking point came one night as Elliot lay awake in bed, the oppressive silence of the apartment pressing down on him. He had avoided the corkboard all day, refusing to glance at it even as he moved through the room. But now, as he stared at the ceiling, he felt an irresistible pull, a compulsion to look at the photograph one last time.

He rose from the bed slowly, his movements deliberate as he approached the corkboard. The sheet he had draped over it was undisturbed, its edges fluttering faintly in the still air. Elliot hesitated for a moment, his breath hitching as he reached for the fabric.

With a sharp tug, he pulled the sheet away, revealing the corkboard beneath. Delyla's photograph was still there, pinned at the center. But this time, her face was unrecognizable.

Her features were distorted, twisted into a grotesque mask of anger and pain. Her eyes, once calm and unremarkable, were now wide and bloodshot, glaring at him with a hatred so intense it made Elliot's stomach churn. Her mouth was open in a silent scream, her teeth bared, her expression frozen in a moment of pure rage.

Elliot staggered back, his chest heaving as he struggled to catch his breath. The room seemed to tilt around him, the shadows in the corners growing darker, more menacing. He turned away from the photograph, his hands clutching his head as he tried to make sense of what he had seen.

When he finally turned back, her face was normal again.

The changes in Delyla's photograph were more than just tricks of the mind—they were a manifestation of the chaos that had begun to consume Elliot's life. Each shift in her expression, each subtle distortion, chipped away at his already fragile sanity, leaving him questioning what was real and what was a product of his own guilt and paranoia.

Elliot knew he couldn't ignore the photograph, but he also couldn't confront it. It had become a living thing, a window into something far darker than he could comprehend. And as the changes continued, Elliot realized that the photograph wasn't just haunting him—it was warning him.

The question now was whether Elliot could face the truth the photograph seemed determined to reveal—or whether it would consume him entirely.

Chapter 5:
The Ghost Appears

The First Manifestation

The night was unusually silent, even for Elliot's apartment. Silence had become a companion to him—a heavy, oppressive presence that mirrored his own guilt. It followed him everywhere, growing heavier with each passing day. Tonight, though, it seemed to hum with anticipation, a tangible tension that pressed against his chest and made the air in the apartment feel thick and unbreathable.

Elliot had retreated to his usual corner of the living room, his knees pulled to his chest as his eyes darted from shadow to shadow. The corkboard loomed across the room like a specter of its own, Delyla's photograph still pinned at the center. He hadn't looked at it in hours, but he could feel her eyes on him all the same, a silent accusation that refused to let him rest. He hadn't slept in days, his body fueled by a toxic mixture of caffeine and fear. Exhaustion gnawed at the edges of his mind, but he didn't dare close his eyes.

And then it happened.

A Cold Presence

It began as a subtle shift in the air, a faint chill that crept across the room like an invisible fog. Elliot shivered, pulling his arms tighter around his legs as he glanced toward the window. The night outside was calm, the streets below quiet and empty. There was no wind, no open window to explain the sudden drop in temperature.

He tried to dismiss it as his imagination, but the chill grew stronger, sinking into his bones. The air seemed to grow heavier, denser, pressing down on him with an almost suffocating weight. Elliot's breath hitched, his chest tightening as his gaze swept the room.

That was when he saw her.

The First Glimpse

She was standing in the corner of the room, partially obscured by the shadows but unmistakably there. Delyla. Her figure was pale and translucent, her form flickering faintly like an image on an old, damaged film reel. She didn't move, didn't speak. She just stood there, her hollow eyes fixed on him.

Elliot froze, his body paralyzed with fear. His mind raced, struggling to make sense of what he was seeing. This wasn't real. It couldn't be real. But no matter how many times he blinked, Delyla didn't disappear. She remained in the corner, her presence undeniable.

Her face was the same as he remembered—yet different. The faint smile that had once graced her photograph was gone, replaced by an expression of pain and anger. Her features were gaunt, her skin pallid, her eyes sunken and rimmed with shadows. They stared at him, unblinking and unyielding, filled with a quiet fury that sent chills down his spine.

A Staring Contest

Elliot's chest heaved as he struggled to breathe, his eyes locked on Delyla's spectral form. She didn't move. She didn't speak. She simply stared, her gaze heavy with accusation. The silence in the room was deafening, broken only by the sound of Elliot's ragged breaths.

"What... what do you want?" he stammered, his voice barely audible. His words hung in the air, unanswered. Delyla's eyes didn't waver, her expression as still and unchanging as a statue. It was as if she were waiting for something, her presence a silent demand that Elliot couldn't understand.

He pressed himself harder against the wall, his body trembling as a wave of cold washed over him. The temperature in the room seemed to plummet with each passing second, frost forming on the edges of the windows and the surfaces of the furniture. Elliot's breath came out in visible puffs, the cold biting at his skin like icy needles.

Memories Flood Back

As Delyla continued to stare, memories of the alley flooded Elliot's mind with a brutal clarity that made him want to scream. He could see her face, wide-eyed and terrified, her body collapsing onto the pavement as his blade struck. He remembered the sound of her voice, pleading for a chance she would never get, and the slick, metallic scent of blood that had clung to him for days.

"You're not real," he whispered, his voice shaking. "You're just… you're in my head."

But even as he spoke the words, he knew they weren't true. Delyla was there. Her presence was undeniable, and the weight of her gaze was more than he could bear.

Elliot's mind raced with questions. Why now? Why her? He had chosen Delyla because she was supposed to be ordinary, predictable, forgettable. She wasn't supposed to haunt him—not like this.

The Ghostly Accusation

The weight of Delyla's stare seemed to press against Elliot's chest, suffocating him with its intensity. Her eyes, hollow and lifeless, seemed to pierce through him, stripping away every layer of his carefully constructed facade. He felt exposed, vulnerable, as though she could see every dark corner of his mind.

"Say something," Elliot pleaded, his voice breaking. "If you're real, then say something!"

But Delyla remained silent, her form flickering faintly in the corner. Her stillness was more terrifying than any words she could have spoken. It was a silent accusation, a reminder of what he had done and the life he had taken.

Elliot clenched his fists, his nails digging into his palms as he fought to steady his breathing.

He wanted to look away, to escape the weight of her gaze, but he couldn't. Her presence held him captive, paralyzing him with fear and guilt.

A Break in the Silence

Hours seemed to pass, though it was likely only minutes. The tension in the room was unbearable, the silence so thick it felt like a physical force. And then, just as suddenly as she had appeared, Delyla began to move.

Her form flickered, her pale figure shifting slightly as she took a single step forward. Elliot's breath caught in his throat as he pressed himself harder against the wall, his body trembling with fear. Her movements were slow, deliberate, and filled with an unnatural grace that made his skin crawl.

"Stop," he whispered, his voice barely audible. "Don't come any closer."

But Delyla didn't stop. She took another step, her eyes never leaving his. Her lips parted slightly, as though she were about to speak, but no words came. Instead, a faint, hollow sound echoed through the room—a soft, mournful wail that sent chills racing down Elliot's spine.

The Disappearance

Just as Delyla reached the edge of the light cast by the desk lamp, her form flickered violently, as though a static charge were running through her. Her features distorted, her expression twisting into something even more horrifying—a mask of rage and pain. Elliot's heart raced as he stared at her, his chest heaving with terror.

And then, just as suddenly as she had appeared, she was gone.

The room fell silent, the oppressive tension lifting slightly as the cold began to dissipate. Elliot remained frozen in place, his body trembling as he struggled to process what had just happened. His mind raced with questions, but no answers came.

He glanced toward the corner where Delyla had stood, his breath hitching as he half-expected to see her there again. But the corner was empty, the shadows undisturbed.

The Aftermath

Elliot didn't sleep that night. He didn't dare close his eyes, afraid that she might return the moment he let his guard down. His mind replayed the events over and over again, searching for some logical explanation, but there was none. Delyla had been there—he was certain of it. Her presence was undeniable, her gaze haunting him even in her absence.

He sat in the corner of the room, his arms wrapped tightly around his knees as he rocked back and forth. The air still felt heavy, the chill lingering in the corners like a ghost of its own. Elliot's eyes darted around the room, scanning every shadow, every flicker of movement, as though expecting her to reappear at any moment.

"You're not real," he muttered, his voice trembling. "You're not real."

But deep down, he knew the truth. Delyla was real. She was here. And she wasn't going to leave him alone.

The first manifestation of Delyla's ghost was more than just a haunting—it was a confrontation. Her pale, translucent form and hollow, accusing eyes were a reminder of the life Elliot had taken and the consequences of his actions. Her silence, more terrifying than any words she could have spoken, was a weight that pressed against him, forcing him to confront the guilt and fear he had tried so hard to suppress.

Elliot's world, already unraveling, was now entirely out of his control. The appearance of Delyla's ghost was a breaking point, a sign that the line between reality and the supernatural had been irrevocably crossed. And as he sat in the corner of his apartment, trembling with fear, Elliot knew that this was only the beginning.

Elliot's Reaction

The ghostly apparition of Delyla standing in the corner of his apartment shattered whatever remained of Elliot's fragile composure. Fear, like ice water, coursed through his veins, freezing him in place as his mind scrambled to process what he was seeing. This wasn't real. It couldn't be real. He'd told himself that countless times since the disturbances had begun, but now, faced with the spectral figure of the woman he had killed, denial was a crumbling fortress.

Elliot's breathing was shallow and erratic, each gasp catching in his throat. His eyes refused to look away, locked on the pale, translucent form that loomed in the shadows. The cold in the room was suffocating, pressing against his chest and making his lungs work harder for air. He was paralyzed, unable to move or even think, his body betraying him under the weight of his fear.

A Feeble Denial

"This... this isn't real," Elliot muttered, his voice barely a whisper. His words hung in the cold air, trembling as much as he was. He blinked rapidly, as though trying to dispel an illusion, but Delyla's form remained, flickering faintly like a dying lightbulb.

His mind grasped at every logical explanation. Exhaustion. Stress. A hallucination born of guilt and sleepless nights. But as much as he wanted to believe it, the ghost's presence was too tangible. Her hollow eyes were locked on him, filled with a quiet, relentless accusation that pierced through the walls he had built to protect himself from his own guilt.

"You're... not here," he stammered, his voice breaking. "You're just... in my head."

But even as he spoke, he knew the words were lies. The air was too heavy, the cold too real. He could feel her presence like a weight pressing against his skin, and the longer he stared at her, the more undeniable it became.

The First Words

Elliot's legs felt like lead, his knees trembling as he struggled to remain upright. He wanted to run, to flee the apartment and leave this nightmare behind, but his body wouldn't obey him. Instead, he found himself speaking, his voice shaky and uneven.

"What... what do you want?" he asked, his words barely coherent. His throat felt dry, his mouth parched as though the very air around him had been sucked away. He took a halting step forward, his hands shaking at his sides.

The ghost didn't respond. Delyla's form remained still, her pale, translucent body flickering faintly in the dim light. Her expression was unreadable, a mixture of pain and anger that made Elliot's stomach churn. Her eyes, though hollow, seemed alive with emotion, and Elliot felt as though she could see straight through him—into the darkest corners of his soul.

"Why are you here?" he tried again, his voice rising slightly, though it still wavered with fear. "What do you want from me?"

Still, Delyla said nothing. The silence was deafening, more oppressive than any sound could have been. It was as though the entire apartment held its breath, waiting for something to happen.

A Desperate Plea

The silence stretched on, unbearable in its weight. Elliot's hands clenched into fists, his nails digging into his palms as he fought to steady himself. His chest heaved with each labored breath, his heart pounding so hard he thought it might burst.

"I didn't mean to!" he blurted out, the words spilling from his lips before he could stop them. "I didn't know—how could I have known?"

The ghost's gaze didn't waver, her eyes fixed on him with an intensity that made him feel as though he were being dissected. Elliot stumbled back, his body colliding with the wall behind him. The cold seeped through the plaster, biting into his skin and making him shiver.

"I wasn't trying to—" he continued, his voice breaking. "It wasn't supposed to be like this."

He wasn't sure what he was saying anymore. The words came in a rush, incoherent and desperate, a torrent of excuses and half-truths that he flung at the ghost in a futile attempt to justify his actions. But Delyla's silence was unrelenting, her presence a quiet condemnation that stripped away every defense he tried to build.

The Breaking Point

Elliot's legs gave out, and he sank to the floor, his back pressed against the wall as he pulled his knees to his chest. His body trembled uncontrollably, his breath coming in shallow gasps as tears streamed down his face. He had spent so much time convincing himself that he was in control, that every action he took was calculated and deliberate. But now, faced with the ghost of his victim, that illusion had shattered.

"Please," he whispered, his voice cracking. "Just… leave me alone."

The ghost didn't move. She remained in the corner of the room, her form flickering faintly as though caught between two worlds. The cold in the apartment grew more intense, and Elliot wrapped his arms around himself, trying to stave off the chill.

"Why are you doing this to me?" he asked, his voice rising in a mixture of anger and desperation. "I… I didn't know you. I didn't mean for any of this to happen."

His words echoed through the apartment, but Delyla remained silent. Her stillness was more terrifying than any words she could have spoken. It was as though she were waiting for something, her presence a demand that Elliot couldn't understand.

Fighting the Fear

Elliot's initial terror began to give way to a flicker of anger—an emotion born not of defiance, but of his own fear and helplessness. He clenched his fists, his knuckles white as he forced himself to stand. His legs trembled beneath him, but he planted his feet firmly on the floor, refusing to let the ghost keep him down.

"You think this is my fault?" he shouted, his voice shaking but louder now. "You think I wanted this? I didn't choose you!"

The words tasted bitter as they left his mouth. They felt wrong, hollow, but he said them anyway, desperate to regain some semblance of control. He took a step toward the ghost, his hands trembling at his sides.

"You were… just a target," he said, his voice faltering. "That's all. Just… a target."

As the words left his lips, Delyla's expression seemed to shift. It was subtle—her hollow eyes narrowing slightly, her translucent form flickering more intensely. Elliot froze, his anger evaporating in an instant as a new wave of fear crashed over him.

"I didn't mean it," he stammered, his voice barely a whisper. "I didn't mean it…"

An Unspoken Answer

The ghost's silence continued, but it was no longer empty. It was heavy with meaning, a quiet accusation that Elliot couldn't ignore. Her presence seemed to fill the room, pressing against him from all sides, suffocating him with its intensity.

Elliot fell to his knees again, his body trembling as he buried his face in his hands. He wanted to scream, to run, to do anything that would make her go away. But no matter how hard he tried, he couldn't escape her gaze.

"I'm sorry," he whispered, his voice breaking. "I'm so sorry…"

For a moment, the room seemed to grow even colder, the air so heavy that it felt like it was crushing him. And then, just as suddenly as she had appeared, Delyla was gone.

The Aftermath

The apartment was silent once more, the oppressive tension lifting slightly as the cold began to dissipate. Elliot remained on the floor, his body trembling and his mind racing. He couldn't make sense of what had just happened. Was it real? Or was it another hallucination, a product of his own guilt and paranoia?

He looked toward the corner where Delyla had stood, his chest tightening as he half-expected to see her there again. But the corner was empty, the shadows undisturbed.

Elliot pulled himself to his feet, his legs unsteady beneath him. He stumbled toward the bathroom, his hands shaking as he splashed cold water on his face. His reflection in the mirror was almost unrecognizable—his eyes bloodshot, his skin pale, his expression hollow and haunted.

"I can't do this," he whispered, his voice trembling. "I can't keep doing this…"

But even as he said the words, he knew there was no escape. Delyla's ghost wasn't just a manifestation of his guilt—it was something far more real, and it wasn't going to leave him alone.

Elliot's reaction to Delyla's ghost was a chaotic mixture of fear, denial, and desperation. Paralyzed by terror, he initially tried to dismiss her presence as a hallucination, but the reality of her spectral form was undeniable. His attempts to speak to her were incoherent, his words a jumble of excuses and apologies that did nothing to ease the weight of her silent accusation.

The encounter left Elliot broken, his already fragile sanity pushed to its limits. The ghost's presence was a reminder of the life he had taken and the consequences of his actions, forcing him to confront the guilt and fear he had tried so hard to suppress. And as the cold air lingered in the apartment, Elliot knew that this was only the beginning of his torment. Delyla's ghost wasn't just haunting him—it was hunting him, and there was no escape.

Delyla Speaks

The silence that had filled Elliot's apartment since Delyla's death had been a relentless torment, but when it broke, it became something far worse. Her voice—the voice of the ghost whose hollow, accusing eyes had haunted him for weeks—cut through the still air with a power that froze him in place. It wasn't a scream, nor was it gentle. It was a voice fractured by sorrow and rage, and its sound made every hair on Elliot's body stand on end.

The First Words

It began with a faint whisper. Elliot was sitting at his desk, the corkboard looming in his peripheral vision like a constant reminder of his failure. He had been trying to piece together what little remained of his shattered routine, avoiding direct glances at Delyla's photograph while feigning focus on his scattered notes.

"Why?"

The single word cut through the air, sharp and unmistakable. Elliot froze, his pen slipping from his trembling fingers. The sound didn't seem to come from any particular direction; it was as though the word had emerged from the air itself, wrapping around him like a cold wind.

He turned slowly, his heart pounding in his chest. At first, the room seemed empty, the shadows in the corners as still and lifeless as they had always been. But then she was there—Delyla, standing just beyond the edge of the light, her pale, translucent form flickering faintly.

Her mouth moved again, her voice low but heavy with emotion. "Why me?"

Elliot's breath caught in his throat. He had spent weeks convincing himself that the disturbances in his apartment were hallucinations, the product of a guilt-ridden mind. But now, faced with Delyla's ghost not just staring but speaking to him, there was no room left for denial.

A Voice of Pain and Anger

Delyla's voice was unlike anything Elliot had ever heard. It wasn't entirely human, not anymore. There was a sorrowful resonance to it, an echo that seemed to carry the weight of her suffering. But beneath the sorrow was an unmistakable anger, a sharp edge that made Elliot's stomach churn.

"You planned it," she said, her words cutting through the stillness like a knife. "You followed me. You watched me. And then you killed me."

Elliot stumbled back, his knees nearly giving out as the accusations struck him. "I-I didn't…" he stammered, his voice trembling. "It wasn't personal. It wasn't supposed to be like this."

Her gaze burned into him, her hollow eyes filled with a fury that made him feel as though he were being flayed alive. "Not personal?" she repeated, her tone incredulous. "You stole my life, and it wasn't personal?"

Elliot couldn't meet her eyes. His hands clenched at his sides, his nails digging into his palms as he fought to keep himself from collapsing under the weight of her words.

The Demand for Answers

"Why me?" Delyla's voice rose, filled with a mixture of pain and accusation. "Out of everyone in this city, why did you choose me?"

Elliot swallowed hard, his throat dry and his chest tight. He wanted to answer her, but the words wouldn't come. How could he explain the methodical coldness of his selection process to the woman whose life he had taken? How could he justify reducing her to nothing more than a target?

"I... I didn't know you," he finally managed, his voice barely audible. "You fit the pattern. You were... predictable."

Delyla's expression twisted, her features contorting in a mixture of disbelief and fury. "Predictable?" she repeated, her voice sharp and venomous. "That's all I was to you? A pattern? A checklist?"

Elliot flinched as her words hit him like physical blows. "It wasn't about you," he said, his voice cracking. "It could have been anyone..."

Her laughter was low and bitter, a sound that sent chills racing down his spine. "But it wasn't anyone. It was me. You made a choice, Elliot. You chose me."

The Moral Reckoning

Delyla took a step closer, her translucent form flickering like a candle in a gust of wind. The air around her grew colder, the temperature in the room dropping so rapidly that Elliot's breath became visible.

"What gave you the right?" she asked, her voice trembling with fury. "What made you think you could decide who gets to live and who doesn't?"

Elliot shook his head, his hands trembling at his sides. "I wasn't trying to—" he began, but she cut him off.

"You weren't trying to what?" she demanded, her voice rising. "To ruin someone's life? To leave their family shattered? To make them a ghost, trapped in the world of the living?"

Her words hit him like a tidal wave, drowning him in a sea of guilt and shame. Elliot stumbled back, his legs hitting the chair behind him as he sank into it, his chest heaving with shallow, panicked breaths.

"I thought... I thought I could do it," he admitted, his voice barely above a whisper. "I thought I could control it. But I was wrong."

Delyla's gaze didn't soften. If anything, her anger seemed to grow. "Control?" she said, her tone dripping with disdain. "You think you had control? You couldn't even control yourself."

The Haunting Memories

As Delyla spoke, memories of the alley flooded Elliot's mind. He saw her face, wide-eyed and terrified, her body crumpling to the ground as his blade struck. He remembered the sound of her voice, pleading for a chance she would never get. The image of her blood pooling on the pavement burned into his mind, as vivid now as it had been that night.

"Do you see it now?" Delyla asked, her voice quieter but no less cutting. "Do you see what you did?"

Elliot nodded weakly, tears streaming down his face. "I see it," he whispered. "I see it every time I close my eyes."

"Good," she said, her tone colder than the air around her. "Because I won't let you forget."

A Moment of Humanity

For a brief moment, the anger in Delyla's voice gave way to something softer—something more human. "Do you know what you took from me?" she asked, her voice trembling with emotion. "Do you have any idea what my life was worth?"

Elliot looked up at her, his own pain reflected in her hollow eyes. "I didn't know," he admitted, his voice shaking. "I didn't know anything about you. And I can never make it right."

Delyla's form flickered, her translucent body seeming to grow dimmer for a moment before brightening again. "You're right," she said softly. "You can't make it right. But you can live with it."

Her words hung in the air, heavy with meaning. Elliot's chest tightened, his guilt threatening to crush him under its weight. He wanted to ask her what she meant, what she wanted from him, but the words wouldn't come.

The Unspoken Warning

As the room fell silent, Delyla's gaze grew more intense. Her eyes, filled with a mixture of sorrow and fury, seemed to pierce through Elliot's very soul. "This isn't over," she said, her voice low and ominous. "You don't get to move on. You don't get to forget."

Elliot's heart raced as her form began to fade, her translucent body flickering like a dying flame. "Wait!" he called out, his voice desperate. "Don't go—please, don't go!"

But Delyla didn't respond. Her figure grew fainter and fainter until she was nothing more than a shadow in the corner of the room. The cold air lingered, a reminder of her presence, but the apartment was silent once more.

Elliot sank to the floor, his body trembling as tears streamed down his face. Her words echoed in his mind, each one a dagger to his already broken soul. He had thought that killing Delyla would give him control, that it would prove something to himself. But now, he realized, it had only left him with questions he could never answer and a guilt that would never go away.

Delyla's voice, filled with a haunting mixture of sorrow and rage, was a reckoning that Elliot couldn't escape. Her accusations stripped away every excuse, every justification, leaving him exposed and vulnerable. Her demands for answers—*"Why me? What gave you the right?"*—were questions he had no way of answering, forcing him to confront the depth of his guilt and the consequences of his actions.

The encounter left Elliot shaken to his core, his fragile grip on reality slipping even further. Delyla's words weren't just a condemnation—they were a promise. She wasn't going to let him forget what he had done, and the haunting was far from over. For Elliot, there would be no escape, no redemption—only the relentless weight of his guilt and the ghostly voice that would continue to haunt him.

Physical Interference

Elliot had convinced himself, until now, that Delyla's ghost was a psychological manifestation—a product of guilt gnawing at the edges of his sanity. The whispers, the flickering shadows, and even her voice—haunting as it was—he could attribute to his unraveling mind. But when Delyla's presence turned physical, there was no longer room for doubt. This was not a hallucination. It was real, and it was far more dangerous than he could have imagined.

The First Shove

It started subtly, as most things in Elliot's nightmare had. He had spent the night pacing the length of his apartment, unable to rest after the confrontation with Delyla's ghost. Her words—*"Why me? What gave you the right?"*—echoed in his mind, drowning out any hope of finding clarity or solace. His movements were erratic, his thoughts fractured, as he tried to piece together a plan to regain control of his spiraling life.

The shove came without warning. As Elliot passed the corkboard, something—an unseen force—pushed him hard against the wall. His shoulder hit the plaster with enough force to send a jolt of pain down his arm, and he stumbled, clutching at the wall for support.

"What the hell?" he gasped, his breath catching in his throat.

His eyes darted around the room, searching for an explanation. The air was still, the apartment silent save for the faint hum of the refrigerator. But the cold was back, seeping into his skin and raising goosebumps on his arms. Elliot pressed his back against the wall, his chest heaving as he scanned the room for any sign of movement.

"You're losing it," he muttered, though the words rang hollow. The force of the shove had been too real, too deliberate to dismiss.

The Corkboard Collapses

The corkboard had become a symbol of everything Elliot had built and everything he had destroyed. It was his anchor, his tool for control, and his reminder of failure. But now, it too was turning against him.

A few days after the shove, Elliot sat at his desk, trying to organize his scattered notes. The corkboard loomed in front of him, Delyla's photograph still pinned at the center. He avoided looking directly at it, but he could feel her eyes on him all the same.

The first sign of trouble was a faint creak, so soft that Elliot might have ignored it if not for the growing paranoia that had taken hold of him. He glanced up, his eyes narrowing as he noticed the corkboard trembling slightly, as though something were pulling at it.

"Stop," he whispered, his voice trembling. "Don't—"

Before he could finish the sentence, the corkboard tore free from the wall, crashing to the floor with a deafening bang. Papers scattered across the room, strings snapping and tangling as the board came to rest at his feet. Delyla's photograph fluttered down last, landing face-up on the shattered remains of his once-meticulous creation.

Elliot stumbled back, his heart racing as he stared at the mess. "What do you want from me?" he shouted, his voice cracking. "Why won't you leave me alone?"

The air around him grew colder, and for a moment, he thought he heard her laugh—a low, bitter sound that sent chills racing down his spine.

The Push into the Mirror

The next escalation came in the bathroom, where Delyla's presence had always been the strongest. Elliot stood at the sink, splashing cold water on his face in a futile attempt to shake the exhaustion that weighed him down. His reflection in the mirror was gaunt and pale, his eyes bloodshot and ringed with dark shadows. He barely recognized himself.

As he reached for the towel, the room's temperature dropped sharply. Frost began to form on the edges of the mirror, the glass fogging over as his breath became visible in the freezing air.

"Not again," Elliot muttered, his voice trembling. He turned to leave, but before he could take a step, an invisible force shoved him forward.

He hit the mirror hard, the glass shuddering under the impact but miraculously not breaking. His hands shot out instinctively, gripping the edges of the sink as he tried to steady himself. The cold against his back was almost unbearable, pressing into him like a solid weight.

"Stop it!" he shouted, his voice echoing off the tiled walls. "Leave me alone!"

The force released him abruptly, and Elliot stumbled back, his chest heaving as he clutched at his ribs. He glanced at the mirror, half-expecting to see Delyla's face staring back at him. But the glass reflected only his own terrified expression, the frost slowly melting into streaks of water.

Objects Become Weapons

The physical interference became more frequent—and more violent. At first, it was small objects: a pen rolling across the desk, a chair sliding out from the table. But soon, the disturbances grew more aggressive.

One evening, as Elliot sat in the corner of the living room, a book flew across the room, narrowly missing his head. It struck the wall with enough force to leave a dent before falling to the floor. Elliot scrambled to his feet, his body trembling as he backed into the corner.

"What do you want from me?" he demanded, his voice shaking. "Just tell me what you want!"

The room remained silent, but the air felt charged, as though the walls themselves were alive. Another object—a framed photograph of his parents—flew off the shelf, shattering against the floor. Shards of glass scattered across the room, glinting in the dim light like tiny, malevolent stars.

Elliot clutched at his head, his fingers tangling in his hair as he sank to his knees. "Stop it!" he screamed. "Just stop!"

But the attacks continued. A chair toppled over, its wooden legs splintering as it hit the ground. The lamp on his desk flickered violently before the bulb exploded, plunging the room into darkness. Elliot cowered in the corner, his arms wrapped tightly around his knees as the chaos raged around him.

The Realization of Power

It wasn't until the force physically grabbed him that Elliot truly understood the depth of Delyla's power. He had been standing in the kitchen, trying to muster the energy to eat, when he felt it—a cold, unyielding grip on his arm. It wasn't a fleeting touch or a spectral caress. It was firm, deliberate, and terrifyingly real.

Elliot froze, his body stiffening as the grip tightened. He turned his head slowly, half-expecting to see Delyla standing beside him, but there was no one there. The cold against his skin was unbearable, seeping into his bones and leaving him trembling.

"Let me go," he whispered, his voice barely audible. "Please… let me go."

The grip released him suddenly, and Elliot stumbled back, clutching at his arm. When he looked down, he saw faint red marks where the fingers had been—proof that her presence wasn't just emotional or psychological. It was physical. It was real.

Elliot sank to the floor, his chest heaving as he tried to process what had just happened. His mind raced with questions, but one thought overshadowed them all: he wasn't safe. Not here. Not anywhere.

The Fear Takes Hold

The realization that Delyla's ghost could touch him—could hurt him—changed everything. The apartment, once his sanctuary, had become a prison. Every object was a potential weapon, every shadow a threat. Elliot spent most of his time in the corner of the living room, his body curled into a defensive posture as he watched the room with wide, terrified eyes.

He spoke to her often, his words a mix of pleas and demands. "What do you want from me?" he would ask, his voice trembling. "Why are you doing this?"

But Delyla never answered. Her presence was felt in every corner of the apartment, but her voice remained silent. It was as though she were punishing him, forcing him to confront the weight of his guilt without offering him the chance to atone.

Delyla's physical interference was the final confirmation that Elliot's haunting wasn't just in his mind. The shoves, the thrown objects, and the cold, unrelenting grip on his arm were undeniable proof that her presence was real—and that she was angry. Her power was not just emotional; it was physical, and it was growing.

Elliot's world, already shattered, had become a place of constant fear and danger. He was no longer the master of his own domain; he was a prisoner, trapped in a battle he couldn't win. And as the disturbances grew more violent, Elliot knew that Delyla's anger was far from spent. This was only the beginning.

The Ghost's Warning

The apartment was shrouded in an uneasy silence, the kind that stretched too thin and carried an unnatural weight. Elliot sat on the edge of his bed, his body tense and trembling.

He hadn't slept in days, and the toll of exhaustion had left his mind raw and fragile. Delyla's presence had become a relentless shadow over his life, her ghost haunting him with whispers, movements, and accusations. But tonight, there was something different in the air—a feeling Elliot couldn't quite place, a charged tension that crackled in the stillness like a distant storm waiting to break.

The Unsettling Calm

Elliot tried to distract himself, pacing the room with uneven steps, muttering to himself under his breath. His mind raced with memories of the past few weeks, of the first subtle signs of her presence, the horrifying reality of her voice, and the physical attacks that had left him bruised and battered. His once-meticulous apartment had turned into a chaotic battlefield, and he was the losing party, reduced to a fearful shell of his former self.

But tonight, none of that chaos was present. The objects in the apartment remained still, the shadows undisturbed, the air quiet but unbearably cold. It was as if the entire space was holding its breath, waiting for something inevitable. Elliot could feel the weight of it pressing down on him, a sensation that made his chest tighten and his skin prickle with unease.

He turned toward the corkboard—the site of so many confrontations. Delyla's photograph still hung at the center, her faint smile frozen in time. Elliot's gaze lingered on it, his hands clenching into fists at his sides. He wanted to tear it down, to destroy it, but every time he tried, a wave of dread stopped him cold.

"Just leave me alone," he muttered, his voice trembling. "Haven't you done enough?"

His words hung in the cold air, unanswered.

Her Appearance

It was past midnight when she appeared, as she always did, without warning. One moment, the corner of the room was empty; the next, it was filled with her pale, flickering form. Delyla's ghost stood in the shadows, her translucent figure illuminated by the faint light spilling from the desk lamp. Her expression was unreadable—a mixture of sorrow and fury that made Elliot's stomach churn.

Elliot froze, his body stiffening as his breath caught in his throat. His pulse pounded in his ears as he stared at her, his mind reeling. He had seen her many times before, but the shock of her presence never lessened. This time, though, there was something different about her. The air around her seemed charged with energy, her form more solid, more real than ever before.

"Why are you doing this to me?" he asked, his voice barely above a whisper. "What do you want?"

Delyla didn't respond immediately. She remained still, her hollow eyes fixed on him with an intensity that made his chest tighten. The silence stretched on, heavy and oppressive, until she finally spoke.

The Warning Begins

"Your suffering," she said, her voice low and resonant, "has only just begun."

Elliot's knees buckled, and he stumbled back, collapsing into the chair behind him. Her voice was like ice, cold and sharp, cutting through the air with a power that left no room for doubt. It wasn't just a statement—it was a declaration, a promise.

"What does that mean?" he demanded, his voice rising with panic. "What are you going to do to me?"

Delyla took a step closer, her translucent form flickering faintly as the temperature in the room plummeted. Elliot could see his breath in the air, each exhale forming a pale mist that dissolved into the freezing stillness. The cold bit into his skin, seeping through his clothes and leaving him trembling.

"You took everything from me," she said, her voice trembling with both sorrow and fury. "Now, I'll take everything from you."

Her words sent a chill racing down Elliot's spine. He gripped the arms of the chair tightly, his knuckles white as he struggled to maintain his composure. "I didn't mean to," he said, his voice cracking. "It wasn't supposed to be like this."

Delyla's expression twisted, her features contorting with anger. "Wasn't supposed to be like this?" she repeated, her voice rising. "You planned it, Elliot. You stalked me. You killed me. And now, you expect pity?"

Elliot shook his head, tears streaming down his face. "I'm sorry," he said, his voice trembling. "I'm so sorry…"

Cryptic Words and Lingering Dread

Delyla's gaze softened for a brief moment, her hollow eyes filling with something that almost resembled sadness. But the moment passed quickly, her fury returning as she took another step closer. Her presence was overwhelming, her form flickering more violently as the air grew colder.

"Sorry isn't enough," she said. "It will never be enough."

Elliot's chest tightened, his breathing shallow as he tried to process her words. "What do you want from me?" he asked, his voice breaking. "Just tell me what you want!"

Delyla didn't answer immediately. Instead, she raised a hand, her translucent fingers trembling as though she were struggling with some unseen force. The lights in the apartment flickered violently, plunging the room into brief moments of darkness. When the light stabilized, Delyla's expression had changed. She looked calmer now, but her gaze was no less intense.

"I don't want your excuses," she said. "I don't want your tears. I want you to suffer."

Elliot's heart sank, a wave of despair crashing over him. He had known, deep down, that there would be no forgiveness, no reprieve from the torment she had brought into his life. But hearing it spoken aloud shattered whatever fragile hope he had been clinging to.

A Final Question

As the silence returned, Elliot found himself unable to look away from her. His mind raced with questions, but one rose above the rest, a desperate plea for understanding.

"Why me?" he asked, his voice barely audible. "Why are you doing this to me?"

Delyla tilted her head slightly, her gaze unwavering. "Why you?" she repeated, her tone heavy with disbelief. "Because you chose me. You decided my life was worth less than your obsession. And now, I'm giving you what you deserve."

Her words were like daggers, each one cutting deeper than the last. Elliot felt his resolve crumbling, his guilt threatening to consume him entirely. "I can't take this," he whispered, his voice trembling. "I can't…"

Delyla stepped back, her form beginning to fade. The room grew colder still, the frost creeping along the edges of the furniture and the windows as her presence ebbed. But before she disappeared completely, she spoke one final time.

"This is just the beginning," she said, her voice echoing through the room. "You will never escape me."

The Aftermath

When Delyla was gone, the room was left in an unnatural silence. The air was still freezing, the frost on the windows glinting faintly in the dim light. Elliot remained in the chair, his body trembling as tears streamed down his face. Her words echoed in his mind, a haunting refrain that refused to be silenced.

"Your suffering has only just begun."

He buried his face in his hands, his chest heaving with sobs as the weight of her warning settled over him. He had thought he understood fear, guilt, and torment, but now he realized that he was only scratching the surface. Delyla's presence wasn't just a haunting—it was a reckoning, and it wasn't over.

A World Forever Changed

In the days that followed, Elliot couldn't shake the feeling that Delyla's ghost was still watching him. The disturbances in the apartment grew more frequent, the cold air a constant reminder of her presence. Objects moved on their own, shadows flickered in the corners of his vision, and the whispers returned, growing louder and more insistent with each passing night.

He tried to leave, packing a bag and stepping out into the hallway, but the air outside the apartment felt just as oppressive, just as heavy. It was as though Delyla's presence wasn't confined to the space—it was tied to him. No matter where he went, she would follow.

The realization left him broken. There was no escape, no salvation. He was trapped, bound to the ghost of the woman he had killed, her warning a constant reminder of the torment that awaited him.

Delyla's warning wasn't just a statement—it was a declaration of intent, a promise of endless suffering that would haunt Elliot for the rest of his life. Her cryptic words left him with more questions than answers, but one thing was clear: his torment was far from over.

As the frost melted and the air grew heavy once more, Elliot knew that he was no longer the master of his own life. He was a prisoner, bound by guilt and haunted by a force far beyond his understanding. And as Delyla's voice echoed in his mind, he realized that his suffering had only just begun.

The Aftermath

Elliot hadn't thought it was possible for his world to unravel any further, but the ghostly warning Delyla had delivered left him utterly shattered. Her voice still echoed in his ears, her final words reverberating through his skull like an unrelenting drumbeat: *"Your suffering has only just begun."* It was a promise, not a threat, and it had burrowed into his mind, leaving him drowning in terror and disbelief.

The apartment was ice-cold, a biting chill that seemed to radiate from the very walls. Elliot sat in the corner of the room, clutching the knife in his hands as though it were a lifeline. The blade, cold and sharp, felt like the only tangible thing left in a world that had grown unrecognizable. He couldn't bring himself to let it go, even as his hands trembled and his muscles ached from holding it too tightly.

A Night Without Rest

Elliot's gaze flickered across the room, darting from shadow to shadow. The apartment was dimly lit by a single lamp, its flickering bulb casting weak, uneven light that only deepened the sense of unease. Every corner seemed alive, every shadow a potential hiding place for Delyla's ghost. He couldn't trust his eyes, couldn't trust the space around him. The apartment had become a foreign, hostile landscape, and Elliot felt like prey trapped in a predator's den.

Sleep was impossible. Each time he closed his eyes, he could see Delyla's face—twisted in anger and pain, her hollow eyes boring into him. Her voice, cold and sorrowful, whispered through his mind, reminding him of the life he had taken and the torment he had unleashed upon himself.

"You'll never escape me," her voice seemed to say, weaving its way through his thoughts. "This is just the beginning."

Elliot's body was heavy with exhaustion, his limbs aching from hours of tension, but his mind was racing. The events of the night replayed themselves in vivid detail, looping endlessly like a nightmare he couldn't wake from. He couldn't stop himself from questioning everything—his decisions, his actions, and the darkness within him that had led him to this point.

The Knife as a Talisman

The knife in Elliot's hands was both a comfort and a curse. It was the weapon that had ended Delyla's life, the tool that had transformed him from an obsessive outsider into a killer. And yet, as he sat in the corner clutching it, it felt like the only thing tethering him to reality. The blade gleamed faintly in the dim light, its edge sharp and unyielding.

Elliot stared at it, his eyes wide and bloodshot, his breath coming in shallow gasps. The weight of the knife in his hands was a reminder of his guilt, but it also gave him a fleeting sense of control. It was the one thing in the room that hadn't been touched by Delyla's ghost, the one object that hadn't turned against him.

"If you come back," Elliot whispered, his voice trembling, "I'll be ready."

The words felt hollow, a desperate attempt to convince himself that he still had power in a situation where he was utterly powerless. Deep down, he knew the knife was useless against Delyla's ghost. She wasn't bound by the rules of the physical world. She was something else entirely, something he couldn't fight or escape.

Memories of the Kill

As the hours dragged on, Elliot's thoughts turned to the night of Delyla's murder. He had tried to bury the memory, to lock it away in the darkest corners of his mind, but now it came rushing back with brutal clarity.

He remembered the way he had followed her, his heart pounding with a mix of fear and anticipation. He had rehearsed every step of the plan, convinced that he was in control. But when the moment came, it had all fallen apart. The hesitation, the panic, the messy, chaotic kill—it had been nothing like he had imagined.

Elliot's grip on the knife tightened as the memory of her eyes, wide with fear and disbelief, burned itself into his mind. He had told himself she was just a target, just another step in his twisted plan. But now, faced with her ghost, he couldn't deny the humanity he had stolen from her.

"I didn't know," he muttered, his voice barely audible. "I didn't know it would be like this."

But the words offered no comfort. They were empty, a futile attempt to absolve himself of the guilt that weighed him down.

Paranoia Takes Hold

As the night wore on, Elliot's paranoia deepened. Every sound, every flicker of light, sent a jolt of fear through his body. The apartment seemed alive, its walls pulsing with an unseen energy. He imagined Delyla's ghost lurking in the shadows, waiting for the perfect moment to strike again.

Elliot's eyes darted toward the corkboard, now lying face-down on the floor where Delyla's ghost had pulled it from the wall. Her photograph had landed a few feet away, and though it was crumpled and torn, her faint smile still seemed to mock him. He couldn't bring himself to pick it up, couldn't bear to see her face again.

The whispers returned, faint at first but growing louder as the night stretched on. They seemed to come from everywhere and nowhere, wrapping around him like a cold wind. The words were indistinct, but their tone was unmistakable—accusatory, condemning, relentless.

"You knew," they seemed to say. "You chose this."

Elliot clutched the knife tighter, his knuckles white as he rocked back and forth in the corner. "Leave me alone," he whispered, his voice shaking. "Just leave me alone…"

But the whispers didn't stop. They grew louder, overlapping and intertwining until they became a deafening cacophony that filled the room.

A Mind Unraveling

By the time the first rays of dawn began to filter through the curtains, Elliot was barely holding himself together. His body was trembling, his mind teetering on the edge of collapse. He hadn't slept, hadn't eaten, hadn't moved from the corner except to shift uncomfortably against the cold, hard wall.

The knife, still clutched in his hands, felt heavier now, its weight a reminder of everything he had done. He stared at it, his vision blurry with exhaustion, his thoughts spiraling out of control. The whispers had subsided with the coming of daylight, but the oppressive silence that replaced them was almost worse.

Elliot's thoughts turned dark as he considered his options. He couldn't go on like this, couldn't continue living in a world where Delyla's ghost haunted his every waking moment. But what choice did he have? She had promised that his suffering was only beginning, and he believed her.

"I can't do this," he muttered, his voice barely above a whisper. "I can't…"

The Cold Remains

Even as the sun rose higher in the sky, the apartment remained cold. The frost on the windows had begun to melt, but the air still carried a chill that seeped into Elliot's bones. He knew it was her. Even in her absence, Delyla's presence lingered, a constant reminder that he was never truly alone.

Elliot forced himself to stand, his legs trembling beneath him as he staggered toward the window. He peered out at the street below, watching as the city began to come alive. People hurried along the sidewalks, oblivious to the nightmare unfolding just a few floors above them.

For a brief moment, Elliot envied their ignorance. He wondered what it would be like to go back to a time when his world was simple, when his mind wasn't consumed by guilt and fear. But that time was gone. Delyla had taken it from him, just as he had taken her life.

The night after Delyla's ghost delivered her warning was a turning point for Elliot. It was the night he realized that his suffering was far from over, that he was trapped in a torment he couldn't escape. Clutching the knife like a talisman, he spent the hours in a state of paralyzed fear, unable to sleep or think clearly. The oppressive cold, the relentless whispers, and the haunting memories of his crime all conspired to unravel what little remained of his sanity.

As the sun rose and the world outside continued on as if nothing had happened, Elliot was left alone in his apartment, a prisoner of his own guilt and fear. He knew that Delyla's warning was not an empty threat. This was just the beginning, and the aftermath of his actions would haunt him for the rest of his life.

Chapter 6: Escalation

Increased Aggression

Delyla's ghost had become more than just an eerie presence lingering in the shadows of Elliot's life. What began as subtle signs of her haunting—faint whispers, fleeting apparitions, and an ever-present chill—had now evolved into something relentless, aggressive, and dangerous. Her appearances became frequent and forceful, her wrath disrupting every moment of Elliot's existence. The haunting had shifted from a psychological battle to an outright war, and Elliot's life was the battlefield.

A Relentless Presence

The first sign of Delyla's escalation came early one morning, just as the first rays of dawn began to creep through the apartment's frost-covered windows. Elliot had spent the night huddled in the corner of his bedroom, his knees drawn to his chest and his knife clutched tightly in his trembling hands. Sleep had eluded him for weeks, but tonight the exhaustion had won, dragging him into a fitful slumber.

He awoke to the sound of footsteps—soft, deliberate, and impossibly close. His eyes flew open, his chest tightening as he scanned the dimly lit room. At first, there was nothing but the faint glow of the streetlights outside. Then, in the corner opposite him, she appeared.

Delyla's ghost was more solid than before, her form flickering less and her edges more defined. She stood motionless, her hollow eyes fixed on him with an intensity that made his stomach churn. Her presence filled the room, suffocating and cold, and Elliot's breath came in shallow gasps as he scrambled to his feet.

"Leave me alone!" he shouted, his voice cracking.

Delyla didn't respond. Instead, she took a step forward, her translucent feet making no sound against the floor. The room's temperature plummeted, frost spreading rapidly across the walls and windows. Elliot's knife slipped from his hands, clattering to the floor as his fingers went numb.

That morning set the tone for what was to come. Delyla's ghost was no longer content to haunt him in silence. She was there, constantly, her presence disrupting every moment of his waking life.

Objects as Weapons

It wasn't long before Delyla's aggression extended beyond her chilling presence. Objects in the apartment began to move—at first subtly, then violently. A chair would slide across the room as Elliot sat in it, forcing him to stand. A glass of water would topple over, spilling its contents just as he reached for it. Then, the objects became weapons.

One afternoon, as Elliot sat at his desk trying to regain a semblance of control, the desk lamp flew off the table, narrowly missing his head. He ducked instinctively, his heart pounding as the lamp shattered against the wall behind him. Shards of glass rained down, glinting like tiny daggers in the dim light.

"Stop it!" he screamed, his voice filled with a mix of anger and terror.

The room responded with silence, but only for a moment. Then, the corkboard—the centerpiece of Elliot's obsession—ripped itself free from the wall, slamming onto the floor with enough force to split the wood. Papers, pins, and string scattered across the room, and Delyla's photograph landed face-up among the chaos.

Elliot stared at the mess, his body trembling as tears streamed down his face. His world, once meticulously ordered, was now a wreckage of fear and despair. He sank to his knees, clutching his head as the cold wind that seemed to emanate from Delyla's ghost howled through the room.

Screams in the Shadows

Delyla's voice, once a whisper that barely reached his ears, had grown into something deafening and visceral. She screamed now—long, anguished wails that echoed through the apartment, shaking the walls and rattling the windows.

The first time it happened, Elliot thought the sound was coming from the street outside. He rushed to the window, his heart racing, only to find the street below eerily quiet. Then, the scream came again, louder this time, filling the room with a sound so raw and guttural it made his chest ache.

"Stop it!" he yelled, his voice drowned out by the ghostly wail.

Delyla's form appeared in the corner, her translucent body shimmering as her mouth opened impossibly wide. The scream seemed to pour out of her, reverberating through the apartment with a force that made Elliot's knees buckle. He collapsed onto the floor, clutching his ears as the sound threatened to tear him apart.

The screams became a regular occurrence, each one more horrifying than the last. They came at all hours of the day and night, leaving Elliot unable to rest or think clearly. The sound followed him even when he tried to leave the apartment, echoing in his mind and driving him to the brink of madness.

Chilling Winds

The apartment had always been cold since Delyla's haunting began, but now the chill had become unbearable. The temperature dropped to near-freezing levels, frost creeping along the walls and forming intricate patterns on the windows. But the worst part was the wind.

It started as a faint breeze, rustling papers and sending shivers down Elliot's spine. Then, it grew stronger, a howling gale that tore through the apartment with a fury that defied logic. Furniture toppled over, books flew off shelves, and the air was filled with a biting cold that made Elliot's skin ache.

One night, as Elliot tried to barricade himself in his bedroom, the wind tore through the apartment with such force that the door to his room was ripped open. Delyla's ghost stood in the doorway, her form shimmering as the wind whipped around her, her hair and tattered clothes flowing like smoke.

"You can't hide," she said, her voice cutting through the roar of the wind like a knife. "You'll never escape me."

Elliot clutched the blanket around his shoulders, his teeth chattering as he backed into the corner of the room. The wind seemed to follow him, swirling around him with a ferocity that left him gasping for air.

Isolation and Despair

The constant attacks left Elliot completely isolated. He stopped going outside, too afraid of what might happen if Delyla's ghost followed him. His phone lay abandoned on the floor, its screen shattered during one of Delyla's fits of aggression. He had no one to call, no one who would believe him even if he tried to explain.

The apartment, once his sanctuary, had become a prison. Every corner held a new terror, every shadow a reminder of Delyla's presence. Elliot spent his days in a constant state of vigilance, his body trembling with exhaustion as he waited for the next attack.

He stopped eating, stopped sleeping, stopped caring about anything beyond surviving the next moment. His reflection in the mirror was unrecognizable—a gaunt, hollow-eyed figure that barely resembled the man he once was.

"I can't do this anymore," he whispered one night, his voice trembling. "Please... just stop."

But Delyla didn't stop. She only grew stronger, her presence more suffocating, her attacks more relentless.

A Desperate Plea

Elliot's breaking point came during one of Delyla's most violent episodes. The apartment was in shambles—furniture overturned, glass shattered, and papers scattered everywhere. The wind howled through the room, and Delyla's screams filled the air, drowning out every thought.

Elliot fell to his knees in the middle of the chaos, his hands clutching at his head as he screamed, "What do you want from me? Just tell me what you want!"

Delyla's ghost appeared before him, her form towering and menacing. Her eyes burned with a fury that made Elliot's chest tighten, and her voice was cold and unyielding as she said, "I want you to suffer."

Her words cut through him like a blade, leaving him trembling and broken. He sank lower to the floor, his body trembling as he whispered, "I'm sorry… I'm so sorry…"

The room fell silent for a moment, the wind dying down and Delyla's form flickering faintly. Then, she leaned closer, her voice a chilling whisper in his ear: "It's too late for sorry."

Delyla's increased aggression marked a turning point in her haunting, transforming Elliot's life into a living nightmare. Her relentless presence, violent attacks, and chilling winds left him physically and mentally shattered. The once-controlled man was now a broken shell, consumed by fear and despair as Delyla's wrath continued to escalate. The ghost's promise of unending torment loomed over him, a constant reminder that his suffering was far from over.

Elliot's Isolation

Elliot's descent into isolation wasn't a sudden drop; it was a slow, suffocating spiral. Each moment of Delyla's haunting—every scream, every chilling touch, every instance of physical interference—pushed him further away from the outside world and deeper into his own despair. The man who once meticulously planned and calculated every step of his life now found himself trapped in a prison of fear, a cage of his own making. Isolation wasn't just his refuge; it was his only perceived means of survival.

Fear of the Outside World

Elliot had always been an observer of life rather than a participant, but after Delyla's ghost began following him beyond the confines of his apartment, the outside world became an unbearable source of terror. It started with small, fleeting encounters—her reflection in a shop window, her translucent figure lingering in an alleyway as he hurried past. At first, he told himself it wasn't real, that it was his imagination playing tricks on him. But then she became bolder, more obvious.

One day, as Elliot walked through a park in a desperate attempt to clear his mind, Delyla appeared on a bench just ahead of him. She didn't move or speak; she simply stared at him with those hollow, accusing eyes. His breath hitched, and he froze, unable to look away. When he blinked, she was gone, but the fear lingered.

He tried to go about his errands that day, but every corner he turned, every reflective surface he passed, she was there. By the time he returned to his apartment, his hands were shaking so violently that he could barely unlock the door. He collapsed onto the floor once inside, his chest heaving as he whispered to himself, "I can't go out again. I can't."

The idea of leaving became unbearable. If Delyla could follow him outside, there was no sanctuary, no escape. Elliot resolved to stay inside, convincing himself that he could at least contain her within the walls of his apartment. But deep down, he knew it was a hollow lie.

Retreating from Human Contact

The isolation grew deeper as Elliot began cutting himself off from everyone he knew. It wasn't as though he had many people in his life to begin with—his solitary nature and obsessive tendencies had ensured that—but even the small, superficial connections he maintained were now unbearable.

His phone was the first casualty. At first, he ignored calls, letting them go to voicemail. Then, the incessant ringing became a source of anxiety, a reminder that the world outside still existed, demanding his attention. One day, after Delyla's ghost knocked the phone off his desk, Elliot picked it up and hurled it against the wall, shattering it into pieces. The silence that followed was both a relief and a weight pressing down on his chest.

Knocks on the door were another problem. His landlord came by to ask about the strange noises coming from his apartment. A deliveryman once knocked for several minutes, trying to hand off a package Elliot had forgotten he ordered. Each time, Elliot pressed himself against the wall, holding his breath until the person outside gave up and left.

"Go away," he muttered under his breath each time, his voice trembling. "Just leave me alone."

Delyla's presence often intensified during these moments, as though she were mocking his attempts to hide from the world. The air would grow colder, objects would shift or fall, and her ghostly figure would appear in the corner, watching him with quiet disdain.

The Apartment as a Prison

Elliot's apartment, once his sanctuary, had transformed into a cage. The walls seemed to close in on him, the air growing staler with each passing day. The mess left by Delyla's physical aggression remained untouched—overturned furniture, shattered glass, and the scattered remnants of his corkboard covered the floor like the wreckage of his mind.

He stopped cleaning, stopped organizing, stopped caring. The once-meticulous man who had prided himself on order and control now lived in squalor, too consumed by fear and paranoia to do anything about it.

Windows became another point of fear. The idea of someone seeing him, of the outside world intruding on his isolation, was unbearable. He hung heavy blankets over the windows, plunging the apartment into perpetual dimness. The sunlight that managed to seep through was cold and lifeless, a pale imitation of the warmth he no longer allowed himself to feel.

Every noise outside the apartment became a potential threat. The footsteps of neighbors in the hallway, the distant hum of traffic, even the sound of birds chirping outside his window—all of it made him jump, his heart racing as he waited for Delyla to make her next move.

The Loss of Time

With no connection to the outside world, time became meaningless to Elliot. Days blurred into nights, and weeks passed without him noticing. He stopped checking the calendar, stopped keeping track of the hours. The clocks in the apartment seemed to mock him, their ticking a constant reminder of the life slipping away from him.

Elliot's routine—if it could even be called that—consisted of little more than sitting in the corner of his bedroom, clutching his knife like a talisman. He slept in fits and starts, jolted awake by nightmares or the chilling presence of Delyla's ghost. Food became an afterthought; he subsisted on whatever scraps he could find in his pantry, too afraid to leave the apartment to buy more.

"Time doesn't matter," he muttered to himself one day, his voice hoarse from disuse. "It's all the same now."

Delyla's ghost seemed to feed off his disorientation, appearing at random intervals that made it impossible for him to anticipate or prepare for her. Sometimes, she would linger for hours, her presence a suffocating weight that made the air in the apartment feel unbreathable. Other times, she would vanish as quickly as she appeared, leaving Elliot to wonder if she had ever been there at all.

Paranoia and Self-Doubt

Elliot's paranoia grew to unbearable levels, consuming every thought and action. He began to question everything—his memories, his senses, even his own mind. Was Delyla's ghost truly haunting him, or was he descending into madness? The line between reality and delusion blurred until it no longer existed.

He started hearing things—soft whispers, faint laughter, the sound of footsteps pacing the apartment when he was alone. Sometimes, he would catch glimpses of movement out of the corner of his eye, only to turn and find nothing there. Each instance chipped away at his already fragile sanity.

"She's everywhere," he muttered one night, his voice trembling. "She's in my head. She's in the walls. I can't get away from her."

Even his own reflection became a source of fear. The mirrors in the apartment seemed to distort his image, twisting his features into something grotesque and unrecognizable. He covered them all with towels and sheets, but he could still feel the weight of his reflection staring at him, judging him.

The Point of No Return

Elliot's isolation reached its peak one night when Delyla's ghost launched her most aggressive attack yet. The apartment was plunged into darkness as every lightbulb shattered simultaneously. The temperature dropped so rapidly that frost formed on the walls, and a deafening wind howled through the space, knocking over furniture and scattering papers.

Delyla appeared in the center of the chaos, her form more solid than ever. Her eyes burned with fury as she screamed, the sound so loud and piercing that it felt like it was coming from inside Elliot's skull.

"You think you can hide?" she shouted, her voice reverberating through the apartment. "You think this will save you?"

Elliot collapsed onto the floor, his hands covering his ears as he screamed back, "I'm sorry! I'm so sorry!"

The wind died down, and the room fell silent. Delyla's ghost stepped closer, her expression cold and unyielding. "Sorry isn't enough," she said, her voice low and menacing. "You don't get to escape."

When she vanished, Elliot was left alone in the dark, trembling and sobbing. He realized then that his isolation hadn't protected him from Delyla—it had only made him more vulnerable. There was no escape from her wrath, no refuge from her torment.

Elliot's self-imposed isolation was born out of fear, but it became its own form of punishment. By cutting himself off from the outside world, he had trapped himself in a prison of paranoia and despair, with Delyla's ghost as his constant warden. The apartment, once a sanctuary, had become a living nightmare—a place where time lost all meaning and the boundaries between reality and delusion dissolved.

As Elliot sat in the darkness of his ruined apartment, he realized that there was no escape from Delyla's haunting, no way to undo what he had done. Isolation, once his shield, had become his cage, and Delyla held the key.

Psychological Torment

Elliot had always prided himself on being methodical, logical, and in control. Even as his life unraveled after Delyla's murder, he clung to the belief that he was still the architect of his own fate. But Delyla's ghost was relentless, and her haunting began to infiltrate the most sacred and private spaces of his mind. Her voice became a weapon, dredging up his darkest thoughts and insecurities, exposing the cracks in his carefully constructed facade. What began as whispers soon became a symphony of torment, eroding Elliot's sanity piece by piece.

The Whispering Begins

The whispers started subtly, barely audible at first, like faint echoes carried on the cold winds that now perpetually haunted his apartment. Elliot often heard them at night, as he lay curled on his mattress in the dark, clutching the knife he had used to kill Delyla. The sound was faint, almost indistinguishable from his own thoughts. At first, he convinced himself that it was his mind playing tricks on him, a side effect of the exhaustion and fear that had consumed him since the night of the murder.

But as the whispers grew louder, more distinct, he could no longer deny their source. Delyla's voice—soft, cold, and filled with disdain—was speaking to him, her words slicing through the silence like a blade.

"You're pathetic," she murmured one night, her voice carrying from the corner of the room. "You think you're strong, but you're nothing."

Elliot froze, his heart pounding in his chest. He sat up, his eyes darting toward the sound, but the corner was empty. The air in the apartment was heavy, oppressive, and he could feel her presence, even if he couldn't see her.

"You planned it all, didn't you?" she continued, her voice a mixture of mockery and venom. "All that research, all that preparation... and you still failed."

The words hit him like a punch to the gut, and Elliot buried his face in his hands. "Shut up," he muttered, his voice trembling. "Just shut up."

But the whispers didn't stop. They grew louder, more insistent, weaving themselves into his thoughts until he couldn't distinguish her voice from his own.

Mocking the Murder

Delyla's ghost began to zero in on the event that haunted Elliot most—the night of her murder. She dissected every detail of his clumsy, botched attack, her voice dripping with scorn as she recounted his failures.

"You thought you were so clever," she sneered, her voice echoing through the room as Elliot huddled in the corner. "Stalking me, learning my routine. Did you think you were a predator? A hunter?"

Elliot clenched his fists, his nails digging into his palms as he fought to block out her words. But they were relentless, cutting through his defenses with brutal precision.

"You hesitated," she said, her tone growing colder. "You hesitated, and I saw it. I saw the fear in your eyes. You didn't even have the guts to do it properly."

Tears streamed down Elliot's face as he shook his head, his body trembling. "I didn't... I didn't mean to..." he stammered, his voice breaking.

Delyla's laughter filled the room, hollow and bitter. "Didn't mean to?" she repeated mockingly. "You meant every second of it, Elliot. You planned it for weeks, months. And when the moment came, you couldn't even finish it cleanly."

The memory of that night played in his mind like a film reel, each frame sharper and more vivid than the last. He saw himself fumbling with the knife, his hands shaking as Delyla screamed and fought back. He remembered the way her eyes widened in fear, the way her body crumpled to the ground in slow motion. And he remembered the overwhelming sense of failure that followed—the knowledge that he had not been the predator he had imagined himself to be.

Exposing His Insecurities

Delyla's voice wasn't content to mock his actions; she delved deeper, exposing the insecurities that Elliot had buried for years. She seemed to know him better than he knew himself, her words striking at the heart of his fears and weaknesses.

"You've always been a coward," she said one night, her voice low and venomous. "Hiding behind your plans, your notebooks, your corkboard. You thought those things made you powerful, but they were just a shield."

Elliot shook his head, his eyes wide with panic as he backed against the wall. "Stop it," he whispered. "You don't know me."

"Oh, but I do," Delyla replied, her voice like ice. "I've seen you. The little boy who was too scared to stand up for himself. The man who watched life pass him by because he was too afraid to live it. You thought killing me would change that, didn't you? You thought it would make you strong."

Her words cut deeper than any physical wound, and Elliot felt his resolve crumbling. She was right—he had thought that the act of taking a life would give him control, power. But instead, it had left him hollow, broken, and weaker than ever.

The Erosion of Identity

As Delyla's whispers grew more persistent, Elliot began to lose his sense of self. Her voice was no longer confined to the apartment; it followed him everywhere, seeping into his thoughts and drowning out his own inner voice. He found himself questioning his every action, his every decision.

"Do you even know who you are anymore?" Delyla asked one day, her voice echoing in his mind as he sat at his desk, staring blankly at the scattered remnants of his corkboard. "You're not a man. You're not even a monster. You're nothing."

The words repeated themselves in his mind, a relentless mantra that left him spiraling into despair. Elliot began to doubt everything he had ever believed about himself. His identity, once built on a foundation of control and intellect, was now a crumbling ruin.

"Who are you, Elliot?" Delyla taunted. "A fraud? A failure? Or just a scared little boy pretending to be something he's not?"

Elliot couldn't answer her. He didn't know anymore.

Guilt as a Weapon

Delyla's most effective weapon was guilt. She wielded it with precision, forcing Elliot to confront the weight of his actions and the lives he had destroyed—not just hers, but her family's, her friends', and even his own.

"You didn't just kill me," she said one night, her voice heavy with sorrow. "You killed everything I could have been. Every dream, every chance, every moment. You took it all."

Elliot buried his face in his hands, his shoulders shaking as he sobbed. "I didn't mean to…" he whispered. "I didn't mean to…"

"But you did," Delyla replied, her tone unyielding. "You knew exactly what you were doing. You planned it, step by step. And now, you get to live with it."

Her words forced Elliot to confront the full scope of his crime. He saw Delyla's life play out in his mind—her childhood, her family, her hopes and dreams. He saw the pain her death had caused, the empty chair at the dinner table, the tears of her loved ones. The weight of it all was crushing, and Elliot felt as though he were drowning in his own guilt.

The Coward's Legacy

Delyla's final weapon was her ability to strip away Elliot's delusions, forcing him to see himself for what he truly was. She didn't just mock his clumsy attack; she tore apart the very foundation of his self-image.

"You wanted to be remembered, didn't you?" she asked one night, her voice laced with mockery. "You thought this would make you someone. But now, you'll only be remembered as a coward. A fraud."

Elliot shook his head, his hands trembling as he clutched at his hair. "I didn't want this," he muttered. "I didn't…"

"But you did," Delyla said, her voice cold and final. "You wanted control. You wanted power. And now, you have nothing."

Her words left Elliot shattered, his mind a fractured mess of guilt, fear, and self-loathing. He had nowhere to turn, no escape from the torment that Delyla had unleashed upon him. Her voice, once an external force, had become a part of him, entwined with his thoughts and insecurities. And as he sat alone in the darkness of his apartment, he realized that the torment would never end.

Delyla's psychological torment was as devastating as it was relentless. By whispering Elliot's darkest thoughts aloud, mocking his failures, and exposing his insecurities, she dismantled every shred of his identity. Her voice, both a weapon and a mirror, forced Elliot to confront the truth of who he was—a coward, a failure, and a man consumed by guilt. Her haunting wasn't just a punishment; it was a reckoning, one that left Elliot a hollow, broken shell of the person he once thought himself to be.

The Ghost Gains Power

Elliot's world was already crumbling, a chaotic ruin of fear, guilt, and despair. His apartment, once a place of control and obsessive order, had become a prison under Delyla's relentless haunting. But even in his darkest moments, Elliot had held on to one hope: that Delyla's ghost was confined to the walls of his home, that her power couldn't reach beyond the apartment. That hope was shattered the first time he saw her outside.

The realization that Delyla's presence wasn't bound by the physical limits of his apartment pushed Elliot further into a spiral of paranoia. She wasn't just a haunting; she was everywhere. Every step he took outside was no longer an escape but a terrifying reminder that there was no refuge from her torment.

The First Appearance Outside

Elliot had been forcing himself to leave his apartment occasionally, if only to avoid complete isolation. The apartment was suffocating, its cold and oppressive atmosphere a constant reminder of Delyla's presence. On a rare outing, he found himself walking aimlessly through the city, his hands buried deep in his jacket pockets as he kept his head down.

The first time he saw her outside was in a shop window. He had stopped to adjust his coat against the biting wind, his breath fogging up the glass as he looked into the brightly lit store. At first, the reflection seemed normal—a display of mannequins, shelves of neatly stacked clothes, and the soft glow of hanging lights. But then, just behind his own reflection, he saw her.

Delyla stood motionless, her translucent form flickering faintly in the glass. Her hollow eyes locked onto his, and for a moment, Elliot couldn't breathe. He spun around, expecting to see her standing behind him on the sidewalk, but the space was empty. When he turned back to the window, her reflection was gone.

The encounter left him shaken. He stumbled into an alleyway, his legs trembling beneath him as he leaned against a brick wall. "This can't be real," he muttered, his breath coming in short, panicked gasps. "She's not supposed to be here."

But the truth was undeniable. Delyla's ghost had followed him

A Growing Presence

After that day, Delyla began appearing more frequently outside the apartment. It started with fleeting glimpses—her figure disappearing around a corner just as Elliot approached, or her face appearing briefly in the side mirror of a parked car. Each time, Elliot's heart raced, his paranoia growing with every encounter.

He began to avoid reflective surfaces, terrified of seeing her again. Shop windows, puddles, even the gleaming metal of elevator doors became potential threats. But no matter how careful he was, Delyla found ways to remind him of her presence.

One afternoon, as Elliot sat on a park bench trying to collect his thoughts, he heard her voice. It was faint at first, blending with the chatter of nearby conversations and the rustling of leaves in the wind. But as he strained to listen, the words became clearer.

"Coward," she whispered, her voice cold and biting. "Fraud."

Elliot shot to his feet, his eyes darting around the park. The people around him went about their day, oblivious to his panic. He scanned the trees, the benches, the pathways, but there was no sign of her. And yet, he couldn't shake the feeling that she was watching him.

Crowded Streets and Empty Alleys

The city streets, once a source of anonymity and escape, became a battleground. Delyla's presence was everywhere, her voice weaving through the noise of crowded sidewalks and bustling shops. Elliot would hear her whisper his name as he passed strangers, or feel the ghostly brush of her hand against his shoulder as he pushed through a crowd.

One evening, as he walked home from a failed attempt at normalcy, he turned into an empty alley to avoid the throngs of people on the main street. The alley was quiet, the distant hum of traffic muffled by the towering buildings on either side. For a moment, he allowed himself to breathe, to believe he was alone.

But then, he heard footsteps behind him.

Elliot froze, his body tensing as the sound grew closer. He turned slowly, his breath hitching in his throat as he saw her standing at the far end of the alley. Her form was more solid than it had ever been, her translucent body glowing faintly in the dim light.

"You can't run," she said, her voice echoing off the brick walls. "You can't hide."

Elliot stumbled backward, his heart pounding in his chest. He turned and ran, his footsteps echoing loudly as he fled the alley. But no matter how fast he ran, he couldn't escape the feeling that she was right behind him.

No Safe Places

The places Elliot once considered safe became tainted by Delyla's growing power. His favorite coffee shop, the small park bench he used to sit on, even the quiet bookstore he visited to lose himself in anonymity—each one was invaded by her presence.

In the coffee shop, as he waited for his order, he saw her reflection in the glass of the pastry display. She stood just behind him, her hollow eyes staring through him. He turned quickly, nearly knocking over a table, but there was no one there.

At the park, as he tried to calm his racing thoughts, he felt her cold touch on his shoulder. He turned, expecting to see a stranger brushing past him, but the pathway was empty. The cold lingered, seeping into his skin and leaving him trembling.

The bookstore was the worst. As he browsed the shelves, trying to distract himself with a novel, Delyla's voice whispered from the pages. "You don't belong here," she said, her tone icy. "You don't belong anywhere."

Elliot dropped the book, his hands trembling as he backed away from the shelf. The other patrons stared at him, their expressions a mix of confusion and concern. He muttered an apology and fled the store, vowing never to return.

The Breaking Point

The constant appearances and whispers wore Elliot down, leaving him a shell of his former self. He stopped going outside altogether, convinced that Delyla would follow him wherever he went. His world became smaller and smaller, his apartment a suffocating prison.

But even in his isolation, Delyla found ways to torment him. Her voice echoed through the walls, her reflection appeared in the windows even though they were covered. She was everywhere, her presence inescapable.

One night, as Elliot sat on the floor of his apartment clutching his knees to his chest,

Delyla appeared directly in front of him. Her form was solid, her expression filled with a mix of anger and sorrow.

"You thought you could run," she said, her voice cutting through the silence like a blade. "You thought you could escape me."

Elliot shook his head, tears streaming down his face. "What do you want from me?" he whispered, his voice trembling. "Why won't you leave me alone?"

Delyla leaned closer, her hollow eyes piercing through him. "You know why," she said. "You know what you did."

The Loss of Hope

Elliot's hope for escape, for redemption, for any semblance of peace, was gone. Delyla's power had grown beyond anything he could have imagined, and there was no longer a place he could go to avoid her. She was everywhere—in the streets, in the reflections, in the voices of strangers. Her haunting wasn't confined to his apartment; it was his entire existence.

The realization left him broken. He stopped trying to fight, stopped trying to run. He accepted that his life was no longer his own, that Delyla's ghost would haunt him until his dying breath.

As he sat in the darkness of his apartment, the sound of her voice filled the room once more. "This is your life now," she whispered, her tone soft but unyielding. "This is your punishment."

Elliot closed his eyes, his body trembling as he whispered, "I'm sorry…"

But Delyla's voice offered no forgiveness, only a chilling promise: "It's too late for sorry."

Delyla's ghost gaining power and following Elliot beyond the confines of his apartment marked a significant escalation in her haunting. The once-safe spaces of the outside world became battlegrounds for her relentless torment, leaving Elliot with no refuge from her wrath. Her presence in shop windows, her whispers in crowded streets, and her solid form in quiet alleys drove Elliot to the breaking point, stripping away any hope of escape. Her haunting was no longer bound by physical limits, and Elliot's world had become a living nightmare from which there was no escape.

Elliot's Ritual Attempts

The haunting had taken over Elliot's life. No longer confined to his apartment, Delyla's ghost followed him everywhere, her relentless torment breaking his body and spirit. Desperate and teetering on the edge of madness, Elliot turned to what he once would have dismissed as superstition: rituals. Late at night, with trembling hands, he scoured the internet, searching for anything that might drive away the ghost. Sage, salt, incantations—anything that offered the faintest hope of relief. But with each failed attempt, Delyla's fury grew, her haunting more aggressive and terrifying than before.

The Search for Answers

Elliot's obsession with control had once been his defining trait, but Delyla's ghost had stripped that away. As her presence grew stronger, his sense of helplessness deepened. The internet became his lifeline, a vast sea of possibilities that might hold the key to ending the nightmare.

He spent hours poring over articles, forums, and blogs, looking for anything that resembled a solution. Ghost stories, paranormal guides, and amateur occultists all offered conflicting advice: burn sage, sprinkle salt, recite prayers, draw protective symbols. Each claim seemed more far-fetched than the last, but Elliot was too desperate to care.

He compiled a list of supplies—salt, sage bundles, candles, chalk, and a printout of a banishment spell written by someone claiming to be an expert in the occult. He knew it was irrational, even ridiculous, but logic had no place in his world anymore. If these rituals offered even the faintest chance of peace, they were worth trying.

The First Ritual

Elliot's first attempt at a ritual was clumsy and rushed, his inexperience with such practices painfully obvious. He followed the instructions from one of the websites, starting with a cleansing ritual that involved burning sage and chanting a prayer for protection.

The apartment was dark except for the flickering candlelight. Elliot moved from room to room, holding the smoldering bundle of sage as wisps of smoke curled into the air. His voice trembled as he recited the prayer, the words unfamiliar and awkward on his tongue.

"By this sacred flame, I cleanse this space of darkness," he whispered. "Let no harm linger here. Let no spirit stay."

As he reached the corner of the living room, where Delyla's photograph had once hung on the corkboard, the air grew colder. The candlelight dimmed, and the sage smoke curled unnaturally, as if caught in an invisible current.

A laugh echoed through the room, low and mocking. "You think that's going to work?" Delyla's voice was a mixture of disdain and amusement, her figure materializing in the corner. "You can't burn me away, Elliot."

The sage fell from his trembling hands, the embers scattering on the floor. Elliot scrambled to stamp them out, his heart pounding as Delyla's laughter filled the apartment.

Salt Circles and Symbols

Undeterred by his failure, Elliot moved on to the next ritual. This one involved creating a circle of salt around himself to act as a protective barrier while he recited another incantation. He carefully poured the salt in a wide circle on the living room floor, his hands shaking as he tried to keep the line unbroken.

Once the circle was complete, he sat in the center, clutching a piece of paper with the incantation written on it. His voice was hoarse as he read aloud, the words promising to banish spirits and cleanse the space of negative energy.

For a moment, the apartment was silent. The air felt heavy, charged with an unnatural energy that made Elliot's skin prickle. He dared to hope that the ritual was working.

Then, the salt line was breached.

A sudden gust of wind tore through the apartment, scattering the salt across the floor. Delyla's ghost appeared within the circle, her form more solid than ever, her eyes filled with anger.

"Do you really think a little salt is going to stop me?" she demanded, her voice echoing in the small space. "You can't contain me, Elliot. You can't control me."

The candles flickered violently before extinguishing, plunging the room into darkness. Elliot cowered in the center of the broken circle, his body trembling as Delyla loomed over him.

The Mirror Ritual

Desperation drove Elliot to try one of the more elaborate rituals he found online. This one involved using a mirror to confront the spirit directly and demand its departure. The instructions were detailed, requiring him to draw protective symbols on the mirror's surface with chalk and light a candle in front of it.

Elliot followed the steps meticulously, his movements slow and deliberate as he drew the symbols and placed the candle. He lit the wick, the small flame casting eerie shadows across the room. Taking a deep breath, he positioned himself in front of the mirror, his reflection pale and haggard.

"Delyla," he said, his voice cracking. "I command you to leave this place. Your presence is no longer welcome."

For a moment, nothing happened. Then, Delyla's face appeared in the mirror, her expression twisted with anger and mockery. Her lips moved, but the words didn't match the sound of her voice, which now seemed to come from every corner of the room.

"Command me?" she said, her tone dripping with disdain. "You don't command anything, Elliot. Not anymore."

The mirror began to vibrate, the symbols smudging and distorting as cracks spread across the glass. Elliot stumbled backward, his heart racing as the mirror shattered, shards flying across the room.

Delyla's Increasing Fury

Each failed ritual seemed to enrage Delyla further. Her attacks became more frequent and violent, her presence more oppressive. Objects flew across the room with greater force, doors slammed shut on their own, and the temperature in the apartment dropped to unbearable levels.

"You're pathetic," Delyla sneered during one of her appearances. "You think you can banish me with these childish games? You don't even understand what you've done."

Elliot's frustration boiled over. "What do you want from me?" he shouted, his voice breaking. "I'm trying! I'm trying to make it right!"

Delyla's laughter echoed through the room, cold and cruel. "Make it right? You can't make this right, Elliot. All you're doing is proving how weak you are."

Elliot sank to the floor, his body trembling as tears streamed down his face. He had thought the rituals might offer him some measure of control, but instead, they had only deepened his despair.

The Final Attempt

Elliot's final ritual was the most extreme, a combination of every method he had read about. He used sage, salt, candles, and protective symbols, layering them in a desperate attempt to rid himself of Delyla's ghost once and for all.

The apartment was filled with smoke from the burning sage, the air thick and suffocating. Salt lines crisscrossed the floor, creating a maze of barriers that Elliot hoped would contain her. He lit the candles, their flames casting a faint glow against the darkness, and began chanting the incantation.

For a moment, the room was still. The air felt heavy, charged with energy, and Elliot's heart raced with a mixture of fear and hope.

Then, Delyla appeared in the center of the room, her form towering and menacing. The flames of the candles flickered wildly, and the symbols on the floor seemed to writhe and shift.

"You still don't understand, do you?" she said, her voice cold and unyielding. "You can't get rid of me, Elliot. I'm not some spirit you can banish. I'm your guilt. I'm your punishment. And I'm never leaving."

The candles extinguished, plunging the room into darkness. The salt lines scattered as an unseen force swept through the apartment, and the sage smoke dissipated into nothing. Elliot collapsed to the floor, his body trembling as Delyla's voice echoed one final time.

"This is where you belong," she whispered. "With me."

Elliot's desperate attempts to rid himself of Delyla's ghost only served to deepen his torment. The rituals, born of fear and hope, became futile gestures in the face of Delyla's growing power. Each failure reinforced the truth that there was no escaping her, no undoing what he had done. Delyla's ghost wasn't just a haunting—it was a manifestation of Elliot's guilt and despair, a punishment he couldn't outrun. The rituals were not a path to freedom; they were another reminder of his powerlessness in the face of his own sins.

Foreshadowing Greater Chaos

Elliot had been living in terror ever since Delyla's ghost began haunting him. Each day brought new horrors, pushing him further into despair and paranoia. But as oppressive as her haunting had become, Delyla's latest words sent a chill down his spine that went deeper than any cold spot or spectral touch.

"This is just the beginning," she had whispered, her voice heavy with promise and menace.

Those words lingered in Elliot's mind, replaying over and over. What did she mean? What was coming next? As he struggled to decipher her cryptic warning, the environment around him seemed to shift. Shadows deepened, whispers grew louder, and the once-familiar walls of his apartment became an alien, threatening landscape. The haunting wasn't just about torment anymore; it was a harbinger of something far worse.

The Ominous Whisper

Delyla's cryptic message—*"This is just the beginning"*—marked a turning point in the haunting. It was no longer a personal vendetta, a punishment for Elliot's crime. It was something bigger, something darker, and it loomed over him like a storm on the horizon.

The first sign came late one night, as Elliot sat hunched on his mattress, staring blankly at the floor. The apartment was eerily quiet, the kind of silence that felt alive, pressing against his ears and chest. He was used to Delyla's voice by now, her scornful whispers and mocking laughter, but this was different.

At first, the whisper was faint, blending into the silence like a thread of smoke. It didn't sound like Delyla, though her presence was unmistakable. The words were indecipherable, a low, murmuring chant that seemed to rise from the walls themselves. Elliot froze, his heart pounding as he strained to listen.

"Who's there?" he asked, his voice trembling.

The whispering stopped abruptly, replaced by a cold, oppressive stillness. For a moment, he thought he might have imagined it. But then, Delyla's voice cut through the silence, sharp and cold.

"You'll see soon enough," she said, her tone almost amused. "This is just the beginning."

The room's temperature dropped suddenly, frost creeping along the edges of the windows. Elliot wrapped his arms around himself, shivering as a deep sense of dread settled over him. He didn't know what Delyla was planning, but he knew it was far from over.

Shadows Come Alive

In the days following Delyla's warning, the shadows in Elliot's apartment began to shift and stretch, as though alive. They moved in ways that defied logic, crawling across the walls and ceilings even when the light sources remained static. At first, Elliot thought it was a trick of his exhausted mind, but the movements became too deliberate to ignore.

One evening, as he sat at his desk trying to piece together what little sanity he had left, he noticed a shadow in the corner of the room. It didn't belong to any object or piece of furniture, and it seemed to ripple like water, growing darker and more defined.

"Not again," Elliot whispered, his voice shaking.

The shadow elongated, creeping across the floor toward him. He backed away, his chair scraping against the hardwood as his breath quickened. The temperature in the room plummeted, and he could see his breath in the air.

"Stop!" he shouted, his voice echoing in the empty apartment.

The shadow froze for a moment, then retreated, merging with the darkness in the corner. But as Elliot stared, he could have sworn he saw two faint, glowing eyes watching him from within the blackness.

The shadows became a constant presence after that, lurking at the edges of his vision, their movements subtle but deliberate. They seemed to pulse with a malevolent energy, a silent reminder that Delyla's haunting was evolving into something far more dangerous.

The Whispers Grow Louder

The whispers that had once been faint and intermittent now became a relentless, oppressive force. They filled every corner of the apartment, a cacophony of indistinct voices that grew louder and more insistent with each passing day. Sometimes they sounded like Delyla, mocking and cold; other times, they were unrecognizable, a chorus of voices speaking in a language Elliot couldn't understand.

One night, as he lay curled on his mattress, the whispers reached a fever pitch. They seemed to come from all directions, overlapping and intertwining until they became deafening. Elliot pressed his hands over his ears, his body trembling as he shouted, "Stop! Please, stop!"

The whispers ceased abruptly, leaving a heavy silence in their wake. But then, Delyla's voice cut through the stillness, low and menacing.

"You can't silence this," she said. "You can't silence me."

Elliot sat up, his body drenched in sweat despite the freezing air. He looked around the room, his eyes wide with fear. The whispers might have stopped, but the oppressive energy in the apartment remained, a constant reminder that Delyla's haunting was far from over.

Hostile Cold Spots

The cold spots that had once been isolated to certain areas of the apartment now seemed to follow Elliot wherever he went. They were no longer just a physical discomfort; they were a manifestation of Delyla's growing power, a chilling reminder of her presence.

One night, as Elliot sat on the couch trying to distract himself with an old book, he felt the temperature drop sharply. The cold seemed to seep into his skin, numbing his fingers and making his breath visible in the air. He pulled a blanket around himself, but it did little to ward off the icy chill.

"Do you feel it?" Delyla's voice came from behind him, sending a shiver down his spine.

Elliot turned, but the room was empty. The cold intensified, and he could hear the faint sound of her laughter echoing through the apartment. It wasn't just cold; it was hostile, an energy that pressed against him, suffocating and inescapable.

"Why are you doing this?" he whispered, his voice trembling.

Delyla didn't answer. The cold lingered, a silent reminder that her power was growing, and Elliot was powerless to stop it.

Visions of Chaos

As Delyla's haunting intensified, Elliot began to experience vivid, horrifying visions. They came without warning, flashing before his eyes like fragments of a nightmare. At first, they were fleeting—images of Delyla's face, twisted with anger and pain, or scenes of the apartment engulfed in flames. But over time, the visions grew more elaborate and terrifying.

One day, as Elliot stood in the kitchen trying to prepare a meal, the room around him seemed to shift. The walls darkened, the air thick with the smell of smoke. He turned, and for a moment, he was no longer in his apartment. He was in an unfamiliar place, a room filled with shadowy figures whose faces were obscured.

The figures turned toward him, their eyes glowing faintly in the darkness. Delyla stood among them, her form flickering like a dying flame. "This is your future," she said, her voice cold and emotionless. "This is what's coming."

The vision ended as suddenly as it had begun, leaving Elliot trembling and gasping for air. He clutched the edge of the counter, his mind racing. What had he just seen? Was it a warning, a glimpse of the chaos Delyla had promised?

The Final Warning

Delyla's haunting reached a new level of intensity one night as Elliot sat alone in the dark, the weight of her presence pressing down on him like a physical force. The air was heavy, the shadows alive with movement, and the whispers louder than ever.

Suddenly, the apartment was plunged into silence. The air grew colder, and Delyla's ghost appeared before him, her form more solid and imposing than ever. Her eyes burned with fury, and the room seemed to tremble with her presence.

"This is just the beginning," she said, her voice resonating with a power that made Elliot's chest ache. "You think you've suffered? You think this is the worst I can do?"

Elliot fell to his knees, his body trembling as tears streamed down his face. "What do you want from me?" he whispered. "What are you going to do?"

Delyla leaned closer, her face inches from his. "You'll see," she said, her voice a chilling promise. "Soon, you'll understand."

With that, she vanished, leaving Elliot alone in the freezing, suffocating darkness. Her words echoed in his mind, a haunting refrain that refused to be silenced.

Delyla's cryptic warning—*"This is just the beginning"*—marked a shift in her haunting, transforming it from a personal vendetta into a harbinger of greater chaos. The environment around Elliot became increasingly hostile, with shadows, whispers, and cold spots conspiring to drive him further into despair. As her power grew, so did the sense of inevitability, the looming promise of something far worse than anything Elliot had yet endured. The haunting was no longer just a punishment; it was a prelude to a reckoning that would leave Elliot questioning everything he thought he knew about fear, guilt, and the nature of his torment.

Chapter 7: Losing Control

Fractured Reality

Elliot's descent into madness was not a sudden plummet but a slow, insidious unraveling. His grip on reality, once steady and assured, now felt like sand slipping through his fingers. Delyla's haunting had shattered the barriers between what was real and what was imagined, leaving Elliot adrift in a sea of confusion and fear. Time warped, perceptions twisted, and the very fabric of his existence seemed to tear at the seams. He no longer trusted his own senses, and the world around him became an alien, hostile landscape.

The First Cracks Appear

The first signs of Elliot's fractured reality were subtle, almost imperceptible. He would misplace objects only to find them later in impossible locations—his keys in the freezer, his shoes under the sink. At first, he chalked it up to exhaustion. The sleepless nights and constant tension had left him foggy, his thoughts scattered.

But the incidents became more frequent, more bizarre. One morning, he awoke on the couch with no memory of falling asleep there.

His apartment, once meticulously ordered, was in disarray—papers scattered across the floor, furniture slightly askew. He began to question his own actions, wondering if he was moving things in a daze or if Delyla was toying with him.

The confusion deepened when he started seeing flashes of movement out of the corner of his eye. A shadow darting across the room, a flicker of light that didn't belong. He would turn quickly, his heart racing, but there was never anything there.

"Just tired," he muttered to himself, trying to convince himself that he wasn't losing his mind. But deep down, he knew it was more than that.

Time Slips Away

Elliot's sense of time began to warp, the days blurring into nights with no clear distinction. He would sit down to eat or read, only to look up and realize that hours had passed without his awareness. His blackouts grew longer and more frequent, leaving him disoriented and panicked.

One evening, Elliot decided to take a walk, hoping that fresh air might clear his head. He left his apartment at dusk, the streets quiet and bathed in the soft glow of streetlights. But when he returned, it was nearly dawn, and he had no memory of where he had been or what he had done.

The blackouts became a terrifying routine. He would wake up in unfamiliar positions—on the floor, in the bathtub, once even standing in the hallway outside his apartment door. Each time, his heart would pound with dread as he tried to piece together the missing hours.

"Where did I go?" he whispered one night, staring at his reflection in the bathroom mirror. His pale, haggard face stared back at him, eyes wide with fear. "What's happening to me?"

The mirror cracked without warning, a jagged line splitting his reflection in two. Elliot stumbled back, clutching his chest as the sound echoed through the apartment.

Delyla Outside the Apartment

The boundaries of Delyla's haunting had always been unclear, but Elliot had convinced himself that she was tied to the apartment. It was his one fragile hope—that if he left, he might escape her torment, even temporarily. That hope was shattered when Delyla began appearing outside.

It started with fleeting reflections. As Elliot walked past shop windows or parked cars, he would catch a glimpse of her behind him. Her figure was faint and flickering, barely there, but unmistakable. Each time, his breath would hitch, and he would spin around, only to find the space behind him empty.

One day, as Elliot waited at a crosswalk, he saw her in the glass door of a café across the street. She stood motionless, her hollow eyes locked on him. Panic surged through him, and he stumbled backward, nearly falling into the street. A passerby caught his arm, steadying him.

"Are you okay?" the stranger asked, their voice filled with concern.

Elliot nodded quickly, mumbling a vague response before hurrying away. His mind raced, his thoughts tangled with fear. She was following him now, invading the spaces he thought were safe. There was no escape.

A World Conspiring Against Him

As Delyla's appearances outside the apartment became more frequent, Elliot's paranoia deepened. He began to believe that the entire world was conspiring against him, that every stranger on the street, every voice in the crowd, was somehow connected to her.

In the grocery store, he heard whispers as he passed the aisles. At first, they were indistinct murmurs, blending with the ambient noise. But as he strained to listen, he could make out words—his name, spoken in hushed tones, followed by faint laughter. He turned quickly, his heart racing, but the other shoppers were absorbed in their own tasks, seemingly oblivious to him.

"She's everywhere," he muttered under his breath, gripping the handle of his shopping cart tightly. "They're all watching me."

Even the sound of his phone ringing became a source of anxiety. He stopped answering calls, convinced that the voice on the other end would be hers, mocking and cruel. The mail piled up, unopened, on the floor by the door. Each letter felt like a threat, a potential message from Delyla.

His paranoia consumed him, leaving him isolated and distrustful of everyone around him. The world felt smaller, darker, and infinitely more dangerous.

The Mind Betrays Itself

Elliot's distrust extended beyond the people around him to his own mind. He could no longer trust his senses, his thoughts, or his memories. Everything felt distorted, fragmented, like a puzzle with missing pieces.

He began hearing voices—faint at first, like a soft hum in the back of his mind. But they grew louder, more insistent, until they became a constant presence. Some were Delyla's, cold and mocking, but others were unrecognizable, a cacophony of whispers and shouts that left him trembling.

"You did this," one voice hissed.
"You'll never escape," another taunted.
"Coward," Delyla's voice cut through the chaos, sharp and piercing.

Elliot clutched his head, rocking back and forth on the floor as he tried to block out the noise. "Stop it," he whispered, his voice trembling. "Stop…"

But the voices didn't stop. They followed him wherever he went, invading his thoughts and filling the silence. His mind felt like a battlefield, and he was losing.

Isolation and Despair

Elliot's growing paranoia and distrust left him completely isolated. He stopped leaving the apartment, afraid of what he might see or hear outside. He stopped answering the door, stopped talking to anyone, stopped trying to maintain any connection to the world beyond his walls.

The apartment, once his refuge, became a prison. The shadows that moved across the walls felt alive, watching him with unseen eyes. The whispers grew louder in the silence, a constant reminder that Delyla was always there.

One night, as Elliot sat in the corner of his bedroom, his knees drawn to his chest, he saw her again. She stood in the doorway, her form flickering faintly in the dim light. Her eyes were hollow, her expression unreadable.

"This is your life now," she said, her voice low and cold. "This is all you'll ever have."

Elliot closed his eyes, tears streaming down his face as he whispered, "Please… just leave me alone."

But when he opened his eyes, she was still there, her presence a constant reminder of his guilt and despair.

Elliot's fractured reality was the culmination of Delyla's relentless haunting, his own guilt, and his crumbling sanity. The lines between real and imagined blurred until they were indistinguishable, leaving him trapped in a world of shadows, whispers, and paranoia. Time slipped away from him, his mind betrayed him, and the world around him became an alien, hostile place. Isolated and utterly alone, Elliot was left to face the inescapable truth: there was no escape from Delyla, no refuge from her torment. His reality was broken, and so was he.

Public Humiliation

Elliot had been teetering on the edge of a breakdown for weeks, his mind battered by Delyla's relentless haunting. He had always kept a tight grip on his emotions, retreating into the safety of his apartment whenever the torment became too much. But even the small solace he found in solitude had been ripped away. Delyla's ghost had begun appearing outside his home, haunting him in public spaces, pushing him closer to the brink.

The day he saw her on the crowded street, everything unraveled. What followed was a catastrophic display of fear and desperation, exposing Elliot's unraveling psyche to the world and marking him as a public spectacle.

The Incident

Elliot rarely ventured outside anymore. The bustling city streets, once a source of anonymity and routine, now felt suffocating and dangerous. But his pantry was nearly empty, and his avoidance of delivery services had left him no choice. With his hood pulled low over his head and his hands shoved deep into his jacket pockets, he forced himself out into the throng of people.

The street was crowded, filled with the usual noise of traffic, footsteps, and chatter. Elliot kept his head down, his eyes fixed on the sidewalk, muttering under his breath as he navigated the chaos. He had almost convinced himself he was safe when he saw her.

Delyla stood motionless in the middle of the crosswalk, her translucent form flickering faintly in the midday light. Her hollow eyes were locked on him, her face pale and contorted with a mix of anger and sorrow. She didn't move, didn't speak—she didn't need to. The weight of her presence hit Elliot like a physical blow.

"No," he muttered, his steps faltering. "Not here. Not now."

People brushed past him, muttering in annoyance as he blocked their path. But Elliot didn't notice them. His entire focus was on Delyla, who remained fixed in his path, her gaze unrelenting.

"Go away!" he shouted, his voice breaking. "Just leave me alone!"

The crowd around him froze, a ripple of confusion and alarm spreading through the bustling street. Strangers turned to look at him, their expressions a mix of curiosity and concern. But Delyla remained visible only to Elliot, her presence a private torment that he couldn't escape.

The Breakdown

Elliot's fear and frustration boiled over. He stepped forward, pointing an accusatory finger at the ghost that no one else could see. "What do you want from me?" he yelled, his voice trembling with desperation. "Haven't you done enough?"

The crowd murmured, the bystanders exchanging glances. A mother pulled her child closer, her eyes wary. A man in a business suit took a step back, shaking his head. But Elliot didn't see them. He was consumed by the sight of Delyla, her ghostly figure unmoving, her presence unyielding.

"Answer me!" he screamed, his voice echoing down the street. "Why won't you just leave me alone?"

A teenage boy standing nearby pulled out his phone, his fingers moving quickly to start recording. Others followed suit, their curiosity outweighing their concern. To them, Elliot was a disheveled man yelling at nothing, his gestures wild, his voice filled with a raw, unhinged energy that made him both pitiable and alarming.

Delyla's ghost finally moved, taking a step closer to him. Her lips curved into a faint, mocking smile, and Elliot's composure shattered completely. He lunged forward, swiping at the air where her form flickered, his hands trembling with fury and fear.

"Stop laughing at me!" he roared. "Stop this!"

The crowd recoiled, a few people gasping audibly. The mother with the child hurried away, pulling her daughter along as she muttered about finding somewhere safer. The teenager filming took a cautious step back, but his phone remained steady, capturing every moment of Elliot's meltdown.

The Aftermath on the Street

Elliot's outburst ended as abruptly as it began. He froze mid-motion, his chest heaving, his hands clenched into fists. Delyla was gone, her ghostly figure vanishing as suddenly as it had appeared. But the damage was done. The crowd was staring at him, their expressions a mixture of fear, pity, and disgust.

"What's wrong with him?" someone whispered.

"Drugs, maybe?" another voice suggested.

Elliot's face burned with shame as he realized the spectacle he had created. He stumbled backward, his eyes darting to the people around him, the phones pointed in his direction, the whispers growing louder. He felt trapped, surrounded, exposed.

Without a word, he turned and ran. His feet pounded against the pavement as he fled down the street, the murmurs of the crowd and the distant sound of laughter following him. He didn't stop until he reached his apartment, slamming the door behind him and collapsing onto the floor, his body trembling with a mixture of exhaustion and humiliation.

The Viral Footage

The teenager's video made its way online within hours. It was shared on social media with captions like *"Crazy guy freaks out on Main Street"* and *"What is he yelling at?"* The clip quickly went viral, sparking a flurry of comments and speculation.

Some viewers were amused, finding Elliot's meltdown entertaining in a cruel, detached way. Others expressed concern, wondering if he was mentally ill or in need of help. A few speculated about the cause of his behavior, weaving elaborate theories about ghosts, conspiracies, or hallucinations.

Elliot didn't need to see the video to know it existed. He could feel the weight of it, the knowledge that his breakdown had been immortalized, that the world was laughing at him. He avoided his phone, avoided the internet, avoided everything that might remind him of the incident. But even in his self-imposed isolation, he couldn't escape the sense of being watched, judged, and ridiculed.

Isolation and Paranoia

The humiliation of the public breakdown and the viral footage drove Elliot deeper into his isolation. He stopped leaving the apartment entirely, terrified of running into someone who might recognize him from the video. The thought of being confronted, of seeing the mockery in their eyes, was unbearable.

The apartment became his prison, its walls closing in around him as his paranoia grew. He avoided the windows, afraid of who might be looking in. He turned off his phone, afraid of the messages he might receive. Every knock at the door sent him into a panic, his heart racing as he imagined reporters, police, or curious strangers waiting on the other side.

"She's ruined me," he muttered one night, pacing the length of his living room. "She's taken everything."

But even in his solitude, Delyla found ways to torment him. Her presence lingered in the apartment, a constant, suffocating force that left him trembling with fear.

Delyla's Triumph

That night, as Elliot sat on the couch staring blankly at the wall, Delyla's ghost appeared before him. She stood in the center of the room, her translucent form flickering faintly in the dim light. Her expression was calm, almost satisfied, as though she were savoring her victory.

"You thought you could escape me," she said, her voice soft but unyielding. "But I'm always with you, Elliot. Always."

Elliot didn't respond. He couldn't. His body was frozen, his mind a whirlwind of fear, shame, and despair. Delyla stepped closer, her hollow eyes boring into him.

"Do you see it now?" she asked. "Do you understand what I can do?"

Tears streamed down Elliot's face as he whispered, "Why are you doing this?"

Elliot's public breakdown marked a turning point in Delyla's haunting, exposing him not only to her torment but to the judgment and ridicule of the outside world. The incident on the crowded street shattered what little composure he had left, leaving him isolated, humiliated, and consumed by paranoia. Delyla's ghost, satisfied with the damage she had caused, returned to the apartment that night, her presence a chilling reminder that her torment was far from over. The humiliation and isolation fed into Elliot's growing despair, leaving him a shell of the man he once was, trapped in a nightmare he could no longer escape.

Delyla's lips curved into a faint smile, her form shimmering as she leaned closer. "Because you deserve it," she said. "And this is just the beginning."

With that, she vanished, leaving Elliot alone in the freezing, oppressive darkness of his apartment. The humiliation of the day, the fear of what was to come, and the suffocating weight of Delyla's presence pressed down on him, leaving him trembling and broken.

Elliot's public breakdown marked a turning point in Delyla's haunting, exposing him not only to her torment but to the judgment and ridicule of the outside world. The incident on the crowded street shattered what little composure he had left, leaving him isolated, humiliated, and consumed by paranoia. Delyla's ghost, satisfied with the damage she had caused, returned to the apartment that night, her presence a chilling reminder that her torment was far from over. The humiliation and isolation fed into Elliot's growing despair, leaving him a shell of the man he once was, trapped in a nightmare he could no longer escape.

Delyla's Power Grows

Elliot had thought the haunting couldn't get worse. He had believed that Delyla's ghost tormenting his mind, her whispers, and her mocking presence were the peak of his punishment. But he was wrong. As her power grew, so did her ability to reach him—not just mentally, but physically. Bruises, scratches, and an increasing sense of helplessness replaced his already fragile grip on reality. Delyla was no longer just a haunting presence; she was a force consuming his entire existence, feeding off his fear and guilt to strengthen her hold over him.

Waking with Wounds

Elliot's first indication that Delyla's ghost was becoming more physically aggressive came when he woke one morning with deep scratches along his forearm. The pain was sharp, the raw red lines vivid against his pale skin. He stared at them in confusion, trying to piece together how they had gotten there.

His initial thought was that he had scratched himself in his sleep. He examined his nails, but they were short, and the marks didn't align with anything he could have done. A chill ran down his spine as a faint whisper reached his ears.

"Do you feel it now, Elliot?" Delyla's voice was soft but filled with malice. "This is just the beginning."

The next morning, he woke with bruises—a deep, purplish imprint across his ribs that ached with every breath. The third night, he woke with shallow cuts along his legs, as though something had clawed at him in the dark. Each wound was a reminder that Delyla's haunting wasn't confined to his mind anymore. She was reaching into the physical world, and he had no way to defend himself.

Memories That Aren't His

As the physical attacks increased, so did the mental ones. Delyla began planting memories in Elliot's mind—visions of her life before he had taken it from her. At first, they came as fleeting images. A young Delyla sitting at a kitchen table with her family, laughing as her father told a joke. A teenage Delyla standing on a stage, holding a trophy as the crowd applauded.

The visions grew more vivid, more immersive. Elliot would close his eyes for a moment and find himself transported into her memories, living them as though they were his own. He saw her as a child, running through a park with her siblings, her laughter echoing in the crisp autumn air. He saw her as an adult, sitting in a coffee shop with a notebook, scribbling furiously as she worked on what must have been a story or a journal entry.

One night, as he sat at his desk trying to focus on something—anything—other than Delyla, her voice filled his mind.

"Do you see what you took from me?" she asked, her tone icy. "Do you feel it?"

The memory hit him like a wave. He was in a small apartment that wasn't his, the walls adorned with framed photographs of family and friends. Delyla stood by the window, staring out at the city below. Her expression was thoughtful, her hands wrapped around a steaming mug. Elliot could feel her contentment, her quiet joy, as though it were his own.

When the memory faded, he was back in his own apartment, his body trembling and his eyes wet with tears. He couldn't tell where her memories ended and his own thoughts began. The lines were blurring, leaving him disoriented and deeply unsettled.

A Mind Splintering

The invasion of Delyla's memories left Elliot questioning his own identity. He began to forget small details about himself—his favorite foods, his childhood memories, even the reason he had chosen Delyla as his victim.

Her memories filled the gaps, crowding out his own until he could barely distinguish between them.

"Was that my memory?" he whispered one night, staring at the ceiling as the room spun around him. "Or hers?"

Delyla's voice answered from the darkness. "Does it matter, Elliot? You're nothing without me now."

Her words rang true in a horrifying way. The more her memories consumed him, the more he felt as though he were losing himself. He started calling himself "Elliot" in his own mind, as though the name belonged to someone else. He spoke less, afraid that his own voice might sound unfamiliar. He stopped looking in mirrors, unable to face the stranger staring back at him.

A Violent Presence

The physical manifestations of Delyla's haunting became more aggressive, her power extending to the objects around Elliot. One evening, as he sat on the couch, a book flew off the shelf and slammed into the wall, its pages fluttering like wings. He jumped, his heart racing, but before he could react, the lamp beside him toppled over, shattering on the floor.

"Stop it!" he shouted, his voice trembling with fear and frustration. "Just stop!"

But the attacks didn't stop. Chairs slid across the room, their legs screeching against the floor. The kitchen cabinets burst open, their contents spilling onto the counter and floor in a cacophony of noise. The windows rattled in their frames, as though an unseen force was trying to break through.

Delyla's ghost appeared in the middle of the chaos, her form shimmering and flickering with an intensity that made the air around her crackle. Her eyes locked onto Elliot's, her expression a mix of fury and satisfaction.

"You think you can ignore me?" she asked, her voice echoing with power. "You think you can escape?"

Elliot fell to his knees, his hands covering his head as he sobbed. "I can't… I can't take this anymore."

Constant Torment

Delyla's presence became a constant in Elliot's life, her energy suffocating and inescapable. She was there when he woke up, her figure standing silently in the corner of the room, her eyes unblinking. She was there when he tried to eat, her voice whispering in his ear, making him lose his appetite. She was there when he tried to sleep, her cold touch brushing against his skin, jolting him awake.

The apartment felt smaller, the walls closing in on him as her energy filled every inch of the space. The air was heavy, the temperature always cold, no matter how high he turned the heat. Even the light seemed dimmer, as though her presence drained the brightness from the world.

Elliot stopped trying to fight. He stopped moving the furniture back into place, stopped cleaning up the messes left by her violent outbursts. The apartment became a reflection of his mind—chaotic, broken, and beyond repair.

A Realization

It wasn't until Elliot stood in the middle of his destroyed apartment, his body bruised and his mind fractured, that he understood the truth: Delyla was feeding off his fear and guilt. Every moment of terror, every pang of remorse, every tear he shed made her stronger.

"You're getting stronger," he whispered, his voice barely audible. "You're... you're feeding off me."

Delyla appeared in front of him, her form more solid than ever. She smiled, a cold, predatory expression that sent a shiver down his spine. "You're finally starting to understand," she said. "But it's too late for that, isn't it?"

Elliot sank to the floor, his body trembling as tears streamed down his face. He realized then that there was no escaping her, no defeating her. She wasn't just a ghost—she was a force of nature, a manifestation of everything he had done, everything he regretted, and everything he feared.

And she wasn't going anywhere.

As Delyla's power grew, so did Elliot's torment. The bruises and scratches on his body were just the beginning; her ability to invade his mind and blur the lines between their memories left him questioning his own identity. Her violent physical manifestations and constant presence turned his apartment into a living nightmare, a prison he couldn't escape. Elliot's realization that Delyla was feeding off his fear and guilt only deepened his despair, leaving him trapped in a cycle of suffering with no end in sight. Delyla's power wasn't just growing—it was consuming him entirely.

A Breaking Point

The dim, suffocating air of Elliot's apartment clung to him like a second skin. Every breath felt labored, as though the weight of his despair had grown so heavy it pressed against his lungs. The once neatly organized space had devolved into chaos: shattered glass littered the floor, papers lay strewn about like fallen leaves, and the walls bore smudges and scratches, evidence of his frenzied attempts to stave off the unrelenting force that was Delyla.

Elliot sat on the edge of his sagging mattress, staring blankly at the knife resting on the table in front of him. Its blade gleamed faintly in the dim light, the same blade he had used to take Delyla's life. It was both a symbol of his deepest regret and a grim solution to his torment. The knife seemed to pulsate with a dark energy, drawing his focus like a magnet.

The haunting had pushed him to the edge of his sanity, and now, in the throes of despair, Elliot believed that death might be his only escape.

The Weight of Despair

Weeks had stretched into months since Delyla's ghost had first appeared. What began as subtle whispers and fleeting apparitions had grown into a suffocating nightmare. Her presence was inescapable, her power unrelenting. She haunted his every waking moment and invaded his dreams, her voice cutting through his thoughts like a blade.

Elliot had tried to fight her in the beginning. He had shouted at her, begged her to leave, even turned to rituals and occult practices in a desperate bid to banish her. But nothing worked. Every attempt only seemed to make her stronger, her haunting more invasive. She had stripped him of everything—his sense of control, his identity, and now, even his will to live.

He hadn't left the apartment in weeks. The outside world felt like an alien place, and the thought of facing it was unbearable. The apartment, once his sanctuary, had become a prison, its walls closing in on him with each passing day. Food went uneaten, his body weakened, and his mind frayed under the constant assault of Delyla's torment.

"This has to end," he whispered to himself, his voice barely audible over the oppressive silence of the room. "It has to."

Writing the Note

Elliot's hand trembled as he reached for a pen and a crumpled sheet of paper. His thoughts were a jumbled mess, but he felt compelled to write—to leave behind some explanation for the act he was about to commit. Perhaps it was guilt driving him, or perhaps it was the faint hope that someone, anyone, might understand his anguish.

The words came slowly, each stroke of the pen labored and hesitant.

To Delyla and her family,

I don't know if you'll ever read this, but I need to say it anyway. I'm sorry. For everything. For what I did to Delyla. For the pain I caused. I know it won't mean anything to you, and it shouldn't. What I did was unforgivable.

Delyla, I didn't know you. Not really. But I know now. I've seen your life, your dreams, your family. You were...you are...so much more than I ever understood. And I took that from you. I took everything.

I don't deserve peace. I don't deserve forgiveness. But I can't do this anymore. She won't leave me alone. She's everywhere, in my mind, my body, my soul. I can't eat, I can't sleep, I can't think. I can't live like this.

I'm not running from what I did. I'm running from her. And I'm sorry.

Elliot's tears blurred the ink as he wrote, the weight of his guilt pressing down on him like an iron shroud. He folded the note carefully, placing it on the table beside the knife. His hands shook as he reached for the blade, its cold surface sending a shiver up his spine.

"This is the only way," he whispered, his voice cracking. "It's the only way to end this."

The Moment of Decision

Elliot sat on the floor, the knife heavy in his hands. His breath came in shallow, ragged gasps as he stared at the blade. Memories of Delyla flashed through his mind—not the Delyla he had known in life, but the Delyla he had come to know through her ghostly torment. Her laughter as a child, her quiet determination as a young adult, her dreams of a future that he had stolen from her.

The weight of it all was too much to bear. His chest tightened, his vision blurred, and his grip on the knife faltered. He raised it slowly, the blade catching the faint light as it hovered over his trembling wrist.

"I'm sorry," he whispered, his voice breaking. "I'm so sorry."

As he prepared to make the final move, the room grew cold—colder than it had ever been. The air seemed to thicken, pressing down on him like a physical force. The light flickered violently, plunging the room into intermittent darkness.

Then, he heard her voice.

"Elliot."

It was a whisper, cold and sharp, laced with a venom that sent a chill down his spine. He froze, the knife still poised in his hand, as Delyla's ghost appeared before him.

Delyla's Intervention

Her form flickered violently, her translucent figure radiating an energy that made the air around her crackle. Her hollow eyes locked onto Elliot's, and he felt the knife slip from his grip as his hands began to tremble uncontrollably.

"You don't get to leave yet," Delyla said, her voice devoid of emotion but carrying a weight that made Elliot's heart pound.

She moved closer, her figure towering over him, her presence overwhelming. Elliot's breath came in shallow gasps as he scrambled backward, his back pressing against the wall. "Please," he begged, his voice trembling. "I can't do this anymore. Just let me go."

Delyla's lips curled into a faint, mocking smile. "You think death will save you?" she asked, her tone dripping with disdain. "You think you can escape me?"

The knife, which had fallen to the floor, rose into the air, held aloft by an unseen force. Delyla's ghost reached out, her fingers curling around the blade as the room seemed to shudder with her presence.

Elliot watched in frozen terror as she wrenched the knife from his reach and hurled it across the room. It embedded itself in the wall with a sharp, echoing thud, the sound reverberating through the suffocating silence.

"You don't get to run," Delyla said, her voice cold and unyielding. "Not from this. Not from me."

The Collapse

Elliot's body gave out. He collapsed onto the floor in a heap, his sobs wracking his frame as he buried his face in his hands. The weight of his despair, his guilt, and the inescapable reality of Delyla's torment crushed him. He had thought death might offer him peace, but Delyla had made it clear that even in death, there would be no escape.

"I'm sorry," he whispered through his tears. "I'm so sorry."

Delyla's ghost stood over him, her form flickering faintly as though she were drawing strength from his anguish. For a moment, she said nothing, her gaze heavy and unrelenting. Then, as suddenly as she had appeared, she vanished, leaving the room in suffocating silence.

Elliot lay there for hours, unable to move, his body trembling and his mind spiraling. The knife remained lodged in the wall, a grim reminder of his failure—not just to escape, but to atone. His note sat on the table, its words a hollow echo of a remorse that would never be enough.

The Realization

As the first light of dawn crept through the window, Elliot's tears had dried, but the weight of his despair remained. He stared blankly at the ceiling, his thoughts a tangled web of guilt and fear. He had tried to end it, and Delyla had stopped him. She wasn't done with him yet.

"She won't let me go," he muttered, his voice barely audible. "Not even in death."

The realization settled over him like a shroud. There was no escape. Delyla's torment wasn't confined to the living world; it was eternal, a punishment that would follow him beyond the grave. His suffering wasn't just a consequence of his actions—it was her justice.

Elliot was a man broken beyond repair, trapped in a nightmare of his own making. And Delyla, feeding off his despair, ensured that his torment was far from over.

Chapter 8:
The Ghost's Ultimatum

The Confrontation

Elliot had been living in a relentless nightmare since the night he took Delyla's life. Her ghost had invaded his every waking moment, haunting him with whispers, physical manifestations, and a suffocating presence that he could neither fight nor escape. But nothing could have prepared him for the confrontation that was to come, an event that would strip him of whatever fragile defenses he had left and plunge him into the depths of his guilt and despair.

It began on a night like any other in his twisted existence—dark, cold, and suffused with the oppressive weight of Delyla's lingering presence. Elliot sat in his ruined apartment, his head in his hands, trying to block out the whispers that had become a constant backdrop to his life. But this night would not be like the others. Tonight, Delyla would make him face her wrath in its full, horrifying force.

A Terrifying Form

The temperature in the room dropped suddenly, a bone-deep chill that made Elliot shiver despite the layers of clothing he wore.

The air grew thick, heavy, as though it were pressing down on him, suffocating him. The dim light flickered violently, casting jagged shadows across the walls.

Elliot froze as the familiar sound of her voice echoed through the room, cold and sharp. "Elliot."

He looked up, his heart pounding in his chest, and saw her. But this was not the flickering, translucent form he had grown used to seeing. This was something far worse.

Delyla stood before him, her body a nightmarish reflection of the final moments of her life. Her clothes were torn and bloodied, her skin pale and bruised. The gaping wound where the knife had entered her chest was dark and jagged, oozing blood that dripped onto the floor in slow, rhythmic splatters. Her face was a mask of fury and pain, her eyes hollow and burning with a vengeful fire.

Elliot recoiled, his back hitting the wall as he tried to distance himself from the horrifying apparition. His breath came in short, panicked gasps, and his hands trembled uncontrollably.

"No," he whispered, his voice barely audible. "No, no, no…"

But Delyla stepped closer, her movements deliberate and unyielding. The room seemed to darken around her, the shadows swallowing the light as her presence filled the space.

"You need to see," she said, her voice cold and unrelenting. "You need to feel."

Reliving the Attack

Without warning, the room dissolved around him. Elliot was no longer in his apartment but back in the alley where it had all happened. The sights, sounds, and smells of that night rushed back to him with a brutal clarity that made his stomach churn.

He stood frozen, watching himself from an outside perspective, the knife trembling in his hand as he approached Delyla. She turned, startled, her face a mixture of confusion and fear. The scene played out exactly as it had that night, but this time, every detail was sharpened, amplified, designed to cut him to the core.

He saw the terror in her eyes as she realized what was happening. He heard her voice, trembling and pleading, as she begged him to stop. He felt the weight of the knife in his hand, the sickening resistance as it plunged into her flesh. And then he saw her fall, her body crumpling to the ground, her life slipping away as blood pooled beneath her.

The scene faded, only to start again. Over and over, Elliot was forced to relive the attack, each repetition more harrowing than the last. He screamed, his voice hoarse and desperate, as he begged for it to stop.

"Please!" he cried, tears streaming down his face. "I can't… I can't do this anymore!"

But Delyla's voice cut through his pleas, cold and merciless. "You don't get to decide when this ends. You don't get to look away."

A Twisted Reality

As the visions faded, Elliot found himself back in his apartment, but it was no longer the place he knew. The walls were warped and distorted, pulsing as though alive. The floor seemed to tilt and shift beneath him, throwing him off balance. Shadows crawled across every surface, their movements erratic and threatening.

The room was a physical manifestation of his crumbling mind, a nightmare brought to life. Objects floated in the air, spinning violently before crashing to the ground. The sound of breaking glass and splintering wood filled the air, a chaotic symphony that mirrored Elliot's inner turmoil.

Elliot fell to his knees, his hands clutching at his head as he tried to block out the sights and sounds around him. "Make it stop!" he screamed, his voice raw with desperation. "Please, make it stop!"

But Delyla was relentless. Her form loomed over him, her presence suffocating and inescapable. Her voice echoed through the room, filled with fury and disdain.

"You think this is pain?" she demanded. "You think this is suffering? You haven't even begun to pay for what you've done."

Her words struck him like a physical blow, leaving him trembling and broken. He had thought he understood the depth of her anger, but now he realized how wrong he had been. This was no longer just a haunting. This was a reckoning.

The Darkness Closes In

The light in the apartment flickered one final time before extinguishing completely, plunging the room into suffocating darkness. Elliot's breath came in shallow gasps as he fumbled blindly, his hands searching for something, anything, to ground him.

But the darkness was alive, pressing against him, enveloping him in its cold, unrelenting grip. He could feel Delyla's presence all around him, her energy crackling like a storm. Her voice echoed through the void, each word filled with unrelenting fury.

"You took everything from me," she said. "You stole my life, my dreams, my future. And now, you think you can escape?"

Elliot shook his head, his tears falling freely as he sobbed. "I'm sorry," he whispered. "I'm so sorry."

But Delyla's voice offered no forgiveness, only a chilling finality. "Sorry isn't enough, Elliot. It will never be enough."

Her figure appeared before him, her hollow eyes boring into his soul. The darkness seemed to swirl around her, amplifying her presence until she was all he could see, all he could feel.

The Final Question

As the room began to stabilize, the shadows retreating slightly, Delyla leaned closer to Elliot, her face inches from his. Her expression was unreadable, a mix of anger, sorrow, and something deeper—something that sent a shiver down his spine.

"Do you think you can ever escape what you've done?" she asked, her voice soft but heavy with meaning.

Elliot couldn't answer. His throat felt dry, his mind a whirlwind of fear and guilt. He shook his head weakly, his body trembling as he collapsed onto the floor, curling into a fetal position.

Delyla stood over him for a moment longer, her form flickering faintly. Then, without a word, she vanished, leaving the room in an eerie silence.

The confrontation left Elliot more broken than he had ever been. Delyla's ghost had forced him to confront the full weight of his crime, stripping away any illusions he had clung to. The attack, relived in excruciating detail, had shattered him, and the twisted reality of his apartment mirrored the state of his mind.

Her final question lingered in the air, a chilling reminder that there was no escape from her wrath, no redemption for what he had done. Elliot was trapped, both in his apartment and in the endless cycle of guilt and despair that Delyla had created. The confrontation was not the end of her torment—it was only the beginning.

The Ultimatum

The air in Elliot's apartment was suffocating, the oppressive energy of Delyla's presence heavier than it had ever been. He could feel her before she appeared, the hair on the back of his neck standing on end as the room grew colder and darker. He had come to dread her visits, each one bringing a new level of torment, a deeper dive into his guilt and fear. But this time was different. This time, Delyla's haunting carried a finality that sent a chill through his body.

As her ghost materialized before him, her figure flickering faintly in the dim light, Elliot's heart raced. He couldn't tear his eyes away from her, the mixture of anger and sorrow on her face holding him in place like a vice. She seemed more solid now, her presence more commanding, her voice cutting through the silence like a blade.

"It's time, Elliot," she said, her tone cold but calm. "You can't run from this anymore."

The Choices

Elliot stared at her, his body trembling as he tried to make sense of her words. "What do you mean?" he asked, his voice barely above a whisper.

Delyla's expression didn't change. "You have two options," she said. "Confess to what you did. Turn yourself in. Face justice for your crime. Or…" She paused, her eyes narrowing as her voice dropped to a chilling whisper. "Continue to endure this. Me. Forever."

Her words hung in the air, a dreadful weight pressing down on Elliot's chest. He couldn't breathe, couldn't think. The idea of confessing was unthinkable—his freedom, his life, everything he had left would be stripped away. But the alternative was equally horrifying. The thought of spending the rest of his existence trapped in this cycle of torment, with Delyla's ghost haunting his every moment, was enough to make his stomach churn.

"I can't," he whispered, shaking his head. "I can't do either."

Delyla's eyes burned with intensity. "You'll have to choose," she said. "Because this... this can't go on."

The Struggle

Elliot's mind raced as he grappled with the implications of her ultimatum. If he confessed, he would lose everything—the fragile remnants of his freedom, the anonymity that had shielded him since that night. He would spend the rest of his life in prison, consumed by the knowledge of what he had done.

But if he didn't confess, if he chose to continue running, he would remain at Delyla's mercy. Her haunting would never end. She would follow him everywhere, invading his mind, his body, his soul. The thought of enduring another day, another hour, of her torment was unbearable.

"You're asking me to destroy myself," he said, his voice trembling. "Either way, I lose."

Delyla's gaze softened, but only slightly. "This isn't about you, Elliot," she said. "This is about justice. For what you did. For the people you'll never hurt if you confess."

Her words hit him like a punch to the gut. He had always thought of her haunting as a punishment, a personal vendetta for the crime he had committed. But now, she was framing it as something bigger, something he couldn't ignore. It wasn't just about her—it was about the lives he might destroy if he didn't stop himself.

Her Pain

For the first time, Delyla's voice softened, the edges of her anger giving way to something more vulnerable. "Do you know what you took from me?" she asked, her tone laced with sorrow. "It wasn't just my life. It was everything I could have been. Everything my family lost because of you."

Elliot's chest tightened as her words sank in. He had seen flashes of her life in the memories she had forced into his mind—her laughter, her dreams, the quiet moments of joy she had shared with her family. But hearing her say it, seeing the pain etched into her expression, was almost too much to bear.

"My parents," she continued, her voice trembling slightly. "My siblings. My friends. Do you have any idea what it's like for them? To wake up every day and know I'm gone? To wonder why? To live with the hole you left in their lives?"

Elliot's tears flowed freely now, his body shaking with sobs. "I'm sorry," he choked out. "I'm so sorry."

Delyla's gaze hardened again. "Sorry isn't enough," she said. "It will never be enough."

The Warning

Delyla stepped closer, her presence overwhelming as the temperature in the room plummeted. "If you keep running," she said, her voice low and menacing, "it will only get worse. Your guilt will eat away at you, Elliot. It will manifest in ways you can't imagine. You think this is torment?" She gestured around the room, the chaos of her haunting evident in every shattered object, every scratched wall. "This is nothing compared to what's coming."

Elliot shook his head, his voice trembling as he tried to protest. "I can't go to prison," he said. "I can't... I won't survive."

Delyla's expression didn't waver. "And you think you'll survive this?" she asked, her voice cutting through his excuses like a blade. "You think you can keep living like this? You can't, Elliot. You know you can't."

Her words struck a chord deep within him. He knew she was right. He couldn't keep living like this. The weight of his guilt, the constant presence of her torment, the endless cycle of fear and despair—it was unsustainable. But the thought of confessing, of facing the consequences of his actions, was equally terrifying.

The Paralysis

Elliot sank to the floor, his body trembling as he buried his face in his hands. The room spun around him, the walls closing in as Delyla's ultimatum echoed in his mind. Confess and lose everything. Run and endure eternal torment. Both options felt like a death sentence, and he couldn't see a way out.

"I don't know what to do," he whispered, his voice barely audible. "I can't do this."

Delyla's ghost knelt beside him, her presence cold and unyielding. "You don't have a choice," she said. "You've run out of time."

Elliot looked up at her, his eyes red and swollen with tears. "Why are you doing this to me?" he asked, his voice trembling. "Why won't you just let me go?"

Delyla's expression hardened once more. "Because you don't get to escape," she said. "Not after what you did. Not until you face the truth."

The Final Question

As Delyla's form began to flicker, her energy radiating through the room, she looked down at Elliot with a gaze that was both unyielding and sorrowful. "This is your chance, Elliot," she said. "Your only chance. Do the right thing. Or live with the consequences."

Her figure shimmered, the room growing darker as her presence began to fade. But before she disappeared completely, her voice echoed one final time, cutting through the silence like a knife.

"Do you think you can ever escape what you've done?"

And then she was gone, leaving Elliot alone in the suffocating darkness of his apartment. Her question hung in the air, a chilling reminder that his time was running out. No matter what choice he made, Elliot knew one thing for certain: there was no escaping the weight of his actions. The ultimatum had shattered whatever fragile sense of control he had left, leaving him paralyzed by the knowledge that either decision would destroy him.

A Glimpse of the Afterlife

Elliot sat on the edge of his ruined bed, the familiar weight of despair pressing down on him. The room around him was dark and suffocating, the air heavy with the unshakable presence of Delyla. She hadn't appeared in hours, but her energy lingered, an oppressive force that never truly left. He knew she would return—it was inevitable. But nothing could have prepared him for what was about to happen.

The first sign was the sudden drop in temperature, a cold that seeped into his bones and made his breath visible in the dim light. The hairs on his arms stood on end, and his chest tightened as the shadows in the room seemed to grow darker, deeper.

Then, she appeared.

Delyla's ghost materialized in the corner of the room, her figure flickering faintly, her hollow eyes locking onto Elliot with an intensity that made his heart race. This wasn't the angry, mocking Delyla he had come to dread. There was something different about her this time—a grim determination that sent a chill down his spine.

"It's time," she said, her voice cold and unyielding.

Elliot swallowed hard, his throat dry. "Time for what?" he whispered, his voice trembling.

Delyla stepped closer, her translucent form radiating a cold energy that made the air around her crackle. "You need to see," she said. "You need to understand what's waiting for you."

The Descent

Before Elliot could respond, the room around him began to dissolve. The walls blurred and shifted, the furniture faded into shadow, and the floor seemed to melt away beneath his feet. He felt himself falling, the sensation both terrifying and disorienting. His stomach churned, and his heart pounded in his chest as darkness enveloped him.

When the falling stopped, Elliot found himself standing in an endless void. The air was thick and cold, pressing against his skin like a tangible force. The darkness was absolute, broken only by faint, shifting shapes that moved like shadows within shadows. A cacophony of chilling screams and whispers filled the space, the sounds weaving together into a haunting symphony that made his ears ring.

Elliot turned in every direction, trying to make sense of his surroundings, but there was no sense to be made. The void stretched endlessly, its depths unfathomable. The shadowy forms writhed and twisted, their movements erratic and filled with anguish. Some reached out with claw-like appendages, their shapes distorted and grotesque, while others seemed to collapse inward, their agony consuming them entirely.

"What... what is this?" Elliot stammered, his voice barely audible over the cries that surrounded him.

Delyla's voice came from behind him, cold and emotionless. "This is what waits for you," she said. "If you die without redemption, this is where you'll spend eternity."

The Weight of Souls

As she spoke, the shadowy forms began to move closer, their shapes becoming more defined. Elliot could see their faces now—twisted, broken, and filled with pain. Some were unrecognizable, their features obscured by the darkness, but others had faces he knew.

Delyla was among them, her ghostly form both familiar and alien, her expression filled with a sorrow that cut through him like a knife. Behind her, more faces appeared, faces that Elliot couldn't place but felt he should recognize. Their eyes burned with accusations, their mouths opening in silent screams that seemed to pierce directly into his mind.

Elliot tried to step back, but there was nowhere to go. The forms closed in on him, their presence suffocating, their energy pressing down on his chest. He gasped for air, his hands clawing at his throat as he tried to breathe. The weight of their anguish was unbearable, a crushing force that made his knees buckle.

"This... this isn't real," he whispered, his voice shaking. "It can't be real."

Delyla stepped closer, her figure flickering faintly. "It's as real as the life you took," she said, her voice filled with a cold finality. "This is where you'll come if you die without making things right. An endless void, surrounded by the cries of your victims."

The Agony of the Vision

The shadowy forms began to touch him now, their ghostly hands brushing against his skin. Each touch sent a wave of pain through his body, sharp and cold, like shards of ice piercing his flesh. The cries grew louder, more piercing, until they drowned out every thought in his mind.

Elliot fell to the ground, his body trembling as he curled into a ball. "Stop it!" he screamed, his voice breaking. "Please, make it stop!"

But Delyla didn't move. She stood over him, her gaze unrelenting. "You don't get to escape this, Elliot," she said. "Not until you understand."

The shadows closed in tighter, their energy wrapping around him like chains. He could feel their anger, their sorrow, their pain, all of it seeping into him, consuming him. It wasn't just physical—it was emotional, spiritual. Every part of him felt their torment, their anguish, their despair.

"I'm sorry!" he cried, tears streaming down his face. "I'm so sorry! Please, just stop!"

The Grim Warning

Delyla's expression softened slightly, but her tone remained cold. "Do you think this ends with you?" she asked. "Do you think your suffering will erase theirs? It won't. But you have a choice. You can face justice now, make things right, and maybe—just maybe—you can avoid this."

Elliot looked up at her, his face pale and streaked with tears. "I can't," he whispered, his voice trembling. "I can't do it."

Delyla's eyes hardened. "Then this is your future," she said. "An eternity in the void, surrounded by the souls you've destroyed."

Her words struck him like a blow, the finality of her warning sinking into his mind. The cries of the shadowy forms grew louder, their shapes pressing closer, their anguish suffocating.

The Return to Reality

Just when Elliot thought he couldn't take it anymore, the void began to dissolve. The cries faded, the shadows receded, and the suffocating weight lifted. He found himself back in his apartment, lying on the floor, his body trembling and drenched in sweat.

Delyla stood over him, her figure flickering faintly. "You don't have much time, Elliot," she said, her voice soft but filled with warning. "Make your choice. Because I won't show you this again."

With that, she vanished, leaving the room in an eerie silence. Elliot lay there for what felt like hours, his body shaking, his mind reeling from the vision he had just experienced. The cries of the shadowy forms still echoed in his ears, their anguish a haunting reminder of what awaited him.

Elliot had thought he understood fear, guilt, and despair. But the vision Delyla had shown him was unlike anything he could have imagined. The endless void, the shadowy forms, the weight of their pain pressing down on him—it was a glimpse into a future he couldn't bear to face. Yet the alternative, confessing and facing earthly justice, seemed just as unbearable.

As he lay on the floor, his body trembling and his mind racing, Elliot realized that Delyla's ultimatum wasn't just a choice—it was a sentence. No matter what he decided, his life as he knew it was over. The vision had left him broken, a man teetering on the edge of madness, knowing that the darkness of the void would never truly leave him.

Chapter 9:
Descent into Madness

Elliot's Collapse

Elliot had always prided himself on his composure. He was a man of order, precision, and control, his life a carefully constructed puzzle where every piece fit exactly as intended. But now, that image was gone, shattered by the relentless torment of Delyla's ghost. The man who had once moved through life with calculated confidence was unrecognizable, replaced by someone broken, erratic, and lost in the chaos of his crumbling world.

The transformation had been gradual, each piece of his identity chipped away by Delyla's haunting. At first, it had been subtle—sleepless nights, a growing sense of unease, and a shadow of fear that followed him everywhere. But as her presence intensified, so did Elliot's unraveling. By the time he realized how far he had fallen, there was nothing left of the man he used to be.

A Ruined Home

Elliot's apartment, once a reflection of his meticulous nature, was now a disaster. The once-pristine walls were scratched and smeared with marks he couldn't remember making. Furniture lay overturned, broken and scattered as though the space had been ravaged by a storm. Shards of glass glittered on the floor, remnants of picture frames, lamps, and mirrors he had shattered in fits of frustration and fear.

The corkboard that had once been his pride and joy, a carefully organized map of his plans and thoughts, was now a chaotic mess. The strings and pins had been ripped down, the photos torn and scattered. Delyla's image, once the centerpiece of his twisted fixation, lay crumpled in the corner, though her presence lingered in every shadow.

The air was heavy with the smell of stale sweat, unwashed clothes, and the acrid tang of fear. The once-warm lighting of the apartment had dimmed, the bulbs flickering erratically as though even the electricity couldn't bear to stay consistent. Elliot's home had become a physical manifestation of his mental state: fractured, chaotic, and beyond repair.

Hours in the Corner

Elliot spent most of his time curled in a corner of the living room, his knees drawn to his chest as he muttered to himself. The words were barely coherent, a jumble of pleas, apologies, and desperate attempts to make sense of his torment.

"Please," he whispered, his voice trembling. "Please, just stop. I'm sorry. I'm so sorry."

He rocked back and forth, his movements mechanical and compulsive, as though the rhythm could shield him from the weight of his guilt. His eyes, bloodshot and hollow, stared blankly at the floor, unfocused and unseeing. Even when Delyla's ghost wasn't present, her absence offered no comfort. She was always there, lurking in his mind, a shadow that he couldn't escape.

At times, he would lash out, his frustration boiling over in violent bursts. He clawed at the walls until his nails were torn and bloody, his screams echoing through the empty apartment. But the relief was always temporary, the rage quickly replaced by exhaustion and despair.

"Why won't you leave me alone?" he cried one night, his voice breaking as he slammed his fists against the floor. "What do you want from me?"

The silence that followed was deafening, a void that pressed against his ears and made his chest ache. It was a reminder that there was no answer, no resolution, only the endless torment that Delyla had brought into his life.

A Failing Body

Elliot's physical health had deteriorated rapidly as he neglected even the most basic needs. His once-strong frame had become gaunt and frail, his skin pale and sallow. Dark circles ringed his eyes, a testament to the countless sleepless nights spent staring at the ceiling, his mind racing with fear and regret.

Food had lost all appeal. He couldn't remember the last time he had eaten a proper meal. The few scraps he managed to force down were tasteless, turning to ash in his mouth as his stomach churned with anxiety. Empty takeout containers and half-eaten meals littered the apartment, their contents rotting and forgotten.

Even water felt like a chore. His lips were cracked and dry, his throat parched as he ignored the growing signs of dehydration. His hands trembled constantly, the weakness in his body a mirror of the fragility of his mind.

Elliot's hygiene had become another casualty of his descent. His hair was unkempt, his face covered in a patchy, uneven beard. The smell of sweat and despair clung to him, a physical manifestation of the torment he couldn't escape.

Voices in the Silence

The silence of the apartment, once a refuge, had become a prison. It was in the quiet moments that Delyla's voice was the loudest, cutting through the stillness with a sharpness that made Elliot flinch.

At first, he thought he was imagining it. The whispers were faint, blending with the creak of the floorboards and the hum of the refrigerator. But as the days stretched into weeks, the whispers grew louder, more insistent. They weren't just in his ears—they were in his mind, an inescapable echo that left him trembling.

"You'll never escape," Delyla's voice hissed, her tone cold and unrelenting. "You'll never be free."

Sometimes, the whispers would shift, becoming mockingly kind, a cruel mimicry of the person Delyla had been before he took her life. "Do you miss me, Elliot?" she asked one night, her voice soft and sweet. "Do you wish you could take it back?"

The contrast between her mocking cruelty and feigned kindness left him reeling, unable to distinguish between her torment and his own spiraling thoughts. He began to question everything—his memories, his actions, even his own sanity. The line between reality and hallucination blurred until he couldn't tell where one ended and the other began.

Losing Everything

Elliot's thoughts grew increasingly chaotic, a whirlwind of fear, guilt, and despair that consumed him entirely. He couldn't focus, couldn't think clearly. Every decision felt like a monumental effort, every thought a battle against the overwhelming weight of his torment.

He had lost control of his mind, his body, and his life. The man he once was—a man of precision, control, and confidence—was gone, replaced by someone he didn't recognize. He was a shadow of his former self, a broken figure lost in the ruins of his own making.

One night, as he lay on the floor staring at the cracked ceiling, a single thought cut through the chaos: *This is who I am now.*

The realization was both devastating and oddly freeing. He had tried to fight, to hold on to some semblance of his old self, but it was futile. Delyla had taken everything from him, and there was no going back.

As tears streamed down his face, Elliot whispered the truth he had been avoiding for so long. "I'm nothing," he said, his voice trembling. "I'm nothing without her."

The words hung in the air, a chilling acknowledgment of his complete and total collapse. Elliot was no longer a man—he was a broken vessel, a prisoner of his own guilt, and a victim of Delyla's unrelenting wrath.

And he knew, deep down, that there was no escape.

Visions of Other Victims

Elliot sat in the dimly lit corner of his ruined apartment, the shadows pressing against him like a suffocating presence. The torment Delyla inflicted upon him had reached unimaginable levels, but now, there was something new. Something worse. The faces had begun appearing days ago—faces that didn't belong in his world but had become an unavoidable part of his descent into guilt and madness.

At first, they were fleeting, barely discernible blurs in reflections or quick flickers in his peripheral vision. But as the days passed, the faces grew clearer, their eyes locking onto his with an intensity that pierced through his fragile psyche. These were not strangers. These were people he had once considered as targets, people whose lives he might have taken if Delyla hadn't intervened and set his world aflame.

The First Face

The first time Elliot saw one of the faces, he thought it was another cruel trick by Delyla. He had been pacing his apartment, muttering to himself, when he caught a glimpse of movement in the cracked glass of a photograph frame. At first, he assumed it was Delyla, her ghostly form returning to haunt him. But when he looked closer, his heart stopped.

The face staring back at him was that of a young man, no older than twenty. His features were soft, unassuming, and filled with an innocence that twisted Elliot's stomach into knots. His eyes, however, were what struck Elliot the most. They were wide and sorrowful, brimming with pain and disappointment, as if the man knew exactly what Elliot had once planned for him.

Elliot staggered backward, his breath catching in his throat. "No," he whispered, shaking his head. "You're not real."

The face didn't move, didn't blink, but the sadness in its expression deepened, and Elliot felt a wave of nausea wash over him. He remembered the man. He had followed him for days, memorizing his routine, noting his predictability. Elliot had decided against him, not because of some moral restraint, but because the man had too many friends who walked him home at night.

As the memory resurfaced, the image in the glass seemed to shimmer, and the man's lips parted slightly, as though he were trying to speak. Elliot couldn't bear it. He turned away, covering his face with his hands, but the sorrowful eyes remained burned into his mind.

The Faces Multiply

After that first encounter, the faces began appearing everywhere. In the bathroom mirror, Elliot saw a young woman with dark, wavy hair and a piercing gaze. She had been a cashier at the grocery store he frequented, her friendly smile making her an easy target in his eyes. She stared at him now with an expression of quiet disappointment, her lips pressed into a thin line, as though holding back words she didn't need to say.

In the reflection of the television screen, he saw an older man with a kind face and glasses. Elliot remembered following him home from the library one evening, noting the man's habit of taking the same quiet path every night. He had dismissed him as a target because the man lived with his wife, who was always waiting on the porch when he arrived.

Elliot's apartment became a gallery of these faces, each one more vivid than the last. They appeared in the windows, the glass of the oven door, the shine of a dropped spoon. Even photographs that had nothing to do with these people began to warp, their original subjects replaced by the mournful figures that now haunted him.

A Silent Confrontation

Unlike Delyla, these apparitions didn't speak. They didn't mock or torment him with words. Instead, they watched him, their expressions filled with a mix of anger, sadness, and profound disappointment. The silence was almost worse than Delyla's scorn. It left Elliot alone with his thoughts, forcing him to confront the depth of his depravity.

He had chosen these people because they were vulnerable, because they were easy to control. He had reduced them to puzzles, problems to solve, without ever considering their humanity. And now, their humanity was all he could see.

In one particularly harrowing moment, Elliot caught sight of a face in the window as he passed. It was a young girl, barely sixteen, her wide eyes filled with fear and confusion. He had never followed her, never gotten close, but she had crossed his mind briefly as he sat in the park, watching people go by.

The realization hit him like a blow. He had considered her—not for long, but long enough. Long enough to see her routine, to wonder if she would have been an easy target. The guilt that surged through him was unbearable.

The Depth of His Obsession

The faces forced Elliot to confront a truth he had tried to avoid: Delyla wasn't his first thought, nor would she have been his last. She was one of many, a name on a mental list of potential victims that he had compiled without remorse.

He saw these people now not as potential targets, but as individuals whose lives he could have destroyed. He imagined their families, their friends, the futures they might have had. He saw the ripple effect of pain that his actions would have caused, a wave of suffering that stretched far beyond what he had initially understood.

Each face was a reminder of how far his obsession had taken him. He had become someone who looked at a stranger and saw not a person, but an opportunity. He had justified it to himself as a game, a puzzle to solve, but now, faced with the silent accusations of these mournful figures, he saw it for what it was: a monstrous perversion of control and power.

A Growing Fear

As the faces continued to appear, Elliot began to feel their weight pressing down on him, suffocating him with their silent accusations. Their eyes followed him wherever he went, their expressions a constant reminder of the lives he could have taken.

At night, he dreamed of them, their figures looming over him, their eyes filled with pain. In the dreams, they didn't speak, but their presence was overwhelming, their sorrow almost tangible. He woke in a cold sweat, his chest tight with guilt and fear.

It wasn't just Delyla who haunted him anymore. It was all of them. Every person he had ever considered, every life he had almost taken. They were with him now, their silent judgment inescapable.

Elliot began to wonder if Delyla had orchestrated this, if her power had extended to pulling these faces from his mind and making them manifest. But the more he thought about it, the more he realized that it didn't matter. Whether they were real or a product of his guilt, they were there. And they weren't going away.

A Growing Realization

The faces forced Elliot to acknowledge a horrifying truth: Delyla might not be the only ghost who would haunt him if he refused to atone. If he continued to run from his guilt, from his responsibility, the weight of his actions would only grow heavier.

He imagined a future where these faces multiplied, where every reflective surface showed him the lives he had destroyed, the people he had hurt. He imagined a lifetime of carrying their sorrow, their disappointment, their pain. It was a future he couldn't bear to face.

For the first time, Elliot began to consider Delyla's ultimatum not as a punishment, but as a chance. A chance to stop this, to find some measure of redemption before it was too late. But the fear of confessing, of losing his freedom, still loomed large.

As he sat on the floor of his ruined apartment, surrounded by the faces of the lives he had almost taken, Elliot realized how far he had fallen. He had lost his sense of control, his sense of self, and now, even his mind. And yet, the weight of his guilt pressed him further, urging him toward a decision he wasn't ready to make.

The faces watched him silently, their eyes filled with pain. And Elliot, for the first time, truly understood the depth of the harm he had caused.

The Final Push

Elliot sat in the corner of his apartment, his body slumped against the wall as if the weight of the world had finally crushed him. The room around him was a ruin, the wreckage of his life reflected in the overturned furniture, shattered glass, and scrawled markings on the walls. It was a visual echo of the chaos in his mind, a place where nothing fit, and everything hurt. He hadn't slept in days, the line between waking and dreaming blurred into an unrelenting nightmare. He knew she would come again. She always did.

And she did.

The air grew colder, the oppressive chill cutting through him like a blade. The dim light flickered violently, casting jagged shadows across the walls. Then, she was there—Delyla's ghost, her form more vivid and commanding than it had ever been. Her eyes burned with a mixture of fury and sorrow, her presence filling the room with an energy that made Elliot's chest tighten.

"You think you can keep hiding?" she asked, her voice a sharp edge that sliced through the silence. "You think you can keep lying to yourself?"

Elliot didn't respond. He didn't have the energy to argue, but he wasn't ready to give in either. He stared at her with hollow eyes, waiting for the torment to begin.

Reliving Every Choice

Delyla didn't waste time. With a wave of her translucent hand, the room around them shifted, dissolving into darkness. Elliot felt the familiar pull of her power, dragging him into the depths of his own memories. He tried to resist, but it was useless. He was a passenger in his own mind, forced to confront the choices that had brought him to this point.

The first memory was of his childhood, a moment he had long buried. He was a young boy, sitting alone in his room, his hands meticulously arranging pieces of a puzzle. The room was silent, the laughter of other children distant and unreachable. He had always been different, always drawn to control and precision. But even then, there had been something darker lurking beneath the surface.

"You never wanted connection," Delyla's voice echoed around him. "You wanted control. You wanted power."

The scene shifted, fast-forwarding to his teenage years. He saw himself studying crime stories, his fascination with the minds of killers growing with every book he read. He had told himself it was curiosity, a harmless interest, but Delyla's voice stripped away the façade.

"You wanted to understand them because you wanted to be them," she said. "You craved their control, their ability to make people's lives and deaths a part of their design."

Elliot flinched, the truth of her words striking him like a blow. He had always framed his obsession as intellectual, a quest for knowledge. But deep down, he had known it was something darker.

The Consequences of His Actions

The memories shifted again, this time to the weeks before Delyla's murder. Elliot watched himself sitting at his desk, the corkboard behind him filled with photos, maps, and notes. Delyla's face was at the center, her routine meticulously documented.

"You didn't choose her because of who she was," Delyla said, her voice dripping with disdain. "You chose her because she was convenient. Predictable. Easy."

Elliot opened his mouth to argue, but the words died on his lips. She was right. He had told himself that Delyla was special, that she was different, but the truth was far simpler and far uglier. She had been a puzzle, a problem to solve, nothing more.

The scene shifted to the night of the murder. He watched himself follow her, the knife heavy in his hand. He saw her turn, the confusion and fear in her eyes as she realized what was happening. He saw his own hesitation, his clumsy attack, the horror of her final moments.

"You took everything from me," Delyla said, her voice trembling with a mixture of anger and sorrow. "For what? To feel powerful? To prove something to yourself?"

Elliot turned away, unable to watch, but the memory continued, relentless and unforgiving. He saw her body crumple to the ground, the blood pooling beneath her, the life leaving her eyes. The weight of it was unbearable, and he fell to his knees, his body shaking with sobs.

Stripping Away the Delusions

Delyla's voice cut through his cries, sharp and unrelenting. "No more lies, Elliot. No more justifications. Say it."

He shook his head, his voice trembling. "I didn't… I didn't mean to…"

"Liar," she spat. "You meant every second of it. Say it."

Elliot clutched his head, his fingers digging into his scalp as he tried to block out her words. But there was no escape. The memories, the pain, the truth—it all pressed down on him, suffocating him.

"You wanted control," Delyla said, her voice softer now but no less powerful. "You wanted power. You wanted to feel like you mattered. And you didn't care who you hurt to get it."

The words tore through him, stripping away the last of his defenses. He had always told himself that he wasn't like the killers he studied, that he was different. But now, he saw the truth. He wasn't different. He was worse. He had lied to himself, to everyone, and now there was nothing left to hide behind.

Admitting the Truth

For the first time, Elliot spoke the words he had been avoiding since the night of the murder. "I deserve this," he whispered, his voice trembling. "I deserve to be punished."

The admission hung in the air, a moment of clarity amidst the chaos. It was a small thing, but it felt monumental. For the first time, he wasn't running, wasn't lying, wasn't trying to justify his actions. He was facing the truth, raw and unfiltered.

Delyla's expression didn't soften, but there was a flicker of something in her eyes—acknowledgment, perhaps, or a faint glimmer of satisfaction. "Admitting it isn't enough," she said. "You have to act on it."

Elliot looked up at her, his eyes red and swollen with tears. "What do you mean?" he asked, his voice barely audible.

"You know what I mean," Delyla said. "Confess. Face what you've done. Stop running."

The words sent a chill through him, but he didn't argue. He couldn't. Deep down, he knew she was right. He couldn't keep running. But the thought of confessing, of losing everything, was almost too much to bear.

Teetering on the Edge

As the room returned to its normal state, Delyla's form began to fade. Elliot was left alone in the silence, his body trembling as he sat on the floor. His mind was a whirlwind of thoughts and emotions, the weight of Delyla's words pressing down on him.

He knew he was at a crossroads. He could continue to run, to cling to the fragile remnants of his life, or he could face the consequences of his actions and try to atone. Either way, he knew his life would never be the same.

As he sat there, staring at the empty space where Delyla had stood, Elliot felt a strange sense of calm amidst the chaos. He didn't know what he would do, but for the first time, he understood the depth of his guilt and the gravity of his choices. And as much as it terrified him, he knew he couldn't avoid the truth any longer.

The room was silent, but Elliot's mind was anything but. He sat there, teetering on the edge of acceptance, knowing that the final decision would define the rest of his life—and perhaps, his eternity.

Chapter 10:
The Final Confrontation

The Ultimate Haunting

Elliot's apartment had become a prison of his own making, a decaying tomb filled with the echoes of his guilt and torment. Over the months of Delyla's relentless haunting, he had endured physical attacks, psychological breakdowns, and the horrifying weight of his own conscience. But nothing could have prepared him for what came next. This was no longer just a haunting. This was the ultimate reckoning.

Delyla Becomes Corporeal

It began with an almost imperceptible shift in the air, a sudden weight that made it hard to breathe. The lights in the apartment flickered and dimmed until the room was bathed in an oppressive gloom. Elliot was used to Delyla's presence, but this felt different. There was a new intensity, an almost unbearable energy that made his skin prickle.

And then, she appeared.

Delyla's ghost materialized in the center of the room, but this time, she wasn't the flickering, translucent figure Elliot had grown to fear. She was fully corporeal, her form solid and horrifyingly real. Her face bore the wounds of the attack, the blood still fresh and glistening. The gaping wound in her chest was a stark reminder of Elliot's crime, and her eyes burned with a fury that seemed to pierce straight through him.

Elliot stumbled backward, his breath coming in short, panicked gasps. "No," he whispered, shaking his head. "This isn't real. This can't be real."

But it was. Delyla's presence was undeniable, her footsteps echoing on the wooden floor as she moved closer. The room seemed to shrink around her, the walls pressing in as if the apartment itself was reacting to her rage.

"You've run out of time, Elliot," she said, her voice cold and unyielding. "There's nowhere left to hide."

Trapped in the Apartment

As Elliot turned to flee, he found the door sealed shut. He clawed at the handle, his fingers trembling, but it wouldn't budge. The windows, too, were impenetrable, their glass thick and unyielding. It was as if the apartment had become a living entity, conspiring with Delyla to keep him contained.

"Let me out!" Elliot screamed, pounding on the door with his fists. "Please, let me out!"

Delyla's laugh was low and bitter, sending a shiver down his spine. "You don't get to leave," she said. "Not until you face what you've done."

The walls began to shift, the paint peeling away to reveal scenes from Delyla's life. Elliot saw her as a child, laughing with her siblings in a sunny backyard. He saw her as a teenager, her face lighting up as she held a trophy aloft on a stage. And then, he saw her as an adult, sitting in a café with a notebook, her expression focused and determined.

Each image was a dagger to Elliot's heart, a reminder of everything he had taken from her. But the scenes didn't stop there. The walls twisted and warped, replaying the moment of her murder in horrifying detail. Elliot saw himself stalking her, the knife trembling in his hand. He saw the confusion and fear in her eyes as she turned to face him. He saw her fall, her body crumpling to the ground as the blood pooled beneath her.

Reliving the Attack

The scenes on the walls dissolved, and suddenly, Elliot was no longer in his apartment. He was back in the alley, standing over Delyla's body. The knife was in his hand, its blade slick with her blood. He tried to drop it, but his fingers wouldn't obey. He was trapped in the memory, forced to relive every excruciating detail of the attack.

"Do you feel it now?" Delyla's voice echoed around him, her tone icy and unrelenting. "Do you see what you did?"

The memory replayed itself again and again, each repetition more vivid and horrifying than the last. Elliot felt the weight of the knife, the resistance of Delyla's flesh as the blade plunged into her chest. He heard her screams, her desperate pleas for mercy, and the sickening gurgle as her breath left her body.

"Stop it!" he screamed, his voice cracking with desperation. "Please, stop!"

But Delyla didn't stop. She wouldn't stop. The scene played out over and over, each detail magnified to emphasize his failure and cruelty. Elliot fell to his knees, his body trembling as he sobbed.

Feeling What She Felt

And then, the torment reached a new level. Delyla stepped forward, her ghostly form radiating a cold, unrelenting energy. She raised her hand, and Elliot felt a sudden, sharp pain in his chest. He gasped, clutching at his heart as the sensation spread through his body.

"This is what you made me feel," Delyla said, her voice low and chilling. "Every moment of fear, every ounce of pain."

Elliot's body mimicked hers as she reenacted the attack. He felt the searing pain of the knife entering his flesh, the suffocating pressure as his lungs filled with blood. He couldn't breathe, couldn't think. His vision blurred, and for a moment, he thought he might die.

"You took my life," Delyla said, her voice trembling with emotion. "And now, you'll feel what it's like to lose yours."

The pain was unbearable, each second stretching into an eternity. Elliot screamed, his cries echoing through the apartment, but there was no escape. He was trapped in her memory, forced to experience her final moments as if they were his own.

A Trembling Wreck

When the pain finally subsided, Elliot collapsed onto the floor, his body trembling violently. His chest heaved with ragged breaths, and tears streamed down his face as he curled into a ball. He was a wreck, broken in every conceivable way.

"Why are you doing this to me?" he sobbed, his voice barely audible. "What do you want from me?"

Delyla stood over him, her expression cold and unyielding. "I want you to understand," she said. "I want you to feel the weight of what you've done. And I want you to realize that there is no escape. Not until you take responsibility."

Elliot shook his head, his voice trembling. "I can't… I can't do this anymore."

Delyla's gaze softened slightly, but her tone remained firm. "You don't have a choice," she said. "This is your reckoning, Elliot. And it's only just begun."

Begging for an End

The relentless haunting left Elliot a trembling, sobbing wreck. He had nothing left to give, no strength to fight, no hope of escape. He lay on the floor, his body shaking as he begged for it to end.

"Please," he whispered, his voice raw with desperation. "I'm sorry. I'm so sorry. Just make it stop."

But Delyla didn't answer. She stood silently, her presence a constant reminder of his guilt. The walls around him continued to shift and twist, replaying her life and death in an endless loop. The pain, the fear, the sorrow—it was all-consuming, a tidal wave of emotion that threatened to drown him.

For the first time, Elliot realized the full extent of what he had done. He hadn't just taken Delyla's life—he had destroyed her future, her dreams, and the lives of everyone who had loved her. And now, he was paying the price.

As the night stretched on, Elliot's cries grew weaker, his body trembling as he teetered on the edge of madness. The ultimate haunting had broken him, leaving him a shell of the man he had once been. And Delyla's ghost, unrelenting in her quest for justice, ensured that his suffering was far from over.

Delyla's Pain

The room was unnaturally quiet. The oppressive silence that filled Elliot's apartment was a sharp contrast to the chaos that had defined his life for months. It was the kind of silence that pressed against the ears, magnifying every tiny sound—a creak of the floorboards, the shallow rasp of his breath, the distant hum of the refrigerator. But Elliot knew better than to trust the stillness. It was never just silence anymore. She was always there, waiting, watching, tormenting him.

Delyla's ghost didn't need dramatic entrances. She didn't need to announce herself with flickering lights or shifting shadows. Her presence was enough. When she appeared this time, it wasn't with the terrifying fury he had come to expect. She didn't rage, and she didn't mock. Instead, she stood quietly in the corner of the room, her translucent form flickering faintly in the dim light. There was a gravity to her now, a depth that made the air in the room feel heavier.

Elliot sat frozen on the floor, his back pressed against the wall. His body trembled as he stared at her, unable to look away. He could feel it—the weight of her suffering, the magnitude of her loss. And he knew this wasn't going to be another one of her punishments. This was something worse.

Unfulfilled Dreams

"You don't understand," Delyla said, her voice soft but unwavering. "You don't understand what you took from me."

The room around them began to change, the walls dissolving into a swirling mist. Elliot felt the now-familiar pull of her power, dragging him into her memories. He fought it instinctively, but there was no use. Delyla was in control.

The mist cleared, and Elliot found himself in a brightly lit room. A teenage version of Delyla stood at the center, holding a gold trophy in her hands. Her face was lit with a radiant smile as she beamed at the small crowd gathered around her. Elliot could feel her pride, her joy, as though it were his own.

"This was my first writing competition," Delyla said, her voice tinged with a bittersweet nostalgia. "I worked on that story for months. Every word, every sentence… I thought it might be the start of something."

The scene shifted, fast-forwarding through the years. Delyla sitting at a café, her head bent over a notebook. Delyla standing on a stage, nervously reading aloud from a manuscript. Delyla laughing with friends as they discussed their dreams and plans for the future.

"You didn't just kill me," Delyla continued, her voice breaking slightly. "You killed this. All of it. The stories I would have written. The people I would have loved. The life I was supposed to have."

Elliot's chest tightened, the weight of her words pressing down on him. He wanted to look away, but he couldn't. The memories unfolded before him with relentless clarity, each one a reminder of the life she could have lived—the life he had stolen.

The Weight of His Crime

The scenes changed again, this time to moments after her death. Her family's anguished faces as they received the news. Her friends standing at her grave, their shoulders shaking with silent sobs. Her mother sitting alone in a darkened room, clutching a photograph of Delyla and whispering her name like a prayer.

"You didn't just kill me," Delyla said. "You killed them too. Their joy, their hope, their sense of safety. You tore a hole in their lives that will never heal."

Elliot felt the weight of her words like a physical blow, his chest heaving as tears streamed down his face. The enormity of what he had done was crushing, suffocating. He had always told himself that it was just one life, that his actions had been calculated and contained. But now, faced with the ripple effects of his crime, he realized how wrong he had been.

"I didn't…" he started, his voice trembling. "I didn't mean for any of this."

Delyla's eyes narrowed, her voice cold and sharp. "You didn't think about any of this. You didn't care. I was just a target to you. A name. A face. A puzzle."

Delyla's Fury and Sadness

Her form flickered, growing brighter and more solid as her emotions intensified. "Do you have any idea what it feels like to have everything ripped away from you?" she demanded, her voice trembling with both fury and sadness. "To know that your story ends because someone else decided it should?"

Elliot couldn't answer. He couldn't even look at her. The truth of her words was too much to bear.

"I had dreams," Delyla continued, her voice cracking. "I had plans. And you took them from me. You stole everything I was and everything I could have been. And for what? To feel powerful? To prove something to yourself?"

Her anger was palpable, a crackling energy that filled the room. But there was something else beneath it—a profound sadness that made Elliot's chest ache.

"I wasn't perfect," she said, her voice softer now. "I made mistakes. I had flaws. But I mattered. My life mattered. And you took it from me like it was nothing."

Admitting Guilt

Elliot's sobs grew louder, his body trembling as he clutched his head in his hands. "I'm sorry," he choked out. "I'm so sorry."

Delyla's gaze didn't waver. "Sorry isn't enough," she said. "It will never be enough. But it's a start."

For the first time, Elliot felt the full weight of his guilt. He had always tried to justify his actions, to frame them as something calculated and detached. But now, stripped of his delusions, he saw his crime for what it was—a senseless, selfish act that had destroyed not just one life, but many.

"I deserve this," he whispered, his voice trembling. "I deserve to suffer."

Delyla stepped closer, her expression unreadable. "Your suffering will never compare to mine," she said. "But it's a start."

The Shattering of Delusions

As the memories faded and the apartment returned to its ruined state, Elliot sat on the floor, his body trembling. His mind raced with the images he had seen, the voices he had heard, the weight of Delyla's loss pressing down on him like an avalanche.

He had spent so long telling himself that he was in control, that his actions had been calculated and justified. But now, those delusions were gone. Delyla had torn them apart, exposing the raw, ugly truth beneath.

He wasn't in control. He never had been. He was a coward, a thief, a murderer. And the weight of his crime was something he would carry for the rest of his life.

As Delyla's ghost began to fade, her voice lingered in the air. "Take responsibility," she said, her tone firm but not unkind. "It's the only way."

Elliot didn't respond. He couldn't. He was too broken, too consumed by the enormity of what he had done. As the room fell silent once more, he realized that there was no escape from his guilt, no way to undo the harm he had caused.

But maybe, just maybe, there was a way to begin making it right.

The Final Decision

Elliot sat in the center of his ruined apartment, his back against the cold wall as he stared at the wreckage around him. The air was heavy, the kind of stillness that pressed down like a weight on his chest. His mind raced with fragments of Delyla's words, her voice cutting through his thoughts even in her absence. He knew she was coming. He could feel it in the way the room seemed to hold its breath, waiting.

And then she was there.

Delyla's ghost materialized before him, her presence as overwhelming as ever. This time, her form was sharper, more solid, and her expression was cold and unyielding. Her eyes burned with the weight of her fury and sadness, pinning him in place as though her gaze alone could crush him.

"This is it," she said, her voice sharp and resolute. "Your final chance."

The Last Ultimatum

Elliot flinched at her words, his body trembling as he tried to process their meaning. "What do you mean?" he whispered, his voice barely audible.

"You know what I mean," Delyla replied, stepping closer. "No more running. No more excuses. You need to confess, Elliot. Face what you've done. Take responsibility."

Her words cut through him like a blade, each syllable sharpening the edges of his guilt. He opened his mouth to respond, but no words came. His thoughts were a tangled mess of fear, regret, and self-preservation, each one pulling him in a different direction.

Delyla's expression didn't soften. "This is your last opportunity to atone," she said. "If you refuse, I'll make sure you never know peace. Not in this life. Not in the next."

Elliot's heart raced, his chest tightening as the weight of her ultimatum pressed down on him. He couldn't breathe, couldn't think. The room seemed to close in around him, the walls warping and shifting as though mirroring the chaos in his mind.

Torn Between Fear and Redemption

For what felt like an eternity, Elliot sat frozen, his mind racing. On one hand, there was the safety of his current existence—a fragile and crumbling safety, but safety nonetheless. Turning himself in meant giving that up, exposing himself to a world of punishment, judgment, and scorn. It meant admitting to the world what he had done, stripping away the last shreds of control he had left.

But on the other hand, there was Delyla's warning. He had seen what she could do, felt the depth of her torment. If he refused, he knew she would follow through on her promise. The haunting would continue, growing more intense, more suffocating, until it consumed him entirely.

"I can't," he whispered, shaking his head. "I can't do it."

Delyla's eyes narrowed, her voice cold. "You can't, or you won't?"

Elliot's breath hitched as her words struck him like a blow. He buried his face in his hands, his mind racing with memories of what he had done, what he had taken from her. The weight of it all was crushing, suffocating. He knew she was right. He knew he deserved to suffer. But the thought of confessing, of giving up his freedom, was almost too much to bear.

The Breaking Point

Delyla didn't move, her presence looming over him as he struggled to find the courage to speak. "You don't understand," he said finally, his voice trembling. "If I do this… If I confess… It's over for me."

Her expression didn't waver. "It was over for me the moment you chose to end my life," she said. "And now, it's your turn to face the consequences."

Tears streamed down Elliot's face as he looked up at her, his body shaking. "I'm sorry," he whispered. "I'm so sorry."

Delyla's voice softened slightly, though her resolve remained firm. "Sorry isn't enough," she said. "Not this time."

Elliot collapsed to the floor, his body trembling as he sobbed uncontrollably. His chest heaved with the weight of his emotions, every breath a struggle. He felt like a child, small and helpless in the face of something far greater than himself.

"I'll do it," he whispered finally, his voice barely audible. "I'll confess."

The Apartment Shifts

As the words left his lips, the air in the apartment seemed to change. The oppressive weight that had hung over him for months began to lift, and the room slowly started to return to normal. The walls straightened, the furniture settled, and the shattered glass on the floor seemed to dissolve into nothingness.

Delyla's form began to flicker, her edges softening as she stepped back. For the first time, her expression showed something other than anger or sorrow. There was a faint glimmer of satisfaction in her eyes, though it was tempered by the pain that would never truly leave her.

"This doesn't erase what you've done," she said, her voice steady. "But it's a start. Don't make me come back, Elliot."

And with that, she vanished, her presence fading into the stillness of the apartment. For the first time in what felt like an eternity, Elliot was alone.

The Final Decision

Elliot sat in the silence, his body trembling as he tried to process what had just happened. The room felt different now, lighter somehow, though the weight of his guilt still pressed heavily on his chest. He knew what he had to do. There was no turning back now.

With shaky hands, he reached for his phone. The device felt foreign in his grasp, its weight heavier than it should have been. He stared at the screen for a long moment, his fingers hovering over the keypad as his heart raced.

"You can do this," he whispered to himself, though his voice was filled with doubt.

Taking a deep breath, he began to dial. Each number felt like a step toward the edge of a cliff, the inevitability of his actions pulling him closer to the void. When the phone began to ring, his breath caught in his throat, his entire body tensing as he waited.

"911, what's your emergency?" a voice said on the other end.

Elliot closed his eyes, his hands shaking as he held the phone to his ear. "I... I need to confess," he said, his voice trembling. "I killed someone."

The words hung in the air, a chilling finality settling over him. He didn't know what would come next, but for the first time in months, he felt something close to peace. It wasn't freedom, and it wasn't forgiveness. But it was a start.

And as he sat there, waiting for the consequences of his actions to unfold, Delyla's final words echoed in his mind: *Don't make me come back.*

Epilogue:
The Haunting Never Ends

Elliot's Confession

The interrogation room was cold and sterile, its walls painted a dull gray that seemed to absorb what little light the flickering fluorescent bulb offered. The table in the center was bolted to the floor, its metal surface scratched and scarred from years of use. Elliot sat in the lone chair, his hands cuffed to the table, his body slouched in a way that made him seem smaller than he was. His clothes hung loose on his gaunt frame, and his hollow eyes stared down at the table as though the answers to his misery lay somewhere within its scratched surface.

The room's silence was oppressive, broken only by the occasional hum of the light above. Elliot had turned himself in hours earlier, walking into the police station with trembling hands and bloodshot eyes. His voice had been flat, almost lifeless, as he confessed to the murder of Delyla—and the obsessive planning and stalking that led up to it. The officers who heard his initial statement had looked at him with a mixture of confusion and disbelief, unsure if the man standing before them was telling the truth.

Now, sitting in this room, Elliot felt the weight of his actions pressing down on him like never before. He had expected to feel lighter, freer, as though the act of confession would lift the crushing burden of guilt that had consumed him for months. But instead, he felt hollow. Delyla's presence still lingered in the back of his mind, her voice a constant whisper that made it impossible to believe her torment was truly over.

Reluctant Liberation

Elliot's mind replayed the moments leading up to his confession. He had sat in his apartment for hours, staring at his phone, his hands trembling as he dialed the number for the police. When the dispatcher answered, he had stammered out his admission in a voice barely above a whisper. The silence on the other end of the line had been deafening, followed by the sound of typing and the dispatcher's calm instructions.

Now, as he sat in the interrogation room, he wondered if he had made the right decision. Confessing hadn't brought him the peace he had hoped for. The crushing guilt that had plagued him since Delyla's death was still there, and the memories of her haunting were as vivid as ever.

He closed his eyes, and for a moment, he thought he could hear her voice. It was faint, almost drowned out by the hum of the light, but it was unmistakable. *You think this is enough?* she whispered, her tone cold and sharp. *You think you've paid for what you did?*

Elliot opened his eyes, his breath hitching as he glanced around the room. But he was alone—or at least, he appeared to be. Her presence, though unseen, was undeniable.

The Police Reaction

The door to the interrogation room opened, and two detectives, Harper Connors and Mark Davis entered, their expressions grim. Detective Connors was an older man with a weathered face and sharp eyes that seemed to take in every detail. Detective Davis was younger, his jaw tight and his hands fidgeting nervously as he carried a file. They sat across from Elliot, their movements careful, as though they were unsure what to expect.

"Mr. Marsh," Detective Connors began, his voice steady but probing. "You've made some serious claims. We need to go over them in detail."

Elliot nodded weakly, his eyes still fixed on the table. "I'll tell you everything," he said, his voice barely audible.

Over the next several hours, Elliot recounted the events leading up to Delyla's murder in excruciating detail. He described the weeks he had spent watching her, learning her routine, and planning every step of the attack. He spoke of the knife, the alley, and the moment he had taken her life. His voice was flat, devoid of emotion, as though he were describing someone else's actions rather than his own.

The detectives exchanged uneasy glances as they listened. The level of detail in Elliot's confession was staggering, painting a picture of a man who had meticulously planned his crime. Yet the man sitting before them was broken, his body frail and his voice trembling. It was difficult to reconcile the methodical killer he described with the hollow shell of a person in front of them.

When Elliot finished speaking, the Detective Davis leaned back in his chair, his expression a mixture of disbelief and discomfort. "Why now?" he asked. "Why confess after all this time?"

Elliot hesitated, his fingers twitching against the cuffs. "Because I couldn't live with it anymore," he said. "And because she wouldn't let me."

The detectives frowned at his cryptic answer but didn't press further. There was enough in his confession to secure a conviction, and they had no desire to dig deeper into the mind of a man who had willingly walked into their station and admitted to murder.

A Quiet Courtroom

The courtroom was silent, the air thick with tension as Elliot stood before the judge. His hands were cuffed in front of him, and his posture was slouched, as though the weight of his guilt was too much to bear. The families of the victims sat in the gallery, their eyes fixed on him with a mixture of anger, disbelief, and grief.

When the judge asked for his plea, Elliot's voice was flat and emotionless. "Guilty," he said, the single word echoing through the room.

There was a murmur among the spectators, a wave of whispers and muffled sobs as the reality of his admission sank in. Delyla's family sat together, their faces pale and their eyes red from crying. Her mother clutched a handkerchief in her trembling hands, while her father stared straight ahead, his jaw clenched tightly.

Elliot didn't look at them. He couldn't. His eyes remained fixed on the floor, his shame palpable as the judge read out his sentence: life in prison without the possibility of parole. The words hung in the air, a final, crushing declaration of his fate.

Sentenced to Life

As the guards approached to escort him from the courtroom, Elliot felt a strange mix of emotions. Relief, fear, regret—they all swirled together in a chaotic storm that left him numb. His last moments of freedom were spent staring at the polished wood of the courtroom floor, his mind racing with memories of Delyla and the life he had taken.

He didn't fight as the guards placed a hand on his shoulder, guiding him toward the exit. His legs felt heavy, each step a struggle as though the weight of his guilt was dragging him down. The murmurs of the courtroom faded into the background, replaced by the sound of his own heartbeat pounding in his ears.

A Whisper in the Shadows

As Elliot passed through the door, leaving the courtroom behind, he thought he heard a familiar voice. It was faint, almost drowned out by the shuffle of footsteps and the creak of the door, but it was unmistakable.

Don't think this is over, Delyla's voice whispered, her tone chilling and resolute. *I'll be watching.*

Elliot froze, his body trembling as the words echoed in his mind. He glanced over his shoulder, half-expecting to see her standing in the shadows, but there was nothing there. The guards nudged him forward, and he stumbled, his breath hitching as he tried to steady himself.

The haunting wasn't over. He knew that now. Confessing might have been a step toward redemption, but it wasn't the end of his punishment. Delyla's voice was a reminder of that—a chilling declaration that her presence would never truly leave him.

As he was led down the hallway toward his new life behind bars, Elliot's mind was filled with her words. The weight of his crime pressed down on him like never before, and he realized that the haunting wasn't just about Delyla's wrath. It was about his guilt, his conscience, and the irrevocable damage he had done.

And as the heavy door to his cell slammed shut, Elliot knew that his suffering was far from over.

Life in Prison

Elliot's prison cell was small, sterile, and devoid of any personal touch. The walls were gray and cold, the metal bedframe unforgiving, and the dim light above him flickered sporadically, casting unsettling shadows. But none of that compared to the real prison Elliot faced: the one in his mind. He had imagined that the weight of his guilt would lessen now that he had confessed, that Delyla's presence might fade with his admission of responsibility. Instead, it had grown stronger, more invasive, her ghost following him even here.

It wasn't the prison bars or the rigid schedules that broke him—it was Delyla. She was always there, a constant reminder of his crime and the life he had stolen. Her presence filled the tiny cell, her ghostly form appearing in the reflective surfaces that surrounded him: the metal sink, the polished floors of the corridors, even the glint of light off his food tray. There was no escape. Not here. Not anywhere.

A Prison of the Mind

Elliot sat on the edge of his bed, his hands trembling as he stared at the small metal sink in the corner of his cell. The surface was dull, marred by scratches and years of wear, but every so often, he saw her face in it. Not the Delyla he had first stalked, not the vibrant young woman with hopes and dreams, but the ghostly version that had haunted him relentlessly—her hollow eyes filled with anger and sadness, her wound oozing blood that never seemed to stop.

"Why are you still here?" Elliot whispered, his voice barely audible over the distant hum of prison life.

The sink didn't respond, but he knew better than to think she wasn't listening. She always was. Her silence was as oppressive as her accusations, an unspoken judgment that hung heavy in the air. Sometimes, Elliot thought he could hear her breathing, a faint, raspy sound that made the hairs on his arms stand on end.

He tried to avoid the reflective surfaces, turning his back on the sink and averting his eyes from the polished floors of the corridor when the guards marched him to and from the mess hall. But it didn't matter. Delyla didn't need reflections to make her presence known. She was always there, lurking in the shadows of his mind, her voice echoing through the empty spaces of his thoughts.

Nightly Visitations

The nights were the worst. When the prison grew quiet and the other inmates settled into uneasy sleep, Delyla would return. At first, she was silent, standing in the corner of his cell, her translucent form flickering faintly in the dim light. She didn't speak, but her eyes said everything: *I'm here because of you. This is your doing.*

Elliot would try to ignore her, pulling the thin, scratchy blanket over his head like a child afraid of the dark. But the blanket couldn't block out the cold that seemed to radiate from her, chilling him to the bone. And it couldn't block out her voice when she finally spoke.

"You think this is justice?" she whispered one night, her tone sharp and cutting. "Do you think a life in here can compare to what you took from me?"

Elliot's body trembled as he clutched the edges of the blanket tighter. "I'm sorry," he whispered, his voice cracking. "I don't know what else to do."

Delyla's laugh was low and bitter, filling the tiny cell with its weight. "Sorry isn't enough," she said. "It will never be enough."

Sometimes, her whispers lasted all night, a relentless stream of accusations and reminders that kept him awake until dawn. Other times, she didn't speak at all, simply standing there and watching him with those hollow eyes, her presence more oppressive than any words could be.

Physical Torment

It wasn't just the mental torment that Delyla inflicted on him. She had found ways to reach him physically, her influence manifesting in bruises and scratches that appeared on his body overnight. Elliot would wake to find his arms covered in faint, red lines, or his ribs aching as though someone had pressed down on them with relentless force.

At first, he tried to dismiss it as self-inflicted, the result of restless sleep or a subconscious need to punish himself. But the marks didn't make sense. They were too deliberate, too precise. And sometimes, they mirrored the wounds he had inflicted on Delyla, a horrifying reminder of the pain he had caused.

The other inmates began to notice. They whispered about him in the mess hall, their eyes darting toward the bruises on his arms and the scratches on his neck. Some laughed, calling him cursed or haunted. Others kept their distance, unnerved by the eerie energy that seemed to surround him.

Even the guards avoided him when they could, their faces betraying a mix of pity and unease. Elliot didn't blame them. He could feel it too—that cold, suffocating presence that followed him everywhere, a constant reminder that he would never truly be alone.

Isolation Deepens

Elliot's erratic behavior only deepened his isolation. He talked to himself constantly, his whispered arguments with Delyla drawing the attention of the other inmates. They mocked him, giving him the nickname "Ghost," a cruel jab at the torment he couldn't escape.

"Hey, Ghost!" one inmate called out during yard time, his voice dripping with mockery. "You talking to your girlfriend again?"

The others laughed, but Elliot didn't respond. He couldn't. His focus was elsewhere—on the faint, translucent figure standing by the fence, her hollow eyes fixed on him as though she were waiting for something.

The guards, too, kept their distance, their interactions with him curt and impersonal. He had become a pariah within the prison walls, a man broken by forces they couldn't understand. And though Elliot hated the isolation, he couldn't blame them for their avoidance. He didn't want to be around himself either.

A Crumbling Psyche

The monotony of prison life, combined with Delyla's relentless presence, began to chip away at what little sanity Elliot had left. The days blurred together, each one marked by the same routine: the clang of cell doors, the march to the mess hall, the whispers of the other inmates. But Delyla was the constant, her presence breaking through the monotony with unrelenting force.

Elliot stopped trying to hide his conversations with her, openly responding to her accusations and whispers. "What do you want from me?" he would ask, his voice trembling. "I've already confessed. I'm already here."

The other inmates watched him with a mixture of amusement and unease, their laughter fading as Elliot's outbursts grew more frequent. He became the subject of rumors, his name whispered in hushed tones as though saying it too loudly might summon the ghost that haunted him.

One night, as he sat on his bed, rocking back and forth and muttering to himself, Delyla appeared in the corner of the cell. "You're losing it," she said, her tone laced with mockery. "Do you really think they'll believe you when you tell them why?"

"I don't care what they believe," Elliot snapped, his voice louder than he intended. His outburst earned him a shout from a guard down the hall, but he didn't care. "You're the one who won't leave me alone!"

Delyla's laugh was cold and cruel, echoing in the tiny cell. "I told you, Elliot," she said. "This doesn't end."

A Failed Attempt at Atonement

In a rare moment of clarity, Elliot tried to make amends in the only way he could think of: by writing letters to Delyla's family. He sat at the small desk in his cell, the paper trembling in his hands as he struggled to find the words.

To Delyla's family, he began, his handwriting shaky and uneven. *I don't expect forgiveness. I don't deserve it. But I need you to know that I'm sorry. I'm sorry for what I did, for the pain I caused, for everything I took from you. I know that doesn't mean anything coming from me, but it's the truth.*

He paused, his pen hovering over the page as he tried to continue. But the words felt hollow, meaningless. What could he possibly say to make up for what he had done? How could a few sentences on a piece of paper ever convey the depth of his remorse?

Frustrated, he crumpled the paper and threw it across the room. "It's pointless," he muttered, his voice trembling. "They'll never forgive me. And I don't deserve it."

Delyla appeared in the corner of the cell, her expression unreadable. "You're right," she said. "You don't."

Elliot didn't respond. He couldn't. He simply sat there, staring at the crumpled paper on the floor, knowing that no amount of words could ever erase the damage he had done.

Elliot's life in prison was defined not by the bars that confined him or the guards who watched over him, but by the unrelenting presence of Delyla's ghost. Her torment followed him everywhere, a constant reminder of the life he had stolen and the pain he had caused.

Though he had confessed and been sentenced, Elliot knew that his punishment was far from over. Delyla's whispers, her accusations, and her cold, hollow eyes would remain with him for the rest of his days. And as he lay in his cell at night, staring at the ceiling and listening to the faint sound of her voice, he realized that the true prison wasn't the one he lived in—it was the one he carried within himself.

The Weight of Other Victims

Elliot's life in prison was supposed to be an end, the final chapter of a long descent into madness and guilt. But the haunting that followed him was far from finished. Delyla's presence, which had loomed over him since her death, began to shift in new and horrifying ways. Her torment, once focused solely on her own pain and the life Elliot had taken, expanded to include the gallery of faces—the people Elliot had once considered as potential victims.

Each face brought a fresh wave of guilt, a new dimension to his suffering. These weren't nameless, faceless strangers anymore. They were real people, individuals with lives, families, and futures. And now, their lives were haunting him just as Delyla's was, filling every corner of his mind with unbearable weight.

A Gallery of Faces

It started with the sink. The small, scratched metal basin in his cell had been Delyla's favorite canvas, her face appearing in its dull surface at the most unexpected moments. But one day, as Elliot approached the sink, he saw a different face staring back at him.

It was a young woman with dark hair and tired eyes, her expression a mix of anger and sadness. Elliot froze, his breath catching in his throat as recognition dawned. He had followed her once, noting the way she walked home from her night shifts at a diner. She had been a fleeting thought, a brief consideration in his twisted mind before he discarded her as a potential target.

Her face was soon joined by others. A young man with glasses and a shy smile who had always walked the same route to his college classes. A middle-aged woman with a kind face who had been too predictable in her routines. A teenager with headphones around her neck, her carefree demeanor making her an easy mark.

Each face stared at him with unflinching intensity, their eyes filled with accusation and pain. They didn't speak—not at first. They simply lingered, their presence growing more oppressive with each passing day.

Accusations in the Night

The voices began not long after the faces appeared. They started as whispers, faint and indistinct, blending with the hum of the prison at night. But as the days stretched into weeks, the whispers grew louder, more distinct, until they became an unbearable cacophony.

"Why me?" one voice asked, trembling with sorrow.

"I had a family," another whispered, filled with quiet anger.

"You almost stole everything," a third voice hissed, sharp and accusing.

Their voices overlapped, creating a chorus of pain and grief that echoed through Elliot's cell. He clutched his head, pressing his palms against his ears, but it was no use. The voices weren't coming from outside. They were inside him, woven into the fabric of his mind.

Even Delyla joined the chorus, her voice rising above the others. "Do you see it now?" she asked, her tone a mixture of fury and satisfaction. "Do you see what you almost became?"

Elliot couldn't respond. His voice was lost in the din, swallowed by the weight of their accusations. He curled up on his bed, his body trembling as he begged for silence. But the voices didn't stop. They never stopped.

A Distorted Reality

The faces and voices weren't the only manifestations of Elliot's guilt. Soon, he began to see flashes of their lives—glimpses of what could have been, of the futures he had almost stolen.

He saw the young woman with dark hair at her wedding, her face glowing with happiness as she danced with her new husband. He saw the young man with glasses walking across a stage to receive his diploma, his family cheering from the audience. He saw the teenager blowing out the candles on her 18th birthday cake, her friends laughing and celebrating around her.

These visions felt more vivid than anything in his real surroundings. The sterile walls of his cell, the rigid structure of prison life—all of it faded into the background as the lives of these almost-victims played out before him. He could smell the food at the family dinners, hear the laughter at the parties, feel the warmth of the celebrations.

And then the visions would twist. The laughter would fade, replaced by silence. The joy would evaporate, replaced by grief. He saw their families mourning their losses, their faces etched with pain. He saw himself lurking in the shadows, a knife in his hand, ready to snatch away their futures.

A New Kind of Torment

Delyla seemed to take satisfaction in these new hauntings. Her ghostly form appeared more frequently now, her presence growing stronger with each new face that joined the gallery. She watched as Elliot crumbled under the weight of his guilt, her expression a mix of triumph and sorrow.

"You thought it was just me," she said one night, her voice cold and sharp. "You thought you could limit the damage to one life. But this is what you really are, Elliot. This is what you were becoming."

Elliot didn't respond. He couldn't. He sat on the floor of his cell, his head in his hands, as the visions played out around him. The weight of what he had almost done was suffocating, pressing down on him with an intensity that made it hard to breathe.

"You should thank me," Delyla said, her voice dripping with disdain. "If it weren't for me, these faces wouldn't just be haunting you. They'd be real."

Her words cut through him like a blade, the truth of them undeniable. He had thought of himself as calculated, in control, but Delyla's haunting had shattered that illusion. He wasn't a mastermind. He was a coward, a broken man who had let his obsession consume him.

A Constant Reminder

Even in the rare moments of silence, the faces lingered in his mind. Their eyes, filled with pain and accusation, were burned into his memory. He couldn't escape them, couldn't forget the lives he had almost destroyed.

The faces followed him everywhere. When he closed his eyes, they were there, staring at him in the darkness. When he walked through the prison corridors, their reflections flickered in the polished floors. Even during the brief moments of respite in the yard, he saw them in the shadows, their presence a constant reminder of his guilt.

Elliot's every thought was consumed by them, every breath weighed down by the enormity of his actions. He couldn't escape the gallery of faces, couldn't silence their voices or erase their pain. They were a part of him now, woven into the fabric of his existence.

No End in Sight

As the days turned into weeks and the weeks into months, Elliot realized that his punishment was far from over. Delyla's haunting had extended beyond her own story, becoming a reckoning for every life he had ever considered taking.

There was no escape from the weight of his guilt, no way to undo the harm he had caused or the harm he had almost caused. The faces, the voices, the visions—they were his new reality, a constant reminder of the path he had chosen and the lives he had destroyed.

Elliot sat on the edge of his bed, staring at the floor as Delyla's voice echoed in his mind. "This is who you are," she said. "This is what you've done. And this is what you'll live with for the rest of your life."

Tears streamed down his face as he whispered, "I know."

And in that moment, Elliot realized the true depth of his punishment. It wasn't the prison walls or the loss of his freedom. It was the weight of the lives he had touched, the lives he had destroyed, and the lives he had almost stolen. It was a burden he would carry forever, with no end in sight.

A Glimpse of Redemption

Elliot had spent countless nights haunted by Delyla's ghost, her torment an unrelenting reminder of his crime. His life had become a cycle of guilt and suffering, every breath a testament to the destruction he had wrought. But one night, something changed. It wasn't the oppressive chill that typically accompanied her appearances, nor was it the flickering lights or the heavy silence that signaled her presence. Instead, there was a strange calm in the air, an almost imperceptible shift that made Elliot sit up and take notice.

When Delyla appeared in the corner of his cell, her form was different. The sharp edges of her ghostly figure were softer, her movements less rigid. Her eyes, though still hollow and filled with sorrow, lacked the fury that had defined them for so long. For the first time in months, she didn't radiate anger. She simply stood there, watching him with an expression that Elliot couldn't quite place.

"You're still here," he said, his voice trembling. "Why are you still here?"

Delyla didn't answer right away. When she finally spoke, her tone was quiet, almost contemplative. "Because your story isn't finished," she said. "And neither is mine."

A Flicker of Peace

Elliot stared at her, his mind racing to make sense of her words. "What do you mean?" he asked, his voice cracking with emotion.

Delyla stepped closer, her translucent form shimmering faintly in the dim light. "I can't forgive you, Elliot," she said, her voice firm but devoid of its usual venom. "What you did... it's unforgivable. But I see your remorse. I see the way it's eating you alive."

Her words struck him like a blow, the weight of her acknowledgment both painful and oddly comforting. For months, he had been drowning in his guilt, consumed by the enormity of what he had done. To hear her recognize his suffering, even without forgiveness, was a flicker of something he hadn't felt in a long time: peace.

Delyla's expression softened slightly, though the sorrow in her eyes remained. "You'll never undo what you did to me," she continued. "But maybe... maybe there's a way for you to make something out of the wreckage."

An Offer of Redemption

Elliot's breath hitched as he processed her words. "What do you mean?" he asked. "How could I ever make this right?"

"You can't," Delyla said, her tone matter-of-fact. "But you can try to prevent it from happening again. You can use your pain, your story, to stop others from making the same mistakes."

Elliot felt a lump form in his throat. The idea seemed impossible, almost laughable. How could someone like him, someone who had committed such a horrific act, ever help anyone? But as he looked into Delyla's eyes, he saw a glimmer of something he hadn't expected: hope.

"If you truly want to atone," Delyla said, "then you'll dedicate yourself to it. Not out of fear of me. Not because you want to escape your suffering. But because it's the right thing to do."

Her words hung in the air, their weight pressing down on Elliot like a physical force. For the first time in months, he felt a faint spark of purpose. It was fragile, barely more than a whisper, but it was there.

A Mission in the Madness

The next morning, Elliot found himself staring at a blank sheet of paper. The pencil in his hand felt foreign, its weight unfamiliar as he tried to think of what to write. He had spent so long consumed by his guilt, his thoughts a chaotic mess of regret and fear. Now, he was tasked with something different: documenting his story.

He started slowly, his handwriting shaky as he recounted the earliest days of his obsession. He wrote about the fascination he had with control, the way he saw people as puzzles to solve. He described the meticulous planning that had led to Delyla's murder, the steps he had taken to stalk her, and the cold, calculated way he had justified his actions.

As the words flowed, Elliot felt a strange mix of emotions. There was shame, of course, an overwhelming sense of disgust at the person he had been. But there was also a faint sense of relief, as though putting his story on paper was a way to release some of the weight he had been carrying.

By the time he finished the first entry, his hands were trembling. The paper was filled with jagged, uneven lines of text, but it was a start. For the first time in months, Elliot felt like he was doing something—not to escape his torment, but to face it head-on.

The Return of Agency

The act of writing gave Elliot a sliver of agency, a feeling he hadn't experienced since Delyla's haunting began. He began keeping a journal, documenting every detail of his obsession and the choices that had led to his downfall. Each entry was painful to write, forcing him to confront the darkest parts of himself, but it was also cathartic.

As the days turned into weeks, Elliot started to think about what he could do with his story. He wrote letters to organizations that worked with troubled youth, offering his journal as a resource. In his letters, he described his descent into obsession, his inability to see people as human, and the devastating consequences of his actions.

The responses were slow to come, but when they did, they were cautious but curious. Some organizations expressed interest in using his journal as a cautionary tale, a way to help young people understand the dangers of unchecked anger and obsession. Others rejected him outright, their responses curt and dismissive. But Elliot didn't let the rejections stop him. For the first time in months, he felt like he was moving forward, even if the path was fraught with obstacles.

Delyla's Presence Softens

As Elliot dedicated himself to his newfound mission, Delyla's presence began to change. She still appeared in his cell, her ghostly form flickering in the corners, but her visits were less frequent. When she did appear, her expression was less angry, her voice less cutting.

One night, as Elliot sat on his bed, writing another journal entry, Delyla appeared beside him. He froze, his pencil hovering over the paper as he waited for her to speak.

"You're trying," she said after a long silence. "I can see that."

Elliot turned to look at her, his heart pounding. "Is it enough?" he asked. "Will it ever be enough?"

Delyla's expression was unreadable. "That's not for me to decide," she said. "But it's a start."

Her words lingered in the air, their meaning both comforting and devastating. Elliot knew that her haunting wasn't over, that her presence would remain with him as a constant reminder of his crime. But he also sensed that she was giving him a chance—a fragile, fleeting chance to prove himself.

A Question of Sincerity

Even as Elliot threw himself into his new mission, doubts gnawed at the edges of his mind. Was he doing this because he genuinely wanted to atone, or was it just another way to escape his torment? Was his remorse real, or was it driven by fear of Delyla's wrath?

He wrestled with these questions daily, his thoughts a constant battle between self-loathing and a desperate desire to find meaning in his suffering. He knew he couldn't undo the past, couldn't bring Delyla back or erase the pain he had caused. But he also knew that he couldn't stay in the prison of his guilt forever.

As he sat in his cell, staring at the pages of his journal, Elliot realized that the path to redemption wasn't about finding forgiveness. It wasn't about earning peace or escaping punishment. It was about taking responsibility, even when it felt impossible. It was about facing the consequences of his actions and dedicating himself to something bigger than his own pain.

And as Delyla's ghost watched him from the corner of his cell, her eyes filled with a mixture of sadness and resignation, Elliot made a silent promise: he would keep trying, no matter how futile it seemed. Because for the first time, he understood that redemption wasn't about being forgiven—it was about never stopping the fight to become better, even when it hurt.

Elliot's journey was far from over, but in the flicker of Delyla's softened presence and the faint purpose he had found, there was something he hadn't felt in a long time: hope.

The Haunting Evolves

Life in prison had become a grim routine for Elliot, a cycle of confinement and torment that offered no respite. He had begun to think that he understood the rules of his existence now, the steady beat of Delyla's haunting a cruel yet predictable constant. But Delyla had always been more than just a ghost. She was a force of reckoning, and as Elliot began to adapt to his surroundings, she changed her tactics. The torment evolved, shifting in ways that broke what little stability he had managed to build.

A New Form of Torment

The first change was subtle, almost imperceptible. Delyla's ghost no longer appeared as often as she had before. The hollow-eyed specter that had stood in the corners of his cell, staring at him with unrelenting judgment, seemed to have vanished. At first, Elliot thought it was over—

that perhaps his efforts to atone had satisfied her in some way. But it wasn't relief he felt. It was unease.

Her voice came instead, slipping into his mind like a whisper on the wind. It was no longer the sharp, cutting tone that accused him outright. Now, it was softer, almost intimate, and it came when he least expected it.

"Do you think this changes anything?" she whispered one night as Elliot sat hunched over his journal, the pencil trembling in his hand. "Do you think you can undo what you've done?"

The sound of her voice made him flinch, his heart racing as he glanced around the cell. But there was no sign of her. She was everywhere and nowhere at once, her presence a shadow in the corners of his mind.

It was worse this way. The absence of her physical form left him unmoored, unable to predict when or how she would strike. Her voice came in moments of vulnerability—when he was tired, when he felt a flicker of hope, when he dared to think he might be making progress. It was as though she could sense his weakest points and press into them, her words unraveling his fragile sense of purpose

The Unseen Presence

Though Delyla's ghost was less visible, her influence permeated every aspect of Elliot's life. Objects in his cell moved without explanation. The pencil he had left on his desk would reappear on the floor, its tip snapped as though crushed underfoot. His blanket would be pulled from his bed in the middle of the night, left crumpled in the corner as though someone had thrown it there.

Strange noises disrupted his attempts to sleep—a faint tapping on the walls, the creak of his bedframe, the sound of footsteps pacing just outside his cell. Each time he checked, there was nothing there. But the noises always returned, persistent and maddening.

Elliot tried to dismiss them as his imagination, the product of a mind worn thin by months of guilt and isolation. But deep down, he knew the truth. Delyla was still there, her presence woven into the fabric of his reality. She didn't need to appear to remind him of what he had done. Her absence was just as oppressive as her presence.

A Test of Will

As the haunting grew more subtle, it also grew more insidious. Delyla began testing Elliot's resolve, creating moments of doubt and fear that threatened to undo his progress. She whispered temptations in his ear, daring him to give up on his path to redemption.

"Why bother?" she said one night as he sat on his bed, staring at the pages of his journal. "Do you really think anyone cares about your story? Do you really think you can make a difference?"

Her words cut deep, stirring the insecurities that had always lingered just beneath the surface. Elliot clenched his fists, his nails digging into his palms as he tried to block her out. "You're wrong," he muttered, his voice trembling. "I have to try."

Delyla's laugh was soft and cruel. "You're not doing this for them," she said. "You're doing it for yourself. You think if you suffer enough, you'll find peace. But you won't. Not ever."

The temptation to give up was strong, her words feeding the hopelessness that had become a part of him. But Elliot knew that giving in would mean letting her win. It would mean accepting that he was beyond redemption. And as much as he doubted himself, he couldn't let that happen.

A Prison Without Bars

Elliot came to understand that his true prison wasn't the cell that confined him or the guards who monitored his every move. It wasn't even the haunting presence of Delyla herself. His prison was his own mind, a labyrinth of guilt and regret from which there was no escape.

The walls of his cell were just a physical manifestation of the barriers he had built around himself. No matter how far he tried to run from his actions, no matter how hard he worked to atone, the weight of his crime was always there, pressing down on him like a shackle he couldn't remove.

Delyla's haunting wasn't about punishment— it was about forcing him to confront every aspect of himself, peeling back his layers until there was nothing left to hide behind. She made him face the darkest parts of his soul, the selfishness and cruelty that had driven him to take a life. And in doing so, she made him question whether redemption was even possible.

Her Ultimate Goal

Elliot began to see Delyla's haunting in a new light. It wasn't just about making him suffer. It was about forcing him to see himself for who he truly was. Each whisper, each subtle shift in his surroundings, was a reminder of the person he had been and the person he was trying to become.

"You don't get to pretend this away," Delyla said one night as he lay awake in his bunk, staring at the ceiling. "You don't get to rewrite the past. But maybe... maybe you can make something of the future."

Her words were both a challenge and an offering, a reminder that his suffering wasn't an endpoint but a beginning. She wasn't just punishing him—she was pushing him, shaping him into someone who could finally take responsibility for his actions.

A Warning for Others

Through his torment, Elliot began to see his story as more than just his own. It was a cautionary tale, a warning to others about the dangers of obsession and the consequences of unchecked desires. Delyla's haunting wasn't just for him—it was a ripple effect, meant to extend beyond his life and into the lives of those who might follow a similar path.

Elliot's journal became a vessel for this warning. He wrote not just about his guilt but about the moments that had led him to his crime. He wrote about the choices he had made, the justifications he had created, and the lies he had told himself. And as he wrote, he began to see his suffering as a necessary step toward something greater.

"I'll never undo what I did," he wrote in one entry. "But maybe, if I tell the truth, someone else won't make the same mistakes. Maybe that's the only thing I can do now."

Elliot's haunting had evolved, but so had he. Delyla's presence, once a source of pure torment, had become something more complex—a force that pushed him to confront himself, to challenge his assumptions, and to find meaning in his suffering.

Though her voice still whispered in the darkness and her presence still lingered in the corners of his mind, Elliot no longer saw her as just a ghost. She was a mirror, reflecting the truth he had spent so long avoiding. And as he faced that truth, he began to understand that his story wasn't just about his own redemption. It was about creating something that might help others avoid his fate.

There was no peace for Elliot, no end to the weight of his guilt. But in the haunting, there was purpose. And for the first time, that was enough.

The Never-Ending Punishment

The cold, gray cell that had been Elliot's home for years was as barren and unforgiving as ever. The concrete walls seemed to press inward, the air always damp with a chill that seeped into his bones. The bedframe creaked beneath his gaunt frame, its thin mattress offering little comfort. Elliot sat at the edge of the bed, his hands trembling as he stared at the blank pages of a new journal. He had filled countless others, pouring out the story of his descent into obsession and the crime that had stolen Delyla's life. Yet, no matter how much he wrote, the weight of his guilt remained.

Delyla's presence was constant. She wasn't always visible now, but she was never far. Her voice returned at the most unexpected times, slipping into the silence of the cell like a knife into flesh. Sometimes, it was angry, filled with the same fury that had haunted him from the beginning. Other times, it was sorrowful, tinged with the echoes of the life she could have lived. But it was always there, a thread woven into the fabric of his existence.

Elliot sighed, his chest heavy with the burden he carried. Redemption was a path he had committed himself to, but it was a journey that seemed endless. Each step forward felt like walking in place, every effort weighed down by the inescapable truth of what he had done.

A Cycle of Torment

The nights were the hardest. Alone in his cell, Elliot would lay awake, his mind filled with memories of Delyla and the haunting that had consumed him since her death. Sleep was rare and restless, plagued by dreams of her hollow eyes and the accusing faces of the lives he had almost taken. And when he did manage to drift off, he often woke with fresh bruises and scratches, physical reminders that Delyla's ghost still held sway over him.

The torment was cyclical, a pattern that repeated itself endlessly. Just when Elliot thought he might find a moment of peace, Delyla's voice would return, cutting through his thoughts with chilling precision.

"Do you really think this will end?" she asked one night, her voice soft but biting. "Do you think you can ever undo what you've done?"

Elliot didn't respond. He couldn't. He had asked himself the same question too many times, and he had never found an answer.

An Unbroken Chain

Delyla's presence wasn't predictable, and that made it worse. There were days when Elliot would go hours without hearing her voice or feeling her cold touch. Those moments gave him a flicker of hope, a fragile belief that maybe her torment was fading. But it never lasted.

She always returned, sometimes with anger that burned through him like fire, sometimes with sorrow that weighed heavier than any accusation. The unpredictability of her haunting gnawed at the edges of Elliot's sanity, leaving him constantly on edge, waiting for the next reminder of his crime.

Her words weren't always harsh. Sometimes, they were cruel in their tenderness, laced with a sorrow that mirrored his own guilt.

"I wanted a life," she whispered one morning as Elliot sat hunched over his breakfast tray. "A real life. Do you even remember what that feels like?"

Her words stayed with him long after her voice faded, haunting him more effectively than any scream or accusation could have.

A Prison Within a Prison

Elliot's cell, small and confining, had become a reflection of his own mind—a prison within a prison. The walls felt closer at night, the air colder, as though the cell itself conspired with Delyla's ghost to trap him. He still woke with bruises, the faint, linear scratches on his arms and legs a chilling reminder of her presence.

Some nights, the temperature dropped so sharply that Elliot could see his breath, his body trembling as he pulled the thin blanket tighter around him. He would hear faint noises—the creak of his bedframe, the sound of footsteps pacing just outside his cell. Each time he checked, there was no one there. But he knew better than to believe he was alone.

Elliot had long stopped trying to explain these events to the guards or other inmates. They wouldn't have understood. How could they? This wasn't their punishment. It was his.

A Haunting Legacy

Though Elliot's suffering was unending, his journals had begun to take on a life of their own. The prison library, small and poorly stocked, had become the resting place for some of his earlier entries. Guards, inmates, and even staff members had read them, drawn in by the raw, chilling account of his crime and the haunting that followed.

The journals were filled with vivid descriptions of Delyla, of the lives he had almost taken, and of the torment that had consumed him. But they were also filled with self-reflection, with insights into the dark corners of his mind and the consequences of unchecked obsession.

Some readers were fascinated, others horrified. A few found cautionary lessons in Elliot's words, using his story to start conversations about mental health, guilt, and the ripple effects of violence. Though Elliot didn't know it, his journals were beginning to ripple outward, touching lives in ways he had never anticipated.

The Unanswered Question

One night, as the prison grew quiet and the faint hum of fluorescent lights filled the air, Elliot sat in front of his sink, staring into its dull, reflective surface. His face stared back at him, hollow and gaunt, his eyes ringed with dark circles that spoke of years of sleepless nights. But he wasn't looking at himself. He was looking at her.

Delyla's ghost stood just behind him, her form faint but unmistakable. Her hollow eyes met his in the reflection, and for a long moment, neither of them spoke. The silence was thick, heavy with the weight of everything left unsaid.

"Will this ever end?" Elliot whispered, his voice trembling.

Delyla didn't answer. Her gaze didn't waver, but there was no hint of forgiveness or resolution in her expression. She was simply there, her presence a constant reminder of the life he had stolen and the debt he could never repay.

A Closing Whisper

As the light in Elliot's cell flickered and dimmed, casting the room into a soft shadow, Delyla's voice echoed one last time.

"This is where you belong."

Her words lingered in the air, heavy and final. Elliot closed his eyes, his breath hitching as the chill of her presence enveloped him. He didn't argue. He didn't beg. He simply sat there, letting the truth of her words sink in.

This was his reality—a life of endless guilt, of torment that would never truly fade. Redemption was a fleeting concept, something he would chase but never fully grasp. And though he continued to write, to document his story in the hope that it might help others, he knew that his own suffering would never end.

As the cell fell silent once more, Elliot opened his eyes and stared into the reflection again. Delyla was gone, but the weight of her words remained.

This was where he belonged. And he knew it.

Printed in Great Britain
by Amazon